JESSICA JEFFRIES
A CERTAIN SUNRISE

A SUPERROMANCE FROM
W🌐RLDWIDE

TORONTO · NEW YORK · LOS ANGELES · LONDON

For Heinz—
with deepest love and respect

Love is not love
Which alters when it alteration finds...
O, no! it is an ever-fixed mark,
That looks on tempests and is never shaken.
Shakespeare, "Sonnet 116"

———————————————◆———————————————

Published July 1983

First printing May 1983

ISBN 0-373-70071-7

Copyright © 1983 by Jessica Jeffries. All rights reserved.
Philippine copyright 1983. Australian copyright 1983.
Except for use in any review, the reproduction or utilization of
this work in whole or in part in any form by any electronic,
mechanical or other means, now known or hereafter invented,
including xerography, photocopying and recording, or in any
information storage or retrieval system, is forbidden without
the permission of the publisher, Worldwide Library,
225 Duncan Mill Road, Don Mills, Ontario, Canada M3B 3K9.

All the characters in this book have no existence outside the
imagination of the author and have no relation whatsoever to
anyone bearing the same name or names. They are not even
distantly inspired by any individual known or unknown to the
author, and all the incidents are pure invention.

The Superromance trademark, consisting of the word
SUPERROMANCE, and the Worldwide trademark, consisting of
a globe and the word WORLDWIDE in which the letter "O" is
represented by a depiction of a globe, are trademarks of
Worldwide Library.

Printed in Canada

CHAPTER ONE

MIST-DAMPENED EARTH squished beneath Marla's insulated rubber boots as she covered the distance from the house to the old, weather-beaten barn. Whickers and resounding kicks from the more vociferous and demanding of the horses greeted her arrival, the familiar sounds making her grin in amusement.

It was the same every morning, Marla mused, setting efficiently and automatically about the tasks of graining and haying the horses. Horses, however innately ignorant about certain matters, were absolutely brilliant at ascertaining the exact minute of feeding time.

"Sorry, fellas," she apologized to the five Thoroughbreds, scooping out grain from a wheelbarrow into each feed bucket. She was an hour late that morning, but that fact was more disconcerting to her than to the mildly offended horses. She'd had every intention of rising before dawn to get a head start on the day, which promised to be a hectic one. But the previous night had not managed to fit into her plans, and she had gone to bed at an absolutely horrid hour, sleeping right through the alarm that morning.

Finishing with at least the preliminary chores, Marla walked back outside, continuing on toward the house for a sorely needed cup of coffee and a bit of breakfast. Her attention captured by the distant, blue-hazed vista, her steps slowed gradually to a halt. Folding her arms across the soft plaid flannel material of her jacket, she turned her head westward, her almond-shaped, ultramarine eyes drawing in the simple magnificence of the surrounding countryside, the picturesque multicolored Blue Ridge mountain range.

Marla breathed in deeply of the pure sweet air, relishing its physically and mentally restoring effects. The sensation, though, was a fleeting one. Unbidden, a prickling apprehension assailed her, marring her peaceful contentment.

The latter, of course, was easily understood, an extension of the satisfaction and happiness she had found here in Keswick, Virginia. Living alone had certainly not been an easy feat, but the deep, soul-pulling kinship she felt for the land and her animals was the culmination of all the risks and day-to-day struggles she faced, the reward that made it all worthwhile.

Expelling the reviving breath of air in a

lengthy, almost wistful sigh, Marla turned and retraced her steps to the small, white-frame house that had been her home for the past year. The sudden apprehension she felt was no mystery, either, she acknowledged wryly. In fact, she had been brooding over the same subject for the entire week—the imminent arrival of Morning Meadows's newest owner, about whom Marla, like the other three tenants presently leasing the various horse-related facilities of the three-hundred-fifty acre estate, possessed only minimal knowledge. She was only certain of one thing: he was a European, more than likely an investor, who, along with others in his exalted financial position, had found the extremely valuable Virginia "horse-country" property a sound investment.

Marla, together with the neighboring inhabitants of Keswick and nearby Charlottesville, could only wait, hoping and praying the new owner had at least a vestige of interest in the horse world. Land in these parts was simply too wonderful, too practical, for the horse industry not to be put to such use. Considering the existing properties for even remotely commercial use was regarded as downright sacrilegious by the traditionalists here—a group in which Marla included herself when it came to horses.

One such case in point had made Marla and

other Keswick residents shake their heads in chagrined disbelief: the dismantling of one of Keswick's wealthier horse farms. The new owners, their interests purportedly tied in with the Virginia-state political machine, had made no attempt to commercialize the area. On the contrary, they lived in detached solitude within the walls of their rambling estate mansion. It was what they were *not* doing that had initiated much concerned and regretful commen.. The lush, gently rolling estate, which had for decades been used as breeding and training grounds for some of the finest stock of Virginia Thoroughbreds, now lay idle, empty of livestock. It seemed a crime that such a flourishing tradition should have been so easily dispensed with. Keswick certainly had no need of any other such unconcerned residents. Hopefully the new owner of Morning Meadows, whoever he might be, would not fit into that dubious category.

Oh, but why, Marla wondered wistfully. Why did things have to change? She knew the question to be childish and futile, but it was there just the same. To change now of all times—just when she was really starting to show if not a tremendous, then at least a noteworthy profit for her efforts in that rather capricious business. What would Carl think of her situation now, she mused sardonically, shaking her head as she remembered his frequent patronizing warnings that she was being nothing short of ridiculous thinking she could manage to support herself in the horse business.

Walking around to the rear of the small cottage, Marla scraped the soles of her boots on the doormat before entering the screened-in back porch. Nik, her three-month-old German shepherd puppy, awakened from one of his frequent siestas to scamper across the gray-painted wooden floor toward her, crying with excitement at her presence.

"Hi, there, Nikiroo." Marla laughed the greeting, bending over to nuzzle the black-and-tan dog she had bought two weeks earlier. When full-grown, Nik would hopefully make an excellent guard dog, but for now she was thoroughly enjoying his puppy stage.

"Here you are," she cooed, reaching for a box of dog biscuits and placing a few on the floor in front of him. Nik's attention was immediately diverted as he hungrily devoured the canine hors d'oeuvres, and Marla took advantage of his momentary inattention to let herself in the back door of the kitchen.

Shrugging out of her flannel jacket and woolen cap, she shook her head, loosening the dark blond, sun-streaked tresses, the static effect spraying wispy tendrils in a golden corona around her head. A short, capped haircut would have been much more suitable for her profession, but Marla had steadfastly rejected the idea, electing instead to wear her thick mane in other reasonably practical styles—either tied back in a simple ponytail or gathered into one long French braid that fell to her upper back But on crisp fall days like this one, when the weather was cold enough to warrant a hat, she simply piled the ample mass on top of her head and pulled the knitted cap snugly over it.

With practiced ease Marla began preparing her breakfast, the heat from the gas range soon driving some of the chill out of the air. Minutes later she was seated at the small maple kitchen table, delving into a plate of scrambled eggs, toast with butter and jam and a large mug of steaming black coffee

Savoring the most important meal of her day. Marla gazed through the green-and-white gingham curtains, reminiscing lazily. How very different her life was from only a year ago....

She had made the most momentous decision of her life at that time, one that might turn out to be the wisest she would ever make. Of course, things were difficult now, uncertain, but regardless of what was to happen to the land that was necessary to her livelihood, she sensed deep inside that she would make it. A well-earned feeling of pride and accomplishment swelled within her. She was secure in the knowledge that she could and would take control of her own life.

A mental image of Carl's condescending expression suddenly loomed before her, and Marla felt the almost forgotten, time-softened stab of hurt. Carl, with his carefully contrived mask of concern, his dire prediction that she would be making a serious mistake. Yet she knew now she would have made a far more serious mistake had she listened to him and not made the decision to leave. But such an admission had not been necessary at the time, for both had known there was no point in continuing their hopeless relationship. Marla had played the graceful role of allowing him to save face, hiding the bitter resentment that gripped her. And he had been relieved; she was sure of it.

Carl's suggestion that they live together before their marriage couldn't disguise his true feelings about their future. In spite of his claims of acceptance and understanding, his love for Marla had not been deep enough to sustain the consequences of her recently discovered medical problem. But regardless of the pain this realization had caused her, Marla had not really blamed him.

Carl had never said as much directly. Nevertheless she knew he wanted children of his own someday—an integral part of his plans, a part she would never be able to give him. A routine yearly visit to her gynecologist had revealed an abnormal formation of her fallopian tubes that had gone unobserved previously. The doctor had recommended exploratory surgery, and she had almost not gone through with it—she hadn't been having any problems and really didn't see the point. But eventually she thought better of the decision and agreed to take her doctor's advice, whereby he found that the abnormality was apparently a congenital defect.

It was the consequence of that abnormality, however, that had shocked and stunned her The problem was permanent, irreparable even with the very latest surgical techniques. The diagnosis was confirmed by a second, even a third medical opinion. She was unquestionably infertile. . . and would always be.

It had taken time to adjust to the cruel discovery, but her own sense of self-worth had stood her in good stead, and she had come to an eventual acceptance of what could not be helped and to the realization that her life would go on, perhaps even improve immeasurably. There were times, though, even now, when despite the acceptance, despite the adjustment, Carl's rejection haunted her. It was a painful thing to bear—rejection based on a physical impairment. She was strong now, stronger than she'd ever been, but she knew she could not withstand such a hurt again. Indeed, she had no intention of ever making herself vulnerable again.

Carl had left his mark on her, and she'd suffered a momentary setback, needed to get away. The unexpected death of her maternal grandmother had coincidentally provided the wherewithal to take that first necessary step in starting fresh. She had been astounded by the sum of money left to her in her grandmother's will. Even though it wasn't exactly a windfall, it was a godsend as far as Marla was concerned. She could finally afford to take the gamble that had always remained a fantasy of sorts—quitting her position as a legal secretary to make a living showing and selling quality Thoroughbred hunters and jumpers.

Since she was a child, Marla had ridden, her adolescent years taken up more with horses than with other "normal" teenage pursuits. Fortunately her parents had been able to provide her with the funds to stable and show a Thoroughbred hunter—not an especially noteworthy horse by anyone's standards, but one that provided hours of learning experience in the saddle, both on the flat and over fences.

Her parents' divorce, when Marla was eighteen, had put a halt to her enjoyment of equestrian sports. Left with two children to care for, her mother couldn't support her daughter's increasingly recognized talent.

Marla had given up riding for four years then, her time occupied with working and putting herself through college. She had worked for another four years after graduation as a legal secretary, her salary just enough to enable her to lease a horse and occasionally show on the unrecognized hunter circuit.

With her inheritance she was able to purchase a small stock of young inexperienced horses to train, in addition to locating an adequate piece of lease property on which to board them. The venture had proved successful thus far, though at times lonely. But what she lacked in close human companionship was, for now at least, compensated for by the rigorous schedule her new career entailed.

In truth, she wasn't completely isolated. Morris, the older experienced farmhand she'd hired to take care of many of the stable chores, particularly those requiring an especially strong set of muscles, was an amicable loyal man who provided a valued combination of friendship and security.

Marla had also formed a network of business and social relationships among her neighbors in

Keswick. Some had evolved into dating situations that were very much to her liking, fulfilling many of her needs yet posing no threat to the independent life-style she had come to enjoy and even prefer. It seemed odd how rapidly the dreams and expectations of the past had faded into insignificance. Like a butterfly, she had emerged from a cocoon of conventionally restrictive thinking into the fully capable and self-reliant woman she was now. She felt free for the first time in her twenty-eight years, and it was a precious freedom that would brook no interference—ever.

But now unpleasant reality intruded on her positive musings. Her hard-earned, peaceful existence was in danger of being upset—by this new owner of Morning Meadows Farm.

The jangle of the telephone jolted her out of her brooding reverie, and she hastily placed her almost empty mug of coffee on the table, pushed back her chair and walked across the kitchen to pick up the receiver of the wall telephone.

"Hello?"

The crackle on the line indicated the call was long distance. "Is this Marla Faraday?"

"Yes." The connection was poor, so Marla raised her voice. "Who's calling? I can't hear you very well."

"This is Sylvan Longworth. Can you near me any better?" The man's voice was extremely muffled, although he seemed to be yelling.

"Yes, a little. Where are you calling from?"

"I'm with my wife and daughter at Kennedy airport. Our flight was just canceled for some obscure reason, so we've been booked on the next available one. That won't put us into Dulles, however, until this evening."

Marla bit her lower lip thoughtfully. The news would definitely change her plans for that day, since she had expected them to arrive in the early afternoon, but on further thought she realized she could still make use of the time.

"We thought we would be better off to stay in a hotel near the airport in Dulles tonight, then drive down to Keswick in the morning. Will that inconvenience you too much?"

"Oh, no," Marla assured her potential customer. "Not at all. Tomorrow is fine. What time do you think you'll be here?"

"Hmm. I imagine around ten-thirty or eleven."

'That sounds great. You don't need the directions again, do you?"

"No I still have the ones you gave me earlier '

"Good. Then I'll see you all in the morning."

"Right. Goodbye."

Marla said goodbye and listened as the other end of the line clicked. Slowly she replaced the receiver, calculating how this unexpected change in the day's schedule should be dealt with. Fortunately she had no other definite plans for the next day, and mulling the situation over for a few more moments, she came to the conclusion things would work out better this way anyhow.

A good long workout that day wouldn't hurt Gambler one bit. In fact, it would make him much more pliable and definitely put him in a nicer frame of mind for the younger Longworth, who would be trying him out. Gambler was only a four-year-old, and although a smooth capable hunter, he was still green. The more exercise he got, the better. A host of other much ignored chores occurred to her as she cleaned up the kitchen before donning hat and jacket and returing to the barn.

The afternoon sun dappled the rolling, colorsplashed countryside, casting a mellow honeyed glow on all that its warming rays touched. Gambler snorted gustily, his lively gait quickening as the ground made a gradual ascent. Marla applied the slightest pressure to the inside rein, reinforcing it with a touch of her heel to the horse's flank, cuing him into a left-lead canter.

Gambler responded automatically, flicking his ears forward expectantly as the first fence came into view out of the turn. He speeded up still more, eating up the distance and causing Marla to lose her eye for the correct takeoff point. Gambler lived up to his name then. Taking his chances, he jumped from half a stride ahead, catching Marla behind the motion as they landed long on the opposite side

"Whoa!" Marla commanded loudly, seesawing on the reins as she jerked the horse to a sudden halt. "That's enough of that, boy."

Expertly she backed the horse up several strides, making sure he was in no doubt about who was in control of this particular lesson. Gambler, however, was feeling his oats that afternoon, and as Marla directed him once more toward the same fence, he took hold of the bit again, lunging forward in anticipation of the jump. Prepared this time, and now quite irritated with the gelding's pranks, she jerked him down before the fence, backing him up until his rear end almost touched the end gate of the arena.

Gambler tucked his head down placing the bit cooperatively between his teeth. Marla put the horse into another canter, and the jump was taken in a much more tolerable fashion. After several more attempts with other obstacles around the course she pulled the now heavily breathing horse to a stop, allowing him to catch his breath as she loosened the reins before putting him into a walk.

Reaching up with one hand to free the long blond mane that had slipped into the collar of her sweater, Marla relaxed now herself, her spine curving slightly as her pelvis and hips rotated in a smooth forward motion, carried by the motion of the horse. Letting her gaze wander, she saw that the traffic was just beginning to build on the two-lane highways skirting two sides of the rectangular piece of land that comprised Morning Meadows. By city standards it was not what one would consider heavy traffic, but it was noticeable just the same, most of it due to the end-of-the-day exodus from nearby Charlottesville.

With her attention focused on the rather mundane science, it was several seconds before Marla paid any notice to the powder-blue Mercedes sedan wending its way down the private road that bisected and connected various parts of the farm. A tiny furrow etched the bridge of her nose. Why did the car look somehow familiar? Then she recalled that, in spite of her concentration a few minutes earlier when schooling Gambler, she had glimpsed the Mercedes from the corner of her eye as it entered the farm's main gate.

The automobile certainly didn't belong to anyone living on the sprawling estate, and since she herself was not expecting any visitors today, it seemed all the more curious. Unconsciously she sat up a bit straighter as it became apparent the vehicle was making its way toward the arena she and Gambler were now in. Deliberately declining to show any particular interest in the visitor, Marla squeezed the animal's flanks, urging Gambler into a perkier walk. They were headed away from the Mercedes, but she could hear the tires rolling slowly over the crunching gravel, coming to a stop just outside the arena, followed by the opening of a door.

As she and Gambler rounded the far corner, she observed the figure of a man, imposingly tall and impeccably dressed, emerging from the car. Slamming the door shut, he glanced slowly around him, then walked toward the arena, his stride easy and unhurried. Stopping at the fence, he propped one foot on the lower rail, elbows resting on the upper, the fingers of his hands linked casually together.

As Marla walked Gambler toward him, she got a better view of the stranger. Oddly, something deep within her stirred as she found herself under intense scrutiny from a pair of striking dark chocolate eyes, their rich color framed by a feathering of sooty lashes many a woman would have envied.

That was the extent of any possible feminine comparison. The rest of his appearance was totally, unequivocally, male. Marla quickly assessed his height at somewhere near six feet three inches. The open black overcoat he wore revealed broad formidable shoulders and arms, a muscular torso tapering down to a hard slim waist, narrow hips joining into long runner's legs—the physique of a man in his prime.

Marla pulled Gambler to a halt just in front of the stranger, and he spoke, his voice deep and resonant.

"You really know what you're doing there," he said, his eyes still holding her own as he nodded briefly, indicating the horse.

Marla was silent for a moment. Gambler chewed on the bit and moved restlessly. Inclining her head slightly, she answered, "Thank you. I didn't know I had an audience."

He laughed, a soft husky sound that sent a mysterious unexpected thrill coursing through her. Her breath caught for a mere second. Yet she could feel the back of her neck warming as she caught the look in his eye, denoting his awareness of her discomfort.

"That says a great deal for your powers of concentration." His eyes left her face then, scanning the surrounding area appreciatively before coming back to focus on her once more. "Allow me to introduce myself. I'm Stefan Gerhardt." His gaze seemed to bore into her, and Marla chafed inwardly beneath the disturbing perusal. Gambler pawed the ground impatiently, and she took advantage of the diversion to walk the horse around in a wide circle. Coming to a stop once more, she lifted her own gaze to the man's face.

"My name is Marla Faraday," she said. "I lease the—"

"Yes, I know," he interrupted her, removing his foot from the fence rail and standing with both feet planted slightly apart, his hands shoved into the pockets of his overcoat. Once more the dark brown eyes left hers to take in his surroundings.

Marla frowned, puzzled. How could he know who she was? Certainly they had never met before.... Suddenly the realization dawned on her, and a streak of dread shot through her with the knowledge. Swallowing deeply, she spoke quietly, her azure eyes becoming hooded.

"You...you are the new owner of Morning Meadows?" It was a question. Yet she didn't doubt the answer.

His eyes swept back to her, and the warmth at her nape spread, her face flushing with the emotion she strove to control. She felt awkward, full of butterflies, like some anxious college student searching the postings of exam finals. She drew in a long breath, awaiting what she was still not prepared for.

He nodded then, one corner of his wide, well-shaped mouth lifting in a paltry grin. "I suppose you've been expecting my arrival."

Marla shrugged. "I really didn't know what to expect. We tenants have been kept pretty much in the dark as to the new owner's—your—intentions." Placing both reins in one hand, she swung out of the saddle, leading Gambler toward the gate and reaching forward to unlatch it.

"I'm sorry to hear that," Stefan said, moving swiftly to hold the gate as she and Gambler walked out of the arena.

"I had hoped you would have been informed as to my intentions for the future use of the property here."

Coming around to face him, Marla placed a hand on the side of Gambler's neck, unconsciously stroking him as she waited with bated breath to hear what he was referring to.

He had expected her to question him, but when she remained silent, he explained, "I will be taking over management of the entire estate fairly soon," watching as her incredibly blue eyes widened ever so slightly.

"I see," Marla replied, absently chewing the inside of one cheek. Sweeping one arm in a backward motion, she asked, "Does that include the barn I'm now leasing for my horses?"

He nodded slowly, his brown gaze direct and uncompromising. "Yes, it does."

Marla's breath rushed out silently, her shoulders slumping as she bent her head. She had half expected this; a change of ownership was bound to bring other unsettling changes with it. Still, the reality of the situation was surprisingly overwhelming. Deliberately she lifted her eyes, not to meet the dark pair still watching her closely but to study the autumn-splashed color of the countryside, the rich tones of the distant Blue Ridge mountain range that she had never once taken for granted. How would she bear it, the thought pierced her. How could she ever replace this land she had come to love and cherish?

Turning slowly, she tugged on the reins. Gambler followed more eagerly now as she started back toward the barn. She was mindless of the effect of her abrupt behavior on the dark-haired man, a frown of perplexity etching his roughly hewn features as he watched her retreating figure.

CHAPTER TWO

WITH EACH STEP Marla felt the weight in her chest expanding, becoming heavier and harder to bear. Swallowing deeply, she held her chin high, forcing back the burning constriction in her throat. An almost overwhelming sense of resentment assailed her, an anger directed at the arrogant man who apparently found it a simple task to casually inform her he would be repossessing the property that had been her home for the past year.

But this is ridiculous, a more reasonable inner voice suddenly chided. *I'm behaving like a child who's just been told she can't have the latest toy she wants.* Chagrined by her uncharacteristic indulgence in self-pity, she stopped and turned back. She might as well say goodbye to him. After all, this was his property now, his to do with as he wanted. She couldn't change the situation, and she should at least have the courtesy to conclude her stay here on a decent note.

Stefan was still standing at the gate of the arena. A faintly annoyed expression had altered the previously puzzled one. As she walked back toward him, the chestnut horse following obediently behind, his eyes took in the full length of her graceful slender form. She wasn't what one would term tall, but her legs were long and lithe, firmly tapered thighs molded by suede tan chaps over faded jeans. Her sweater had also seen better days—a natty, dark green woolen pullover that ended just at the waistband of her jeans. Not exactly the picture of haute couture, he mused, yet without a doubt one of the sexiest outfits he'd ever seen on a woman.

And a woman she was, he thought, a muscle in his jaw working in response to the stimulating realization. From the moment he'd seen her astride the recalcitrant animal he'd been impressed with the way she rode, exhibiting a style that was fluid and controlled, her skill in making her demands understood to the horse obvious even to an untrained observer—which he, of course, was not. That skill, no less than her obvious physical attributes, had left an indelible impression on him, one that sparked a certain interesting idea....

As she reached him, she spoke, and he cocked his head slightly. "Mr. Gerhardt...." Marla hesitated for a fraction of a second before continuing. She held her head almost regally, the afternoon breeze fingering the sun-kissed locks, twisting the gently curling ends around one another.

"I apologize for walking away like that just now," she said. She shrugged, and a tiny grimace lifted the corners of her mouth. "I . . . I just wasn't prepared for your visit—so soon, I mean. If you'll excuse me, I need to get Gambler back to the stable now." She paused. "There is something I would like to ask you, however."

Stefan nodded. "Certainly." He regarded her intently, disturbingly, but her brilliant azure eyes boldly held his gaze.

"How soon do I have to leave?" she inquired, successfully quelling the telltale quaver in her voice.

His eyes narrowed, whether from the lowering rays of the strong afternoon sunlight or in contemplation of her question, she could only guess. When at last he responded, she was surprised and puzzled by the answer.

"Perhaps that is something we can discuss."

Marla frowned. "What do you mean?" she asked. Certainly he had some idea of when he wanted to take over the premises she was leasing. It was important information to her. She'd need to get started as soon as possible looking for some other home for herself and her horses.

He appeared to hesitate before replying. "Why don't you take your horse back to the stable and I'll follow you in the car," he suggested. "I would like to speak to you further—if you don't mind," he qualified.

Marla's brows lifted in mild bemusement. "No, of course not," she answered, turning and starting once more toward the barn.

Stefan watched her walk away for a moment, almost mesmerized by the unaffected sway of her jean-clad hips. Distractedly he raked a long-fingered hand through his thick ebony hair and started toward the car. As Marla and the horse walked on, he slid onto the smooth leather driver's seat, switched on the engine and maneuvered the sedan back onto the gravel road that wound up a gentle incline toward the stable.

Marla's curiosity about what Mr. Gerhardt wanted to discuss with her was abruptly forgotten. She was greeted by Morris as soon as she led Gambler into the stable. Seeing her, he leaned the wide-brushed broom he'd been sweeping the floor with against one wall, pulled out a handkerchief and proceeded to blow his nose resoundingly.

"I think you better have a look at Badger," he said in a nasal tone, indicating the bay gelding's stall with a backward nod. From where Marla stood it appeared empty.

"Where is he?" she asked, removing girth and saddle from Gambler's back and handing the reins over to Morris.

"He's in his stall—lying down." Slipping the bridle over Gambler's head and replacing it with a halter, he led the horse to the enclosed concrete washstand at one end of the stable. Securing the halter to the crossties, he returned to where Marla now stood, just outside Badger's stall door.

"Been like that for the past hour or so," Morris commented, a worried frown etching his deeply lined brow, echoing the concern evident in Marla's expression.

Unlatching the stall door, she bent over to slip Badger's halter around his head, then backed up and pulled on the attached lead rope. After several tugs the horse reluctantly heaved himself up onto his unsteady legs, his head drooping wearily.

"He didn't finish his breakfast," Marla commented, eyeing the half-filled feed bucket.

"Uh-uh." Morris shook his head.

Marla grimaced, then whistled between her teeth. This was all she needed. Illnesses in horses could very easily turn into expensive problems, and the symptoms Badger was displaying right now certainly indicated he was ill. Like most horse owners she was acquainted with a variety of veterinary treatments. It was a necessity both from a practical as well as a medical point of view.

"Hmm.... Let's bring him out into the aisleway, Morris. I suppose it wouldn't hurt to medicate him at this point. He looks as though he could use something for the pain."

Morris grunted his agreement and led the ailing horse out of the stall, jerking repeatedly on the lead rope to move the unwilling animal along.

Preoccupied now with Badger's condition, Marla walked back down the aisleway and stepped into the tack room. The sound of a car pulling up just outside the stable doors made no impression on her. Rummaging through the contents of the medicine cabinet, she located the vial she was searching for and placed it in the pocket of her jacket. Standing on tiptoe, she reached up to the top shelf for a syringe and needle, almost dropping them both as a deep voice from behind startled her.

"Is something wrong?" Stefan asked.

Marla gasped and whipped around to see him standing in the doorway, his dark eyebrows raised in open curiosity as he eyed the syringe and needle.

Marla could barely hide the exasperation she felt toward the man for unnerving her so. Her answer was curt as she pulled the paper wrapping from the syringe and withdrew the vial from her pocket. "One of my horses is showing signs of colic," she said, moving past him and into the aisleway.

Stefan turned to see Morris walking the drooping horse slowly toward the end of the aisleway. "How long has he been like that?" he asked, turning back to Marla, who was now drawing some of the amber liquid into the syringe.

"Morris noticed him while I was schooling Gambler. I suppose for an hour or so."

Stefan's dark brows drew together in what Marla could only define as a disapproving expression. Her assumption was supported by his comment. "And you are already medicating him?" he asked skeptically.

The tone of his question rankled Marla even more than the question itself, as if he doubted she knew what she was doing. Who was he to question the manner in which she treated her own horses?

"That seems to be what I'm doing, doesn't it?" she replied, her sweetened tone laced with sarcasm.

Bringing his arms up and folding them

against his unbuttoned overcoat, Stefan snorted lightly. "You Americans are certainly quick with the needle, aren't you?"

Marla glared up at the man, her sea-blue eyes sparkling with annoyance at the impertinent remark. Her attention was caught by something else, too. For the first time she detected the barest hint of an accent in his voice, the slanted remark apparently having brought it out more distinctly.

"And what exactly is that supposed to mean?" she bristled, fixing the cap over the needle of the prepared syringe.

One corner of his mouth lifted in unconcealed amusement at the response he'd provoked in her, calling her attention to the wide firm mouth, compelling her eyes to focus there for only a second, yet long enough to stir a certain warming sensation along the base of her neck.

"Just what it implied," he answered smoothly, the black-framed eyes glinting knowingly as he gazed down at her beautiful vexed face. "Most of the Americans I have observed have been much too eager to medicate their horses at the first sign of anything wrong. Many times the problem can be handled from another perspective, one that doesn't involve drugging the horse unnecessarily."

"Such as?" Marla taunted, her sarcastic tone belying the patient smile she managed.

Stefan turned, giving an upward nod as he glanced pointedly at Morris, who continued to walk the horse up and down the aisleway. "Such as what is being done now," he replied readily. "As you can see, there has been a change in the animal since we've been talking. No doubt he will recover on his own if he is simply walked for a while longer."

It was true. Badger's gait was already becoming perkier just from the few trips up and down. Grudgingly Marla silently admitted that Stefan might have a point. Frequently a horse suffering from an intestinal ailment could be hastened toward a rapid recovery simply by being exercised until the symptoms disappeared.

Ignoring the tall man by her side, she slid the syringe back into her pocket and approached Morris, who stopped, Badger coming to a halt just behind him.

"What do you think, Morris?" Marla asked speculatively, her hands on her hips as she considered the animal's slightly improved demeanor. "That walking seems to be bringing him out of it."

Morris nodded. "You thinkin' about holdin' off on the medicine?"

"Yes. For now. Why don't we keep him walking for another twenty minutes or so? If he feels better by then, you can turn him out in the paddock and let him graze for a while.''

"All right," Morris said, turning the horse around in a half circle and leading him back down the aisleway. Marla was encouraged now by Badger's definite willingness, his iron-shod hooves clopping against the asphalt in a quicker cadence as he followed Morris outside. She turned, half expecting to face Stefan's superior, self-satisfied expression. Instead she was surprised to see him ambling toward the opposite end of the barn, his head turning slowly from side to side. He seemed to be studying the structure of the sturdily built wooden stalls, as indeed was his privilege now, wasn't it, Marla thought with irrepressible ire.

Walking into the tack room, she returned the vial and syringe to the medicine cabinet, her irritation increasing with the new owner's continuing presence. He'd said he wanted to talk to her. She could only assume he wished to discuss how soon he would require her to vacate the premises. The peevishness she felt toward him deepening the sun-tinted glow of her features, darkening the azure depths of her eyes, Marla strode decisively from the room, resolving to get the subject out in the open.

A slip of paper that had fallen from the cork

message board on a wall near the door caught her eye, and she bent over to retrieve it, frowning as she tried to recall the identification of the lone telephone number.

"Oh!" The gasp escaped her lips as she straightened, slamming into the hard wall of Stefan Gerhardt's chest. Dismayed to find the fingers of both hands grasping the lapels of his black overcoat, she pushed against him, rocking back on her heels for an instant before finding her balance and releasing him. Stunned by the unexpected collision, she swallowed spasmodically as she glanced up sheepishly at him.

"Excuse me," she gulped, all too aware of the painful blush staining her cheeks, embarrassed by her obvious clumsiness. Flustered, she reached down to pick up the dropped note, turning to secure it with a pin on the cork board.

"I seem to have a knack for surprising you," Stefan said, his eyes focused on the shimmery blond tresses that had slipped across her shoulder in the scramble, one long strand curving along a corner of her full sensuous lips. He was struck full force with the natural beauty of her. There was a quality to her that seemed to define the word "femininity." He doubted that he'd ever been so affected by a woman on first meeting. Indeed, it was difficult to restrain the hand that longed to reach out and lift the gilded lock from her face, to feel its silkiness between his fingertips. . . .

"Yes, you do," Marla bit out, more perturbed by her own ridiculous reaction to him than by the actual incident. Shoving her hands in the back pockets of her jeans, she longed for some particularly acrimonious words to put him in his place. Yet strangely none came to mind. Instead she found her reluctant gaze drawn in admiration to the jutting rugged line of his jaw, an evening's shadow of beard already shading it. Unable to stop herself, her eyes wandered slowly across the angular planes of his face, upward across the strong bronzed forehead, the lightly curling ebony hair that fell away of its own accord in an off-center part. He had placed his hands on his hips, spreading wide the overcoat to reveal his solid physique. The masculinity he exuded was of an elemental nature. It was only natural that she should react to him, she thought defensively, gathering her composure in an effort to dispel the gawking expression that must surely be written all over her face.

"How long have you been here?" he asked, his pleasant tone allaying, for the moment, some of Marla's antagonism.

"A little more than a year," she answered, then added brusquely, "Excuse me," and moved past him, stepping back into the aisleway. Going to the washstand where Gambler still waited, she picked up a bar of saddle soap and a sponge, dampening the latter and stroking it against the bar to work up a lather. Walking toward the dangling overhead hook and removing the reins from the suspended bridle, she then worked the sponge against them in a gentle cleaning motion. The habit provided a convenient opportunity to avoid, at least for a few moments, the disturbing pair of eyes that watched her so closely.

"You've done a good job in keeping the place up," Stefan commended, his gaze riveted now on the pair of slender delicate hands, expertly stroking the fine-grained leather to shiny smoothness.

The comment further irritated Marla, already disturbed enough by the man's overwhelming physical presence that anything he said or did practically drove her to distraction. "What you really mean is you wonder how in the world I've managed, right?" she retorted daringly.

He cocked one dark eyebrow in deference to her astuteness and inclined his head. He'd been speculating on just that. In truth, he'd known about the young woman who leased part of the property he'd decided on purchasing ever since he'd made the first offer on the place. The fact of a young single woman living alone there had intrigued him, but the last thing he'd expected to encounter was the extraordinary face staring back at him, the sensuous body poised, openly hostile.

"Actually, I have to give Morris credit for a great deal of the work that has gone into keeping up the place," Marla said, not bothering to disguise the haughtiness in her tone. Suddenly overcome with impatience at all this unnecessary small talk, she clucked her tongue and threw the loop of the reins back over the suspended hook. Holding the soap bar and sponge in one hand, she wiped the other over her hip and reached up to loop back the blond curtain of hair that had escaped from behind one ear.

"Look, Mr. Gerhardt, why don't we just get to the point here? You said you wanted to talk to me about something. I assume it has to do with how soon you want me to leave. Well?" She spread her hands in an expansive gesture.

Sliding his hands inside his pockets once more, he lowered his head for a moment and chewed thoughtfully on his lower lip.

Glancing at her, he finally said, "Actually, I was going to extend an offer to stay."

Marla blinked in total amazement. "I...I don't understand. I thought you said you were going to be taking over the entire estate."

"I am, but I'll only be needing the larger facilities for the time being."

'Oh?" Marla frowned in confusion.

"I'll be using the property as a Trakehner breeding station. I'm importing a selection of horses from Germany that have taken me quite some time to acquire. Are you familiar with the breed?"

"Yes, of course," Marla answered, her tone softer now, her interest certainly sparked by this bit of news So the property would remain in the hands of horse owners, she mused. To her knowledge, this would be the first Trakehner breeding station in that part of Virginia. She had a cursory knowledge of the West German warmbloods. Originally bred by inhabitants of eighteenth-century East Prussia, the coveted, highly successful performing horses were rapidly establishing a solid foothold in North America. Crossbreeding with the American Thoroughbred was being attempted, and although concrete results of the venture were at least a couple of years away, so far the experiment was considered by most authorities to be quite positive.

"The first of the horses will be arriving toward the end of the month," Stefan said, watching as Marla placed the bar of soap and sponge back on the shelf in the washstand. "I would not be averse to your staying on here," he continued, "with certain stipulations, of course."

The prospect of remaining had begun to sound inviting, but now she cast him a wary glance. "What sort of stipulations?"

Stefan inhaled deeply of the cold late-afternoon air, taking a few leisurely steps toward the opened doors at the end of the stable. He stared out for a moment, then turned slowly back toward Marla. Once again he was provoking her impatience by purposefully keeping her in suspense.

"In lieu of monetary payment for the lease of the property—both the house and the stable—I would be willing to accept your services as one of my staff."

Marla's spine straightened automatically, her eyes widening slightly as she took a step or two toward him. "I see. In other words, Mr. Gerhardt, what you're saying is that I remain on the property as long as I agree to work for you. Is that correct?" She spoke in an interested straightforward manner, eliciting just the response she would have expected from the man.

"Yes," he answered, obviously pleased with her apparent interest. "From what I have observed you are well acquainted with training young horses. I should think your American techniques could adapt quite well to the young Trakehners I'll be showing and selling.''

Inwardly Marla scoffed at his outrageously prejudiced attitude toward American equestrianism, but she quelled the biting reply she longed to hurl at him in favor of carrying this preposterous proposal a little further. Inclining her head to one side, she raised one eyebrow and commented, ''Mmm-hmm. And I would be allowed to keep my horses here?''

''Yes, of course.''

''But a good deal of my time would be taken up working for you, right?''

Stefan shrugged. ''Naturally. Your free time would of course be yours to use as you see fit.''

Marla paused in pretended thoughtfulness for a moment, looking down as she absently kicked a piece of hay with the toe of one jodhpured foot. What was it about a man, she silently fumed, that made him think every woman was waiting for his direly needed protection and advice? Mr. Gerhardt had already doled out his share of the latter, and now—unbelievably—he was attempting to offer the former. It was almost hilarious, she railed. She'd never met the man before in her life. Yet his character was as obvious to her as the sight of the sun now sinking below the western horizon.

Slowly she lifted her cool blue eyes to meet

the dark brown gaze studying her so expectantly. Her answer was delivered with careful politeness, though her disdainful expression betrayed
her true feelings.

"I appreciate your offer, Mr. Gerhardt, but
I'm afraid I'm not interested. I simply have no
desire—no need—to work for anyone other
than myself. If the conditions of your lease demand that I work for my board, then I will
simply have to look elsewhere."

As she spoke, Marla noticed the unmistak-
ably self-assured expression dissolve from his
handsome face. Her attention was diverted,
however, when Morris walked back into the
stable, leading a much healthier looking
Badger.

"Excuse me," Morris called out, "but I
thought it might be a good idea to turn out In-
trepid with Badger. She hasn't been out all day
and she could keep him company."

Marla nodded. "All right. Just a minute,
Morris. I'll be right there "

Lifting the cleaned bridle from the hook, she
slung it over one shoulder and walked toward
the tack room, stopping for a moment as she
passed Stefan. "I'll let you know as soon as I
find another place." She hesitated, smiling
tightly as she added, "It won't be long, I assure
you."

Stefan searched the lovely face for a long moment, as if wondering how in the world he had so completely misread her. "Are you sure about this? There's no need to make up your mind so hastily. I can wait if you'd like to reconsider."

Blue fire flashed from the ultramarine depths of her eyes, exposing a degree of willfulness he had never before observed in a woman. Marla's response was equally unyielding.

"There *won't* be a change in my answer, Mr. Gerhardt. I'm not interested—period. Now if you'll excuse me, I have work to do."

CHAPTER THREE

THE PIPES SANG LOUDLY as Marla turned on the taps in the bathtub. She was more than ready for a good long soak and didn't care one iota if she used up every drop of hot water in the process of filling the oversize, claw-footed tub.

The day had been long and strenuous and more than a little disappointing. Neither Gambler nor any of her other horses had proved satisfactory to Emilia Longworth, with whom Marla had spent the majority of the day either demonstrating or helping the young girl adjust to the idiosyncrasies of each horse. Emilia, whether from nervousness or simple inexperience, had somehow managed to make every one of the talented Thoroughbreds confused and totally uncooperative.

Releasing a weary exasperated sigh, Marla shrugged out of her sweater and tossed it on the bed, shivering slightly from the lingering chill of the air. After crossing the room to the wall radiator to turn it up, she went back to the bed, plopped down on the end of it, unzipped her jeans and slid them off each slender, well-toned leg, finally removing the knee-high socks underneath.

Mechanically she reached up and began to unfasten the dark blond braid that reached to just below her shoulder blades. Running her tapered fingers through the thick mane, she fell back across the patchwork-quilt-covered bed, crossing one arm over her eyes as she gave in to the demands of her overworked body. The running bathwater had a lulling effect, but Marla had no fear she would fall asleep before it overflowed. While her body begged for respite, her brain reacted in opposition, keeping her nerves taut, sharply reminding her that the day's disappointment paled in comparison to the demands of what lay ahead.

Marla pressed her rose pink lips tightly together, the muscles in her jaw working in a way reminiscent of someone else...whose face suddenly loomed across the darkened screen of her closed eyes. *Him,* the umbrageous thought assailed her. Stefan Gerhardt was the cause of this untimely upheaval in her life. Of course she had meant every word she'd said yesterday about finding a new place for herself and her horses, but she'd be nothing short of a fool to believe it would prove an easy task. She had lucked into Morning Meadows. To locate another, even remotely similar place would take more than a large amount of luck; it would require a miracle.

"Damn!" Marla muttered, pushing herself up on her elbows and staring unseeingly straight ahead. She would have to start making a few telephone calls—and soon.

One look at the steaming bath was enough for her to set her priorities straight, though. Bending over, she swept her long hair into a knot on top of her head, discarded panties and bra and slipped into the water, the drastic change of temperature raising goose bumps from head to toe. The porcelain tub was so deep that, unlike its modern counterparts, it completely concealed her body, until the only part of her still visible was her head, with its golden topknot.

She closed her eyes, and the whirl of agitating thoughts began to evaporate, her body becoming heavier and heavier as slowly her taut muscles relaxed, releasing a tension that was as much emotional as physical. With each breath Marla began to lose herself to the hypnotic effects of the soothing bath, her mind drifting into a state of half awareness akin to that of the last few minutes before awakening. She was conscious only of her own breathing, of the water lapping gently just below her neck.

The sound of a fist against wood made no impression on her; the subsequent creaking of floorboards evoked no response....

STEFAN SHIFTED THE MERCEDES into park and glanced at his watch. Surely she should be back by now. The stable had appeared closed up for the night when he'd driven past earlier, and he'd assumed she'd gone back to the house. The light was on in two rooms of the small, wood-frame cottage, he noticed as he opened the door and stepped out of the car. He pulled up the lapel of his jacket as the gusty, cold evening air assailed him from every direction, playing havoc with his hair, blowing it haphazardly across his forehead. Keeping his head down, chin tucked into the front of his down-filled, navy-and-beige parka, he took long rapid strides to the front of the house. He mounted the steps to the tiny porch and withdrew his fisted hand from his pocket, poising it just over the outer screen door. Hesitating, he peered inside the glass insets of the heavier inner door. The living room looked empty, and Stefan frowned as the thought crossed his mind that perhaps she was not alone. Perhaps he should have called first. He narrowed his dark eyes for a moment, mulling over this possibility. The only other light came from the corner window of the house—undoubtedly a bedroom. A curious sensation gripped Stefan at the unbidden picture of her in there with someone— Ridiculous, he chided himself, lowering his clenched hand to his side, absently rubbing his knuckles against his corded navy slacks.

But then, he'd been ridiculous ever since he'd first laid eyes on the woman. Strange and disturbing, he reflected, that after a lifetime of developing expertise in fending off overardent females who, given the opportunity, would have made immediate and all-consuming demands on his attention he now found himself in quite the opposite position. His captivation with this bewitchingly attractive woman was rapidly reaching uncontrollable proportions. To say he'd been jolted by her immediate fiery rejection of his offer yesterday would be a ludicrous understatement. In all his thirty-eight years he'd rarely been refused by a female. . . for anything. Of course, any European with a cosmopolitan outlook was well aware of the distinction between American women and their continental contemporaries. Indeed, he'd come up against more of them than he'd cared to in his years of residing in the States—relationships that tended to be conducted, due to family business in Germany, on a part-time basis. Yet Marla Faraday was clearly different, altogether intriguing. . . .

The last thought was enough to sharpen his resolution, and without further consideration he landed three sharp raps on the loosened screen door. Pulling it open, he knocked against the inner wooden door and, after waiting several seconds, again on one of the glass window-panes. Still no response. Frowning, Stefan waited, listening for a responsive sound from within. He lowered his hand to the knob of the door, pondering how many more times he should knock before giving up. Perhaps she *was* with someone. The frown deepened just as a sudden vicious gust of wind blasted from behind, the impact pushing him forward. At once the door opened, the chilling wind pulling it out of his grasp and slamming it with a muffled thud against the rubber doorstop.

Stefan stepped into the tiny, softly lit living room, curious to know why Marla had left the door unlocked. His gaze swept the room, taking in the modest furnishings, the general air of neatness and cleanliness.

The thick worn carpet muffled the sound of his heavy steps, but the straining wooden floor beneath loudly announced his presence. Surely that would get her attention.

"Hello?" he called out, still shivering from the cold and rubbing his hands together briskly. The house was none too warm, he noted wryly.

His eyes came to rest on the small fireplace situated in the middle of the outer wall of the room. From the looks of it it had seen only occasional, if indeed any use at all. Casually bending over to pick up the lone periodical lying on top of the low pecan coffee table, he flipped through it absently for a moment, then set it back down. What in the world was she doing back there? His bronzed forehead creased contemplatively; by now it was apparent that she simply hadn't heard him. But why had the door been left open? The question nagged at him. Living in the country was certainly no guarantee against intruders, and from what Stefan had observed Miss Faraday was not what one would judge the careless type.

The possibility of foul play suddenly loomed ominously before him, mobilizing him. He strode quickly through the living room, across the empty dining room and into the kitchen. Unlit and empty.

"Miss Faraday?" he called out. Surely the sound of his footsteps alone would be enough to alert anyone to his presence. Covering the distance down the hallway in a few strides, Stefan entered the bedroom, glanced around the sparsely though tastefully decorated room and noticed the discarded clothes lying on top of the somewhat rumpled bedspread

A partially opened door to his right caught his attention and he moved toward it, pushing it back with one hand while bracing himself against the door frame. He had only a glimpse of the wispy golden hair rising above the edge of the tub before Marla's shriek pierced the air.

Water splashed over the sides of the tub as her toes pushed against the far end. The sound of the door creaking open had finally jolted her from the semitrancelike state she had lapsed into. Both arms came up to shield herself, her blue eyes widened in genuine terror as she gazed disbelievingly at the man peering around the door. Her scream had been instinctive but foreign sounding, as if it came from someone else. It was a brief cry, though, aborted as she suddenly realized who the man was.

"It's okay. It's me," Stefan said, rapidly stepping back and closing the door. "Stefan Gerhardt."

Marla could hardly find her tongue, quivering as she was with a mixture of rage and relief at the sound of his voice. "My God...." Her own voice quavered, her eyes closing tightly as she came to a sitting position in the tub. She seriously doubted her legs would be strong enough to support her at the moment. "What in the world are you *doing* here?"

"Please... forgive me. I knocked several

times and called out, but you didn't answer. Your front door was open, and I honestly thought something was wrong.'' The apology sounded feeble to his own ears. He'd never felt more like an ass. He'd completely terrified the woman.

'Well, as you can see, *nothing* is wrong,'' came the stinging retort. Drawing in a composing breath, Marla stood up, reached for a thick oversize bathtowel and wrapped it around her as she stepped onto the oval bath mat. ''God,'' she muttered to herself, glistening locks escaping the topknot and tumbling down against her neck as she shook her head. ''I can't believe this.'' In a more distinct tone she added, ''I'll be out in a minute. Do you think you would mind waiting for me in the living room?''

''Of course, Stefan replied, raking a hand through his windblown hair and retreating from the bedroom

SEVERAL MINUTES LATER he glanced up from where he sat on the beige-and-brown, corduroy-covered sofa. He'd picked up the equine journal once more and was slowly scanning its contents. Marla's appearance in the doorway was like a physical assault, the knot in his stomach seeming to tighten into a burning constriction as he stared mutely at her.

Hands on both hips of the wine-colored velour robe she was wearing, Marla glared back at the handsome man sitting so casually on her sofa. Lord, she thought disgustedly, she'd assumed he would give her more time than this to leave. She stepped into the room, unaware of the fetching picture she presented. She'd hastily thrown on what she would have normally been wearing at this time of the evening, still too shaken by Stefan's unexpected appearance to think of dressing in anything more appropriate.

The softly burning lamp shed a candlelike glow around the room, its amber rays tinting her complexion, accentuating the gold-tipped locks of hair that fell around her shoulders in disarray. The lapel of her robe dipped suggestively, hinting at the creamy rounded breasts that swelled beneath. The plush material was belted snugly at her tapered waist, then flowed in gentle folds down the curving line of her hips, lightly defining supple lissome thighs before it fell away to brush the floor.

Stefan absently reached out to set the magazine back on the coffee table, his eyes seemingly glued to her.

Crossing her arms over her chest, Marla cocked her head to one side as she stared disdainfully at him.

"I must say, Mr. Gerhardt, you must have

certainly enjoyed Halloween when you were a child.''

Lifting a questioning eyebrow, he replied, ''I'm afraid you're completely wrong about that, Miss Faraday. Germans don't celebrate such an occasion, and I fail to see the point if it was so.''

''The point,'' Marla replied smartly, blue sparks flashing in a now familiar way, ''is that you seem to take an inordinate amount of pleasure in scaring the living daylights out of people—which you have managed to accomplish rather well tonight.''

Rolling his tongue along the inside of one cheek, Stefan appeared to mull this over for a moment. ''Believe me, Miss Faraday,'' he said finally, his gaze reflecting the sincerity of his tone, ''I had no intention of alarming you. I knocked several times, even called out your name, but you didn't answer. Your door was open, and after several minutes I started to think that something might be wrong. I had no intention of walking in on you that way, and I do apologize for frightening you.''

Marla couldn't help but be impressed by the earnestness of his words and tone. Her shoulders lost some of their tension as her gaze shifted to the front door. ''I thought I locked it when I . . . .'' She frowned, obviously perplexed, then turned back to him. "But why are you here, Mr. Gerhardt?" she asked bluntly.

Placing one arm along the back of the sofa, Stefan crossed one ankle over the knee of the other leg. A provocative posture, and Marla felt irritation rise within her at her own response to it. He seemed so at ease, so at home here in the middle of her living room. But, then, it really wasn't her living room, was it? Her irritation grew as she sat down on the edge of the recliner opposite the sofa, trying against all odds to regard the man as casually as he did her.

"I've done some thinking since our conversation yesterday," he was saying, "and I've decided to allow a continuation of the lease you have here—on your terms."

Momentarily taken aback by the unexpected offer, Marla could only murmur, "You have?"

His mouth widened in amused pleasure at her nonplussed response. "That's right," he answered.

"But why?" She was wary now. "What made you change your mind?"

He shrugged, lifting his hand from the back of the sofa. "I have no real need for this part of the property—not yet at least. I see no reason to let it go idle, and since you're not exactly eager to accept the position I offered, I thought it would be more profitable to simply continue

leasing it—at the same rate you're paying now,"
he added generously.

Marla's frown deepened as she shook her
tawny head slowly from side to side in consternation. She would have never thought.... The
news seemed too good to be true, but then she
knew enough not to look a gift horse in the
mouth, as the saying went. Elation and relief,
especially after such a disheartening day, flooded through her.

"You seem really surprised," Stefan said, his
firm mouth softening still further.

"I am," Marla answered truthfully, smiling
weakly herself. She shrugged bemusedly. "I
guess I didn't expect you to change your mind.
Especially so quickly."

"Then you accept the offer?"

"Yes, of course," Marla answered. "It...it
will definitely make a lot of things a good deal
simpler for me."

"Good." His penetrating gaze seemed to take
in every inch of her face and hair—a close,
almost intimate appraisal that was powerfully
disturbing. Abruptly he brought both hands
down to slap his thighs.

"So," he said, raising himself from the couch
with a pantherish litheness and grace. He began
to fasten the snaps of his parka. "I guess that
settles it, then. I'll have a lease drawn up within

the week. If you like, we can make it for an extended period of time instead of the month-to-month agreement you've had. Six months, a year—whatever you prefer.''

Marla nodded and stammered her answer. "Y-yes, that will be fine." Somehow she hadn't expected him to leave so soon, and she found herself searching for a reason—anything—to keep him there awhile longer. There was no justifying this unexpected desire, but she was helpless to stem it.

Stefan took a step toward the door, prompting Marla to stand. "Mr. Gerhardt...."

He turned. "Please, I would prefer you call me by my given name—Stefan. Since we're to be neighbors now, I see no reason why we can't be on less formal terms.'

"Well, all right, then," Marla agreed, abruptly crossing her arms and rubbing them briskly. "Brrr, it's a little chilly in here. I'll have to turn up the heat.... Listen, can I offer you a drink before you leave?''

"I appreciate the offer, thank you, but I have an appointment in a few minutes." He smiled, straight white teeth adding a new dimension of handsomeness to his rugged features. "But thanks just the same.''

He walked the few steps to the front door, put his hand on the knob and looked back, his gaze wandering around the room, then settling on Marla's slender figure a few feet away.

"How long have you lived here...alone?" he suddenly asked.

Her sea-blue eyes widened in surprise at the question, and she wrinkled her brow. "For as long as I've leased the property. Just over a year. Why do you ask?"

Rubbing his palm along his rigid jawline in a contemplative gesture, Stefan sighed, his ebony eyes lambent and somehow whimsical. "I don't know," he ventured quietly. "It just seems hard to believe you actually live here alone." He half laughed. "Somehow I just can't help thinking that several towheaded toddlers hanging on to your skirts would be a more fitting picture."

Marla's hands gripped the flesh of her upper arms reflexively, her posture stiffening with unwonted resentment. Bristling inwardly, she managed a forced smile, her tone devoid now of its former warmth.

"Contrary to what you may think, Mr. Gerhardt," she said, reverting to the more formal mode of address, "not all women are cut out for a career in raising a pack of screaming little monsters."

Stefan chuckled, entirely missing the conviction in her words. "True, true," he agreed, appraising her knowingly. "I would imagine, though, that you could handle the task quite well.''

Marla gritted her teeth in silent reproach as he opened the door, allowing the stiff blustery winds to whip into the unheated room. Shoving his hands into the pockets of his parka, Stefan stepped quickly onto the outside landing, turning back once more. ''Good night—'' he smiled winningly ''—and don't forget to lock the door this time.''

Marla's eyes narrowed almost imperceptibly, her lips compressed into a mechanical smile as she shut the door behind him, applying a bit more pressure than the action required. Clicking the dead bolt into place, she stood beside the door for a moment, castigating herself for allowing his chauvinistic comment to get to her in such a way. Of what possible consequence was his opinion of her personal life anyway?

None, Marla told herself firmly. None whatsoever.

CHAPTER FOUR

THE SCREEN DOOR SLAMMED SHUT as Marla stepped onto the back porch, her appearance eliciting an immediate response from Nik. Awkwardly he heaved himself up on all four huge feet and lunged playfully at her, yapping and crying simultaneously. Marla grinned at the picture he presented—not at all her staunch protector, the fierce German shepherd whose mere presence should effectively discourage any would-be intruders. Not yet at least. In time.

"Good morning, Nikiroo," she cooed in a singsong tone.

She set about filling his plastic bowl with a generous portion of puppy chow, adding a tablespoonful of cottage cheese—Nik's favorite. Shaking her head, she chuckled lightly as she mumbled affectionately to the puppy, knowing he wouldn't eat a bite until she left him alone again. Once he was a little older she planned to put him through at least basic obedience training and then let him have the run of the place. But for now she felt it best that he grow up right here on her back porch—his and her own territory—for which he would develop a natural protectiveness.

Inside the kitchen she cast a glance at the wall clock and decided she had enough time this morning to sit down and enjoy her breakfast. She was expecting another potential customer shortly before noon, a Mr. Jerald Rastbend. He'd been referred to her by a trainer on the summer show circuit who'd taken note of her performances in the pregreen hunter division. Hopefully Mr. Rastbend would get along with at least one of her horses—unlike Emilia Longworth. Although she had a special affection for each of her animals, she couldn't deny that the money from a sale would come in handy. Especially now, just before the winter months, it would be beneficial to have one less mouth to feed.

As she moved around the kitchen, preparing her usual morning meal, she acknowledged that the necessity of exercising such prudence with her small, moderately successful horse operation was particularly irksome in light of what was occurring elsewhere on Morning Meadows. For the past two weeks she had striven to ignore the flurry of activity at her landlord's place, but it was impossible to ignore the fact that Stefan Gerhardt was establishing his Trakehner breeding farm with none of the limits she imposed on herself.

From what she had observed so far, Marla assumed that most if not all his horses had arrived. Broodmares grazed on the slopes of all three pastures, and the turnout paddocks were almost always occupied by the young two- and three-year-olds. Despite her animosity toward the man, Marla's curiosity was aroused by the sight of the gorgeous graceful animals. On more than one occasion she had been tempted to cruise down the gravel road that skirted closer to the hubbub, but a sense of caution and a fair degree of shyness had circumvented the impulse.

Instead she had focused on her own business, marshaling every last reserve of strength to obtain as much benefit as possible from the rapidly diminishing fair days of autumn.

Once winter began in earnest she would have to lay off training for a while. At the moment the young geldings and mares she'd shown all last summer and into early fall were at peak fitness.

As Marla stepped out the front door of the cottage, she glimpsed Morris's ancient battered Chevy pickup, parked on the far side of the stable. How fortunate she was to have acquired his services, she thought for the umpteenth time. Others in Keswick's horse community hired him on a part-time basis, but he did spend a good deal of his time working for her, and she found it difficult to speculate on how well her operation would run without him.

"Good morning, Morris," she called out as she walked into the barn, her presence eliciting a neigh from one of the horses. Smiling, she stopped in front of Badger's stall, running one slender hand down his face and velvety muzzle in an affectionate greeting.

"Mornin'," Morris rumbled in his deep gravelly voice. He was standing inside Gambler's stall, forking manure into the red wheelbarrow blocking the opened door. He stopped for a moment, resting an elbow on the handle of the pitchfork and wiping his brow with his flannel shirt sleeve.

"You've already grained and hayed?" Marla asked, noting that the horses were munching on the hay from the individual bags in each stall.

"Mmm-hmmm," Morris replied, lifting the pitchfork once more to sift through the shaving-padded stall.

Marla frowned as she placed both hands on her hips. "But you didn't have to do that, Morris," she admonished softly. "Morning feedings are my chore."

"I don't mind doing it if I get here early. And besides, don't you have customers coming today?"

"Yes, but...." Her frown cleared as she realized the fruitlessness of any further argument. When Morris was set on some matter or other, he rarely changed his mind. Inexplicably, he was devoted to the place, had made himself as much a part of the scheme of things as she herself. If he insisted on taking over for her at times, she should thank her lucky stars she had such a kindhearted companionable groom.

"Well, all right," she concluded, smiling as she edged past him to the tack room. She reached for a plain snaffle-bitted bridle for Gambler and a pair of draw reins. It was going to be a long and hopefully successful day, and she'd best get started.

THE DAY PROVED TO BE even more successful than she could have hoped for. Jerald Rastbend not only liked her chestnut four-year-old mare, Whisper, but proceeded to make an offer far above her intended asking price.

In a considerably lighter frame of mind, Marla decided to use the rest of the afternoon after Mr. Rastbend's departure to drive into

Charlottesville. The feed supply was in need of replenishment, and she could also take the opportunity to stop by the tack shop she frequented.

Morris walked with her to the pickup. "You sure you don't want me to make the trip?" he asked.

"No, really, Morris." Marla smiled back at him. "I don't mind, and besides I'm stopping by Susie's on the way back." Susie Johnson, one of her good friends, owned the tack shop, and Marla's visits were as often for social purposes as anything else. Her solitary life was quite acceptable by now, but there were times when a healthy dose of gossip was very much in order. And today seemed perfect for just such an indulgence.

"Well, all right, then," Morris agreed, stepping back as she started the engine, then turning to walk back to the barn.

RAYMOND FULVER'S FEED STORE was doing a record amount of business, Marla discovered as she browsed around the warehouse-size building, waiting her turn behind the other customers putting in their orders for feed and hay. Reaching out, she picked up what appeared to be a new brand of worming medicine, turning over the oblong container to read the list of active ingredients. A deep voice calling her name startled her, and she turned—too quickly, she thought later—to see Stefan Gerhardt standing a few steps behind her.

Swallowing self-consciously, she schooled her features into impassivity with an inordinate degree of effort, camouflaging the volatile reaction the man's mere presence evoked in her.

"Mr. Gerhardt," she said, tilting her head quizzically to one side. What was he doing there, she wondered. Certainly he had enough hands to take care of such mundane matters as purchasing feed for his horses.

"Stefan, please," he said quietly, his dark eyes moving almost imperceptibly down the length of her. Had she not been observing him so closely herself, she might have missed the look altogether But she *had* noticed, and it rankled that he could disturb her so deeply. She was fairly used to appreciative glances from members of the opposite sex, indeed even a certain amount of leering. Why should the briefest flicker in this man's eyes affect her so? Undeniably he was an extremely attractive man, and she was not totally immune to the type....

Her eyes held his evenly. "Stefan," she agreed quietly. She replaced the tube of medication on the shelf, then turned back to him he' braid swinging against her back as she moved. She stood facing him with her hands in the back pockets of her jeans, the cream-and-black parka she wore unzipped halfway to reveal a beige flannel shirt beneath.

"What brings you here?" she asked.

Stefan gestured toward the parking lot in front of the store. "Your truck. I was in town on business and was driving by when I thought I saw you getting out. I came in to see if I was right."

Marla frowned slightly. It seemed more than a little odd that he lived on the same piece of property as she did but only decided to seek her out at the local feed store.

"Why?" she asked bluntly.

Stefan shifted his weight, crossing both arms over his broad chest. What he was wearing was hardly more formal than what she had on, Marla noted. The parka was the same one he'd had on the last time she'd seen him—at her house that windy night a couple of weeks earlier. His jeans were not exactly designer variety. Clean yet well-worn, they had been faded by time and wear to a washed-out blue, and they fit so snugly they drew attention to his narrow hips and long muscular thighs.

He pursed his lips for a moment before answering. "I wanted to check and see if things are going all right for you."

Marla relaxed. "Of course they are," she replied curtly. "Couldn't be better, as a matter of fact. I sold one of my four-year-olds today." Damn, she thought, chastising herself for tacking on that bit of information. He didn't need to know anything about her personal or business life, and her remark had had a decidedly defensive ring to it. Somehow she suspected that that was exactly the position he wanted to put her in.

"Congratulations," he said, his smile confirming all too clearly the condescension in his tone. "I must say, you seem to be doing very well for yourself, in spite of the circumstances."

Marla glared coldly at him, her features tightening as she shot back, "And what does that mean? Circumstances?"

Stefan maintained the same casual posture but cocked his head to the side as the corners of his mouth drooped. "Living alone the way you do, running everything by yourself. It's quite extraordinary, you know."

Marla winced at his patronizing tone. "Actually, it's not that bad once you learn the ropes of the business," she answered lightly, refusing to be baited. Stepping to one side, she peered around him to the front of the store, where Raymond Fulver was ringing up the customer ahead of her.

"Excuse me," she said, producing a plastic smile and a preoccupied expression. "I have to place my order now." She started to walk away then but had progressed only a few steps before she felt long steady fingers on her elbow. Turning, she glanced up at him quizzically. "Yes?"

His look at that moment, mystifying in its intensity, shook her to the core, making her quiver inside. Her sharp intake of breath was noticeable in the slight flaring of her nostrils, and Stefan's eyes, which had been focused on the fullness of her lips, did not miss the telltale physical reaction. His lips parted then in a wide leisurely smile, lending his aristocratic features a disarming sort of appeal.

"There was another reason for my stopping by," he said, his fingers still gripping her arm. "I wanted to ask you a favor."

Surprised, Marla lifted her chin slightly as she said, "Oh?"

"Yes." He released her elbow and shoved both hands into the pockets of his jacket. "I wondered if perhaps you might have the time to come by the stable and take a look at one of my four-year-old geldings. Apparently he displays a great deal of jumping ability—at least that's what Roy's been trying to convince me of. Anyway, I'd like a second opinion.''

This, of course, would provide a perfect opportunity for her to satisfy her curiosity about the goings-on up the hill. Tempering her response, she said, ''Who's Roy?''

''My stable manager. Roy Valmire. He also does some training for me.''

''I see.'' She chewed thoughtfully on her lower lip.

''Well?''

Marla lifted her eyes to his. ''When would you like me to come?''

''Whenever is convenient for you. Are you busy the rest of today?''

''I'm stopping by Dover Saddlery after I leave here, but after that I'm pretty much finished for the day.''

''Then why don't you come by when you get back? I should be there in an hour or so, and Roy will be there until around seven.''

Marla wrestled with the request for a moment longer, then answered hesitantly, ''All right, then. I'll be there in about an hour and a half.''

''Good. See you then.''

Marla nodded, then turned and walked toward the front desk to place her order. She inhaled deeply, an unavailing attempt to quell the paroxysm of nervous tension, the strange sort of excitement that suddenly seized her.

THE PICKUP GRADUALLY DECELERATED as Marla turned into the gravel drive leading toward the long, immaculately kept stable. Like her own smaller facility, it was some thirty years old. But every other aspect highlighted the one ingredient necessary to maintain it so admirably: money.

The sturdy, solid-oak exterior was painted a dark nunter green; the trim, windows and shutters around each outer stall door a light gray. Marla stepped out of the truck and slammed the door shut, her gaze scanning the rolling vista of hunt fields, paddocks and pastures occupied by the gorgeous Trakehner horses she'd so far watched only from a distance.

Voices rang out from the interior of the stable, but as she moved inside she could see no one. Strolling slowly down the wide center aisleway, she stopped beside the doors of each occupied stall. Marla, who had spent the major portion of her career working with American Thoroughbreds, was truly impressed with the East Prussian breed. Her attention was caught for a moment as she studied a handsome, dark brown gelding. Like his stall mates, his hindquarters were relatively flat in comparison to the sloping angle of Thoroughbreds, his tail placed somewhat higher and the crest of his neck nearer the poll. Suddenly her perusal was interrupted by the staccato clopping of hooves, signaling someone entering from the opposite end of the long barn.

She looked around to see a sandy-haired young man leading a horse to the washstand in the center of the barn. He had noticed her, also, and as he fastened the crossties to the horse's halter, he called out, "Hello, there. Be with you in a minute."

Marla walked toward him and the horse, waiting as he hosed down the dirt-covered hooves. The animal was a magnificent specimen, and her expression revealed her sincere admiration.

"He's a looker, isn't he?" the young man said, his tone friendly and open. This close up Marla judged him to be about her own age, and although not what one would term handsome, he did possess a certain all-American attractiveness. His sandy brown hair was trimmed neatly just below the ears, and the jeans and pullover he wore accentuated his lean build. The beige leather leggings hugging his calves were worn down to a slick brown shade.

"Yes, he is," Marla agreed. She stood with her hands in her jacket pockets as her gaze moved appreciatively over the chestnut gelding's classic conformation.

Finished with the chore, the man turned off the water and looped the end of the hose onto its metal holding stand. He wiped his hands briskly on a towel and stepped away from the concrete washstand, extending his hand to Marla.

"I'm Roy Valmire," he introduced himself, smiling as she accepted his handshake. "You must be Marla Faraday." At her nod he continued, "Stefan told me you would be coming by this afternoon to have a look at Rudi here. He said to tell you he'll be a little late. He's tied up in his office for a while."

"That's all right," Marla said, moving aside as she watched Roy curry and brush the chestnut, his movements practiced and efficient. Instinctively she decided she liked him.

Roy was neither shy nor affected, and his relaxed manner set her at ease immediately. He spoke with a distinct upper New York accent, and she remarked indirectly on it.

"How long have you lived in Virginia, Roy?"

Chuckling, he picked up a well-shod hoof and scraped out the depression in the sole with a steel hoof pick. "Guess I'll never be mistaken for a native, will I?"

Marla smiled. "No, I don't think so."

"I'm from Albany originally, although I've

lived in several other cities in New York throughout my life. I've been here for as long as Stefan has. How about yourself?''

Marla offered a brief description of her background, and from then on the conversation flowed smoothly and effortlessly. Roy explained how he'd met Stefan the previous year at an international jumping derby and auction in Newport, Rhode Island. He was an accomplished equestrian and exhibitor himself, although an injury to one knee a few years earlier had placed certain limits on his riding and training ability. Stefan had viewed his all-around horse sense with enthusiasm and had snatched him up immediately for the position of manager at Morning Meadows.

''Rudi here has had basic dressage for the past year and a half,'' Roy was explaining as he fitted bridle and saddle on the horse, adjusting the sheepskin saddle pad before tightening the leather girth. ''Stefan really likes the way he jumps, though. He believes that's where his potential lies.''

''Yes, that's what he was telling me.''

''Well, I've been working with him over fences. He's good all right, but we've been having a few problems.'' He turned the horse around and led him into the aisleway. ''You can see for yourself what I mean.'' Marla followed as he walked the horse outside, then stopped to lower the stirrups and swing himself up into the saddle. "I'm gonna walk him over to the hunt course and hack around for a few minutes. Why don't you join me there?"

"All right," Marla agreed, watching from behind as horse and rider clopped away from her. Even at a walking pace she could discern that Rudi had a wealth of potential as a show hunter or jumper. He tracked with a straightness that was fluid and eye-catching, and from any angle his conformation was faultlessly classic.

The afternoon sun was descending rapidly. A chilly breeze had picked up, so Marla pulled her jacket snugly around her neck, flipped up the back collar and shoved her hands inside her pockets. She climbed up onto the top slat of a section of fence bordering one side of the enormous hunt field, hunching her shoulders a bit and positioning her booted feet on the rail below for balance.

Rudi was certainly a very talented horse, she decided, observing as Roy put the Trakehner through his paces. His trot was light on the forehand, his hindquarters well engaged, providing an overall picture of obedience and response to the rider's aids. Transitions into canter, including lead changes—flying ones at that—were automatic and effortless. Marla was impressed—very impressed.

After some twenty minutes of flat work Roy began trotting Rudi over a small crossrail schooling fence. Here Marla's trained eye picked up on the first of the gelding's problems. Even over the simple uncomplicated obstacle the horse had a tendency to overreact, jumping higher than was necessary and leaving the ground from a spot much too far away. He was consistent in doing so; Roy's efforts to hold him back or make him more responsive to his commands were unsuccessful. The problem only became compounded when Roy decided to set up an obstacle consisting of brush box and a small gate.

Frustration was evident in the trainer's face, Marla noted, but it seemed to result from more than just his irritation with the recalcitrant horse. As he slackened the reins after another unsuccessful attempt to get the message across to Rudi, allowing the horse to have his head as he put him into a walk, Marla saw Roy grimace with pain.

A few minutes later Roy brought the horse to a halt in front of her and dismounted, his sudden wince confirming her suspicions. Marla frowned as she watched him toss the reins back over Rudi's head and stride toward her with a discernible limp. "Roy, are you okay?" she asked.

"Damned knee," he muttered, shaking his head impatiently. "It gets to acting up like this at times—usually when I'm jumping." Heaving a resigned sigh, he changed the subject. "But do you see what I mean about Rudi?"

"He's loaded with talent—that's for sure," Marla said enthusiastically, patting the gelding's sleek neck. "Do you mind if I try him out?" The words just popped out of her mouth, but any chagrin or embarrassment she might have felt at being too forward was quickly put to rest as Roy responded eagerly, "Sure, go ahead."

He handed the reins over to her, and she walked the gelding around in a circle, then threw the reins back up over his head and lowered the stirrups once more. Swinging up into the flat English saddle as Roy kept Rudi still, she then adjusted the length of each stirrup. Satisfied, she slid the reins through her fingers and started the horse off at a walk, letting him get the feel of her weight and legs. After a minute or two she cued him into a trot, immediately realizing that the fluidity of the horse's gait was as impressive in the saddle as it had been from an observer's perspective.

Marla continued to work Rudi on the flat,

assessing the length of his stride in the canter. His stride was long, covering perhaps fourteen or fifteen feet of ground instead of the average twelve. That could easily be part of Roy's problem in getting the horse to the correct takeoff point. As she began trotting over the crossrails, Rudi insisted on jumping from an unnecessarily long spot, expending enough energy to clear a three-foot vertical instead of the two-foot-high obstacle he was presented with. The same thing occurred over the other, slightly higher fences. But Marla didn't attempt to correct the horse. She let him choose his own—albeit slightly off—jumping point, giving him the opportunity to discover the miscalculation for himself.

Rudi had a long way to go, but she liked what she felt over the fence. Knees tucked up high and square, head and neck arched beautifully, he exhibited flawless form and an eagerness and willingness to jump that was priceless. To Marla's mind, the horse was every inch an athlete. With work and polish there was every reason to believe Rudi would make one fabulous show horse.

Her concentration, as always when she was riding, was so complete she was unaware of another person joining Roy as he watched. Only slightly winded by the exertion, she turned

Rudi toward Roy and was startled to see Stefan standing there beside him. A sense of déjà vu crept over her, and she wondered why she felt she had experienced this same thing, or a version of it, before. Then she remembered—she had. The first time she'd met Stefan she'd been schooling Gambler. And now, as then, some chord within her was struck by the man's powerful physical presence.

As she walked the horse toward the two waiting men, she was acutely aware of blushing under Stefan's unwavering gaze. She was grateful for Roy's presence.

"So how did you like him?" Stefan asked her, stepping forward to grasp the reins as she dismounted and handed them to him. The scent of his cologne wafted across the small space between them, its musky odor heady and definitely disturbing.

"He's quite talented," Marla answered, reaching up to pull the collar of her jacket back up. Her braid had slipped out, and she pushed it back inside. "He could use a lot of work, but I'm sure he'd be a quick study."

"What kind of talent?" Stefan asked, handing Roy the reins. "Roy, do you mind taking him back over? We'll follow."

"Sure," Roy replied, adding, "You looked really good on him, Marl "

Marla smiled but answered modestly, "I'm sure Rudi could make any rider look good."

Roy raised both eyebrows noncommittally, then began walking the slightly panting horse ahead of them. "Well, see you back at the barn."

"So," Stefan repeated as he and Marla followed at a much slower pace. "What sort of things were you speaking of in regard to training Rudi?"

"Oh, plenty of things—exercises that will help a young green horse learn what he's supposed to do, how to use himself better and become a little scopier when it comes to approaching individual jumps."

Marla gestured with one hand as she warmed to her subject, momentarily forgetting her nervousness with Stefan. "I would start out with cavelleties, of course, then move on to gymnastic exercises to help his balance. And flat work, naturally—lots and lots of that. Most good jumpers are—"

"Marla."

Stefan had stopped, and Marla halted a few steps ahead of him and turned back. Her eyes widened with curiosity as she asked, "Yes?"

"I apologize for not having met you when you arrived. I had unexpected business to attend to."

Marla frowned slightly. "Yes, I know. Roy explained."

"I would like to make up for my rudeness," Stefan said, one corner of his mouth lifting into a charming grin. "I would like to take you out to supper tonight."

"But really, it's not necessary." Marla felt the warmth in her neck spreading upward and was even more embarrassed by the telltale physical reaction.

"And I would like to discuss further your suggestions concerning Rudi," Stefan added. He glanced pointedly at his watch. "It's almost five o'clock, and I have several things to attend to yet. I could pick you up at seven."

Marla compressed her lips and studied the ground at her feet. Glancing back up, she released a small sigh. Still she hesitated as she mulled over the situation. She was impressed by Stefan's apparent sincerity. He really did want to know more about her thoughts on Rudi, and she would be lying if she denied that she was captivated by the gorgeous animal. Quite frankly, she had never been fortunate enough to try out such an athletic, talented horse. What an irreparable shame if he and Roy continued getting nowhere with their current useless techniques.

She shrugged and smiled slightly. "All right, then. Seven it is."

"Good," Stefan said, grinning confidently as he resumed walking beside her to the stable.

They conversed about inconsequential matters on the way, but Marla's mind was preoccupied with her own dawning realization of the far more compelling reason for her acceptance of Stefan's dinner invitation—a reason that had nothing at all to do with a discussion of various training techniques. . .and everything in the world to do with the man himself.

CHAPTER FIVE

THE PARKING LOT of the Boar's Head Inn was filled to capacity, as was typical for practically any night of the week at the popular Charlottesville hotel and restaurant. Stefan avoided the problem of limited parking by passing through the circular drive fronting the entrance, getting out and handing over the keys to the attendant. Then he came around to Marla's side of the car and held the door open while she stepped out.

Marla had been here previously, though usually with a group of friends, contemporaries in the horse world. Such occasions had been fun and relaxing, the atmosphere and charm of the rustic historical setting barely noticed amid nonstop banter and general camaraderie. Tonight, however, was an entirely different situation. Marla's stomach was tied up in anxious knots, the sensation not entirely caused by the hunger pains she'd managed to ignore for most of the day.

She felt ridiculous, like some silly schoolgirl

on her first date. She reflected with chagrin on how she'd fiddled around in her closet, unable to decide what to wear—something she hadn't done for literally years. Opportunities for dressing up were few and far between; Marla's demanding schedule didn't allow for it. But there was no harm in it, and besides, what difference did it make if she devoted a little time and energy to her appearance for once? Her analysis of her own rather uncharacteristic behavior stopped just short of examining the real reason for it.

Stefan held open one of the heavy oak doors, and she preceded him inside. The plushly furnished lobby, which before had merely suggested a certain friendly warmth, now seemed to exude a more potent atmosphere, one of unmistakable intimacy. As the two of them waited behind a partition of blue velvet rope that separated the lobby from the dining areas, Marla looked around the foyer as if seeing it for the first time. Various sketches of hunt scenes graced the timeworn walnut paneling, which, in combination with the thick gray blue carpeting, reduced the murmur of voices and the tinkling sounds of sterling flatware against fine china to a respectable hush.

"Mr. Gerhardt?" Stefan nodded as the maître d' spoke his name. The stately, silver-haired man detached the rope to allow them to pass through, Stefan cupping Marla's elbow in the palm of his hand. It was a simple un- affected gesture, carried out with finesse and a certain old-world charm. In some ways Stefan was delightfully correct, but under the cir- cumstances Marla's reaction to the gesture definitely wasn't. Despite the thick cashmere of her cowl-necked sweater, she felt as if Stefan's fingers were burning through to the flesh beneath. She had never experienced such a sen- sation before. It was strangely thrilling, totally mystifying.

Fortunately he dropped his hand as he waited while she took the seat the maître d' indicated. He seated himself then, and both accepted the menus and wine lists. Grateful for the diversion, Marla began studying the menu immediately, hiding her nervousness behind it and the idle discussion that ensued. Stefan ordered Riesling that he declared was of a particularly worthy vintage. They were silent for a few minutes as they read over the delectable choice of entrées.

"So...now," he said after giving their orders to the waitress dressed in Colonial costume, "I'm very much interested to hear what you have in mind for Rudi."

Marla picked up her wineglass, brought it to her lips and sipped, then set it carefully back down. Stefan definitely knew his wines; it was excellent.

"All right," she said, thankful he'd opened the conversation with the one subject with which she felt truly at ease. "First of all I'd like to ask you a question or two."

One dark eyebrow raised inquisitively, Stefan gave a barely perceptible nod.

"I'd like to know what exactly you have in mind for Rudi. I mean, how far do you intend to develop his jumping ability? That's a very important consideration, you know."

"Yes, I know. One reason I wanted to get your opinion was that I was concerned that perhaps I was making more of his ability than is actually there."

Marla shook her head and smiled softly. "Oh, no. You were perfectly correct in your estimation. Just from observing him today, I would have said his talent is very apparent. And after riding him myself, I'm convinced. I can't be positive at this point, of course, but my feeling is that he could go preliminary jumper, say, by next summer. But I don't know...." Her voice trailed off, and absently she pinched at the edge of the white linen tablecloth.

"What is it you don't know?" Stefan prompted, his attention equally divided between the subject of Rudi's athletic potential and the softly tantalizing appeal of the woman sitting across from him. Her hair shone, the silvery gold streaks highlighted by the single burning candle at their table, her tanned complexion as warm and mellow as butter...or honey....

"Well," Marla continued, lifting her pre-occupied blue gaze to his expectant one, "Rudi is just such an excellent mover. He carries himself naturally, the way most horses take years of constant training to achieve. My hunch is that he would make a fantastic show hunter—with the appropriate amount of work and attention, of course." She hesitated, then tilted her head to one side. "I must tell you, Stefan, I was *very* impressed with Rudi. My knowledge of Trakehners is limited, to say the least. I had no idea they had such tremendous show potential."

Stefan grinned slowly and raised his glass to sip at his wine. "Ah, yes. Then you are quite uneducated when it comes to the Trakehner."

Marla lifted one shoulder in a shrug and smiled self-deprecatingly. "I can't deny that." She hesitated, then asked, "How did you become so interested in the breed, Stefan? Did you have them in Germany?"

Stefan shook his head. "I never owned any of them, if that's what you mean. But yes, my interest in the Trakehner did originate there. I suppose I've always been fascinated to some degree by the animal. They have quite an interesting background, you know.''

"I do know they were originally bred in East Prussia,'' Marla said, "but I'm afraid that's about as far as my knowledge extends.''

Marla listened intently as Stefan imparted general information about the history of the German warmblood, inserting a question herself now and then on a point that particularly caught her interest.

"And so you think Rudi will need a great deal of work,'' Stefan commented, reverting to the original discussion.

"Oh, yes,'' Marla acknowledged emphatically.

"Such as?''

Marla launched immediately into detail on her earlier suggestions for proper training and schooling techniques, her animated features and enthusiastic tone evidence enough that she was in her element. Stefan listened raptly to what she had to say. Being a horseman himself, he was not unacquainted with what she was referring to, but he readily admitted to himself that Marla's knowledge exceeded his own when it came to the best methods to be used in the training of young inexperienced horses. And he had already seen for himself a demonstration of that knowledge.

At length Marla finished her discourse. Stefan nodded, his lips pursed in silent contemplation for a few moments. He looked up suddenly, about to speak, but just then their meal arrived, and their attention was diverted for the time being. They chatted lightly throughout, and Marla now began to actually enjoy being with the man. Her initial tension was still there, but she found it a good deal easier to cope with in light of the interesting conversation, not all of it having to do with horses.

Little by little Stefan drew out of her details of her past, and she found herself discussing her background in an easy uninhibited fashion. Stefan was more reserved about himself, however, although Marla's curiosity was appeased to a certain degree.

Obviously reticent to disclose any information concerning his personal life, he did make it clear at one point that he had never been married. This was definitely food for thought, from Marla's point of view. It seemed unlikely that a man with such eligible qualities had escaped the skillful snare of some willful enamored female.

Stefan's parents still resided on the outskirts of Würzburg, a Bavarian university town, he told her. But when Marla inquired about other family members, a puzzling closed expression stole over his handsome features for a fleeting moment. His only brother, Rolf, he finally answered, had been killed, along with his wife, in a car accident six years earlier.

Marla was somewhat embarrassed at having provoked him into revealing such an obviously painful part of his past, and an uncomfortable silence ensued for several moments.

Finally Stefan broke it, steering the conversation back to Rudi.

"Marla, I want to ask you something, and I want you to be candid."

Marla's blue eyes registered her surprise, and she raised both eyebrows curiously. "Yes?"

"I want to know what you think of Roy."

Marla smiled then. He'd sounded so serious; she'd expected a more alarming comment.

"What is it exactly that you want to know?"

Stefan lifted his hand from the table and turned it palm outward. "Your impression of him."

"Well...he's really very nice, but I'm sure—"

"That's not what I'm referring to," Stefan interrupted her, tracing an indiscernible pattern along the stem of his wineglass.

"Then...."

"I want your honest opinion of his riding ability."

Marla slanted her eyes away, watching as a party of four was escorted into the dining room. She was trying to think of an appropriate reply.

"What you *really* think," Stefan added somberly.

Marla's gaze shifted back to his. "He rides well."

"But is he a trainer?" Stefan asked uncompromisingly.

Placing her elbow on the table, she ran her knuckles across her chin for a thoughtful moment. "All right, I'll tell you what I think," she said finally, praying that her frankness wouldn't undermine Roy professionally.

"I think he could do more harm than good as far as Rudi's concerned. I'm sure he had the ability to train at one time—perhaps even now. But it's obvious the injury to his knee has messed him up rather badly."

"Hmmm." Stefan scratched his jaw thoughtfully. "I was fairly certain of that myself."

Marla hesitated, then ventured to ask, "Did you hire Roy to train all your horses?"

"I hired him to manage my stable and to work with the horses I intend either to show or sell as show horses."

Marla nodded and looked away again. Stefan peered at her intently. "I think you are right about him and Rudi. He is not doing the horse any good."

Her face brightened somewhat as she turned back to him and suggested enthusiastically, "There are quite a few good trainers around here who would be delighted to work with Rudi. I don't know if you're aware of it or not, but this area is home for some of the most talented equestrians in the United States. Marti Stenback himself lives only a few miles from here, and—"

"I'm not interested in having Marti Stenback train my horse." Stefan's interruption was almost brusque. "I want you to do it."

The proposition was so unexpected Marla was taken off guard. She stared at him, slightly shocked, for several seconds. "But...but Rudi needs someone like Marti, someone who—"

"I've seen what you can do with him," Stefan stated firmly. "He responded very well to you. That is the most important thing, is it not?" His dark liquid eyes insistently held her own. "I'm willing to pay you well for training him."

She was speechless when he named the salary he was prepared to pay. All she could do was blink and swallow deeply. It wasn't the fact that again he was asking her to work for him; this was different, entirely different. In the other arrangement she would have been working for her room and board. Now, however, her services would be those of an independent trainer—the personal trainer of a horse like none other she had ever ridden or worked with in her life. It was a tempting offer...very tempting. Yet still unsure, she hesitated.

The disquieting undercurrents that flowed beneath the surface rapport of their relationship made her wary, undercurrents felt so strongly at times—at least by her—that they were positively frightening. Yet the urge to accept the offer was fast becoming irresistible. Absentmindedly she fiddled with the stem of her coffee spoon.

"Well?" Stefan asked, his tone quietly demanding.

"I...I just don't know," she stalled.

"It would be a shame, don't you agree, for Rudi's talent to go to waste."

Marla glanced up at him shrewdly. The man didn't waste time playing games—that was certain. He had hit home, and very expertly, with that last calculated statement. He recognized the fact that she had been captivated by Rudi, and he had capitalized on her admiration for the horse. If it was true—and she really had no way of knowing for sure—that he would hire no one but her to train the horse, then of course he had hooked her. Marla couldn't abide the thought of such potential being ignored.

"All right, then," she said finally, a strange

fluttering sensation beginning deep inside her chest as she uttered the words. "I'll work with him."

Stefan's eyes held a gleam of triumph, a hint of satisfaction that Marla suspected stemmed from more than simply acquiring the trainer of his choice for his favorite Trakehner. But his elusive reactions were inconsequential anyway. She had made her commitment, and it would stand.

Stefan ordered liqueurs for them both, and they began to discuss the details of the arrangement. Marla was surprised when Stefan said he wanted Rudi to board at her place, but after mulling it over, she realized it was the best thing to do. It would certainly make working with the horse a good deal more convenient for her.

Perhaps the delicious food and drinks had put her in a much mellower frame of mind, but whatever the reason, on the drive back to Keswick, she found she was a good deal more at ease with Stefan. Pulling into the small driveway that led to the back of the house, he slid out from behind the wheel and helped her out of the car. As before, in the restaurant, Stefan cupped her elbow in his hand as he escorted her to the back porch. Nik heard them both and yapped, his high-pitched bark at first a warning, then a greeting as Marla assured him it was only her.

"He thinks he's a guard dog already," Marla commented, laughing lightly.

They were standing at the screen door, and Stefan's expression indicated he did not see any particular humor in her comment.

"You need a grown animal, not a puppy, for a dog to be of any use around here."

His condescending tone irritated her, and she answered defensively, "He won't always be a puppy. I got nim young on purpose, so he would grow up knowing me. That will ensure his protectiveness toward me."

"And what do you do in the meantime?" Stefan's dark gaze surveyed the perimeter of the isolated house, then leveled on her face. She was clearly annoyed. "I find it hard to believe you are not fearful of living alone this way. It is very unusual for a young unmarried woman not to have a family—or someone—to take care of her."

Marla scowled as she answered, "Yes, I believe you've mentioned something like that before. How old-fashioned you are in some ways, Stefan. Actually, I really shouldn't even bother to answer, but since you seem to find my situation so hard to understand, I will. I've been living here—and doing quite well at it—for more than a year now. Difficult as you may find it to believe, which apparently you do, I enjoy living by myself, making it on my own with no help from anyone else. And as for the safety factor, I've never found reason to be afraid, and I doubt I ever will. Keswick is not exactly the crime capital of the country, you know.''

"Crimes can occur anywhere, not just in big cities,'' he countered.

Exasperated, Marla pulled the collar of her coat up around her neck and cheeks. Things had been going so well between them. Why did he have to bring up a subject it was obvious they were never going to agree on? She hated to think the matter would crop up on a regular basis, especially considering the change in status of their relationship. Perhaps if she just ignored it.... "Look, it's getting rather chilly standing here. Thank you, Stefan, for the evening and the job. I—''

His movement was so sudden then, yet so smoothly and efficiently executed, that she never got a chance to finish her sentence. Her lips parted unconsciously as Stefan took a step forward, his body so near her own that the flaps of his open overcoat slapped against her thighs. She caught the blaze in the dark brown depths of his eyes just before his arms came up to rest lightly on her shoulders. She swallowed, her throat feeling raw and parched as he lowered his head, slowly, deliberately.

Her mind screamed a silent protest, but crazily her body didn't heed the warning. The feel of his own body against hers as he held her close within the circle of his arms was magnetizing. Marla realized in a blinding flash that she was powerless to stop what was about to happen, because she didn't want to stop it. . . .

The chill of the autumn night was forgotten as Stefan pulled her even closer, nestling her slender body within the protective cover of his overcoat. His lips brushed softly against her own at first, flesh against flesh joining in tentative exploration. Reason, which made a last-ditch effort to object, was abandoned completely as Marla surrendered to the need this man summoned within her, gave in to the physical attraction she had felt for him from the very first moment she'd seen him.

As their mouths parted, searching tongues seeking the heady depths within, Marla had one fleeting, crystal-clear thought: *just this once. What harm will this one little kiss do just this once?*

It was a simple question, implicitly demanding compliance.

At length Stefan released her, brushing back a stray wisp of her hair before stepping away to watch her turn and open the back door to the cottage. He spoke quietly into the silence between them. "I will talk to Roy tomorrow. We will make arrangements for delivering Rudi as soon as possible."

"All right," Marla said, surprised at the smoothness with which she spoke. She opened the door to the porch and moved inside, bidding him good-night and watching as he walked back to his car and backed out of the driveway. She bent down to cuddle Nik, who whined with delight.

It was well past the puppy's bedtime, as well as her own, but she remained on the chilly back porch, petting and talking to Nik for far longer than she would have otherwise. But she was in sore need of some—any—distraction to dispel the telltale clutching pain that still gripped her long after Stefan's departure.

CHAPTER SIX

SHE AWAKENED with a start, jerking up to a half-sitting position as she leaned on one elbow, reaching up with one hand to wipe the film of perspiration covering her upper lip. What had she been dreaming about? She stared at the wall opposite her bed, stared hard as she strained to remember what had obviously been a disturbing dream.

Yet she could not summon up even the theme of it. Slumping back onto the pillow, Marla threw one arm across her forehead as she drew in a deep breath, then let it out slowly. Her mind remained blank for a moment, but gradually a certain undefinable image appeared, slowly shedding its fuzzy camouflage: the image of a man, tall, dark-haired with deeply penetrating ebony eyes.

"Damn!" she muttered aloud. Would she ever manage to get him out of her mind? For the past two weeks she'd been plagued like this, dreaming of Stefan Gerhardt almost every night, thinking of him far more than was necessary during the daytime.

And why? Surely one kiss, albeit one that should have never occurred in the first place, should not have made this much of a difference in the way she conducted her life. But somehow it had, in spite of the fact she hadn't seen him at all since the night they'd had dinner and he'd asked her to train Rudi.

Roy had telephoned her the next day and on the following day had delivered the horse to Marla's stable, his new home for the next few months. Marla had been concerned that Roy would be angry or offended by Stefan's decision to take the responsibility of training his most talented horse out of Roy's hands. But the enthusiasm he had displayed toward the new arrangement dispelled her fears.

"I've seen what you can do," Roy had told her. "Whatever needs to be done with Rudi, I'm sure you're as capable as anyone in seeing to it."

He'd also alluded to the problem with his knee, and Marla had sensed, though he didn't quite put it onto words, that he was actually relieved to be rid of the responsibility for Rudi. Although she was curious to know why Stefan didn't come with him to deliver the horse, she carefully avoided bringing this up. Roy, how ever, answered the unasked question by informing her Stefan had had to make immediate overnight arrangements to fly to Germany—some family matter, he surmised.

He hadn't indicated how long his employer would be gone, but Marla had dismissed the matter mentally—or at least pretended she had. Her relationship with Stefan was strictly business. His personal comings and goings were of no concern to her.

Marla, of course, had developed an immediate fondness for Rudi the first time Roy had handed her the reins. But what she came to learn about the animal during the following days, transformed that initial fondness into a distinct sense of kinship with the beautiful chestnut gelding. Rudi's attributes extended well beyond the talent and potential that Marla had immediately appreciated. His overall manners were nothing short of charming, if such a description could be applied to an animal. Even Morris enjoyed working around and handling the young Trakehner.

And Marla soon discovered that Rudi was an incredibly quick study. She had begun working him the very first day he'd arrived, taking him out for a casual familiarizing hack around the pasture and along the road before bringing him into the arena for a more structured lesson.

They had followed essentially the same pattern every day since then—first a ride or a simple walk around the property, then half an hour to forty-five minutes' worth of dressage in the arena. Every third day Marla worked the willing Trakhener over fences, making use of the techniques she had covered with Stefan.

Marla knew, both from her own experience and from observing others in the business of training and showing hunters and jumpers, that one could quite easily become jaded after a while, looking on the animals as merely a means of making a living, possibly a very lucrative one. If Marla's attitude had been in danger of changing in such a way, it wasn't any longer— not since Rudi's arrival. He was simply the most marvelous horse she'd ever known, and each and every time she rode him served to strengthen the ever-expanding thread of communication and mutual understanding that seemed to bind the two of them together. She was, after all, a genuine horse lover, but knowing and working with Rudi had emphasized that deeply ingrained facet of her personality, re-awakened the appreciation and respect she had always reserved for the animals.

In this regard she had reason to be grateful to Stefan, above all. In spite of her resolve to discourage any further activities that might put them in a situation like the one that had led to that highly charged kiss, she felt a compelling urge to at least speak with him about the progress Rudi was making.

So far she hadn't had any such opportunity. Roy came by on a regular basis and agreed with her that Rudi was improving dramatically. But he still made no mention of when Stefan would be returning from Germany, and Marla had to put her impatience on hold.

SHORTLY AFTER NOON she began exercising Sassy, her five-year-old mare, on a longe. It usually took the young horse several rounds of playful bucks to settle down to the workout routine of fifteen minutes' longeing followed by half an hour's work on the flat.

"Whoa, whoa," Marla commanded gently, purposely leaving the longe on the ground until Sassy settled down a bit more. "That's a good girl," she said soothingly as the mare put her head down and bucked once more before easing into a working trot.

The sun was angled directly overhead, warming Marla's back against the chill of the late October day. The blue sky was absolutely cloudless, and as she kept the mare in a trot on the longe, she let her gaze wander to the backdrop of the Blue Ridge range. Another coat of color had been added to the already changing leaves, deepening the golds and russets and burgundies to dramatic generous tones. Marla breathed in deeply. How she loved this place. If only.... The wistful thought flitted across her brain.

She brought herself up sharply. If only what? Feeling the stirrings of an odd inner excitement, she chewed thoughtfully on her lower lip as she directed her gaze back to Sassy. At a loss to explain the unbidden inexplicable emotion pulling at her, she passed it off as merely a peculiarity of the season itself. Autumn had always had this effect on her. It seemed as though most of the events that had led to major changes in her life had occurred at this time of year. That same expectancy, a feeling that something was going to happen, was strongly affecting her now, that was all.

"Enough of that," she muttered aloud. The next instant Morris shouted her name, and she turned, calling back, "Yes?" The mare was still trotting in a circle around her.

"Telephone," Morris yelled "You want me to take a message?"

"No, that's okay. I'm coming back over now anyway." Turning to the mare, she gave her a verbal command to halt and tugged on the longe. Drawing it in toward her and looping it neatly around her elbow, she stood still, making the horse walk toward her. She detached the line from the snaffle bit, reached up and pulled the reins back down over the horse's head, then started back for the barn, leading the mare behind.

The sound of her boots rang out on the asphalt-covered aisleway, which Morris was sweeping. "The sun's really bright out there," she said. "I need my visor."

"Here, I'll take him." Morris leaned the wide-brushed broom against the wall and took the reins.

"Thanks," Marla said, continuing on toward the tack room. "Has Rudi been turned out yet?" she asked as she opened the door.

"Badger's out now, but I'm getting ready to bring him in. Rudi's next."

"Good," Marla commented, walking into the tack room and picking up the telephone on the desk.

"Hello?"

"Marla, baby, how's it going?"

"Scotty? Is that you?" Marla's voice sang out with incredulity.

"Sure it's me. Who else do you know with such a sexy voice?"

"You're crazy," Marla said with a laugh, perching on the edge of an old wing-back chair next to the desk. "When did you get in? I didn't think you could make it back that fast from Harrisburg."

"Dark Crystal came up lame on the second day. We weren't doing so hot otherwise, so George and I left a day early."

"Oh, that's too bad Is he hurt badly?"

"No, just a strain. No tendons or anything serious."

"Well, that's good. And Mary? Is she back, too?"

"No. Believe it or not, she and her mare were stars this time—pinned second in a couple of classes and won the under saddle class. She stayed for the classic—and you know how much money rides on one of those competitions."

"That's fantastic! Well, I'm glad you called anyway. I want to hear all about it."

Marla's friends Scotty Hamlinson and George and Mary Slater, the latter a brother-and-sister trainer-rider team, generally made the circuit of East Coast indoor shows every year. Marla's financial situation at the moment and the fact that her horses were too young and inexperienced precluded any possibility of her attending, but someday she planned on making them all on a regular basis. For now she had to content herself with hearing the details from those who could compete in the upper echelon of the show circuit.

"Well, what are you doing for supper tonight?" Scotty interrupted her reverie.

"Tonight?"

"Why not? You said you wanted to hear all about it."

"Oh, I do. Are you sure you're not too tired....?"

"Hell, I'm too keyed up to be tired," Scotty said with a wry chuckle. "What I need is a good steak and a stiff one—or two—or three."

Marla laughed. "You sound like it. All right, then. What time?"

"Pick you up around seven?"

"Okay. I should be ready."

"Sounds good. See you then."

Marla hung up the phone and smiled to herself. She was glad Scotty was back. She would love nothing more than to sit down and listen to all the juicy details of the shows she had missed. And if anyone was worth listening to in the relating it was Scotty Hamlinson.

Born and raised in Charlottesville, he had ridden since he was old enough for his mother to put him on a pony and lead him around. He was a consummate rider, and Marla had known and admired him from a distance during her years as a junior exhibitor. In the past year she'd got to know him even better. The two of them had become good friends, and Marla visited the farm he lived on with his parents fairly often, as did quite a number of other equestrians from around the country. Scotty's reputation as a trainer was also well established, his knowledge in such demand that he gave frequent, highly profitable clinics at his place.

The more she thought about it, the more Marla's spirits lifted at the prospect of the evening ahead. Scotty, along with most of her other friends in Keswick and Charlottesville, would be leaving again rather soon to continue on the indoor circuit—the Washington National in Landover, Maryland, then on to New York at Madison Square Garden. With his busy schedule, tonight might be the only time she would have to see him for quite a while.

Marla was every bit as pleased with the evening as she'd anticipated. Scotty, in spite of the fact he'd been awake for more than twenty-four hours, was in fantastic form. He had Marla in stitches half the night, his somewhat rounded boyish face used to comical advantage as he accompanied his vast supply of stories with his usual share of animated facial expressions.

The Junction was jumping that evening, packed to the walls, the boisterous crowd competing with the ridiculously loud background music. Under other circumstances Marla felt sure she wouldn't have been able to stand the bedlam, but that night she felt as relaxed and at ease as if she were dining at the Boar's Head. As usual, Scotty's popularity drew others to their table, and before the evening was over they had to move to one that would accommodate their group of eight.

It was late...very late by the time Scotty deposited Marla on her doorstep. The car reached the house just as Marla let out a peal of laughter that rippled through the cold night air.

"Scotty, you're crazy!" She shook her head at another of his silly jokes, opening the door to get out. He kept the motor running.

"I know. That's what the doctor told my mother when I was born, but she decided to take her chances."

Marla laughed again as she stepped out of the car and held the door open while she leaned back inside. "I had a fantastic time—as usual. Call me before you leave for Washington, all right?"

"Of course. I can't leave town without saying goodbye to my favorite woman."

Marla waved at him. "Get out of here, Scotty. The day you have a favorite woman will be the day they bury you."

Scotty produced an exaggerated pout and

lifted his shoulders expressively. 'Nobody ever takes me seriously. It's a shame, a real shame.''

"Bye, you nut. Talk to you later.'' She slammed the door shut, and Scotty waved and smiled. But he didn't drive off until he saw Marla open the front door.

Stepping inside, she turned to shove the door closed just as the outer screen door bounced into place. Her hand was on the wall switch, ready to flip it on, when she heard a rustling behind her. Instantly her senses were alert, fear shooting through her like an electric shock. She remained completely still, every muscle in her body tensed, ready for fight or flight—or both.

Further rustling intensified the fear that seemed to have invaded every cell of her body. Frantically she tried to decide whether to jerk back the lock and run for her life or flip on the lights and perhaps scare whoever—or whatever—was rummaging around in her house. The former was probably the more intelligent choice, and her hand had just moved for the lock as a light came on behind her, the small lamp beside the living-room couch.

In the same instant that she half jumped, half turned, a deep masculine voice cut into the silence, and the scream that threatened to erupt from her throat came out as a desperate whimper.

"One o'clock seems a rather late hour for one with such important responsibilities, don't you agree?"

Stefan Gerhardt stared back at her from his half-reclining position on the couch. His dark eyes met her angry glare evenly, then traveled slowly, insultingly, down the length of her body.

"Damn it!" Marla hissed, bringing one hand up automatically to her throat. "*What* is wrong with you? Do you make a living scaring the hell out of people, or is this just a little hobby of yours?"

His expression remained unmoved; she could have been a kitten trying out her claws for all the concern he displayed. His gaze covered every inch of her body as she stood there, rooted to the spot with impotent rage at this incredible man, ensconced on her couch as if he owned it— which of course he did, a derisive inner voice reminded her.

The thought fired her anger even more, and she spat out, "I would like an explanation, dammit! What in the hell are you doing in my living room? At one o'clock in the morning!" she flung one hand out behind her. "And how did you get in? I know I didn't leave the door open this time."

Stefan regarded her silently for a moment,

then pulled himself upright. The suede jacket he wore had slipped back to reveal a snug white turtleneck tucked into a pair of obviously custom-made, untinted pigskin slacks. He ran a hand though his hair, and as Marla waited, fuming, for his reply, she noticed for the first time that his face was creased with lines, adding a haggard quality to his craggy features.

"I let myself in," he said, his gaze slanting to indicate a ring of keys lying on her coffee table.

Marla frowned as she eyed the set. "But...." Her voice trailed off, and she frowned in confusion. Her heart was only now resuming a more reasonable beat, but her anger hadn't abated one iota—wouldn't until she found out what in heaven's name had possessed the man to invade her privacy this way.

"I have a key to all the buildings I own," he explained matter-of-factly, then got up and walked into the adjoining dining room. "Where do you keep your liquor?" he asked, opening one of the doors in the narrow maple hutch that stood in one corner.

At his action Marla lost her temper completely, which finally gave her the impetus to move from the spot she'd remained practically glued to. "So what does that mean—you have a key to all your own buildings? Do you conduct nightly inspections of all your tenants on a regular basis?'' Her voice positively dripped with heavy sarcasm.

Stefan turned casually back to her, a half smile curving his mouth. "You're the only tenant I have.''

Marla placed both hands on her hips and glared back at him. "A most unfortunate circumstance, I'm beginning to believe.'' Her frown deepened as she asked, "Where's your car? I didn't see....''

"In the back,'' Stefan answered smoothly, opening yet another door to tne hutch. "Ah. here we are.'' Glasses clinked as he chose from among the few bottles of liquor she kept there. "Good. You have at least a passable Scotch.'' Withdrawing the bottle, he set it on the table. "And where can I find a glass?''

Marla cast him an arch look. "You mean you don't know? I would have thought you'd make that your business, too.'' She walked into the dining room and opened another of the small cabinet doors, extracting a highball glass and setting it down next to the bottle of Scotch. "Here. If you want ice and water, you'll have to get it from the kitchen.''

"No. Neat is just fine,'' he replied easily, emptying some of the golden liquid into the glass, then taking it with him back into the living room. His actions were carried out with such aplomb, such utter disregard for the fact that he was an intruder in her home, an intruder who had yet to explain his presence, that it was all Marla could do to keep from ranting at him. Yet she was loath to reveal the depth of emotion he provoked in her when he seemed to treat all this as a rather normal situation.

Mustering up every ounce of composure possible, she shrugged out of the navy pea coat she'd been wearing over a pair of cream wool slacks and a heavy, lavender cable-knit sweater. Hanging the coat over the back of a dining-room chair, she walked back into the living room, stopping to stare at Stefan as he perused a magazine from her coffee table. Bringing up both arms, she wrapped them around her chest as she watched him for a moment. Finally, heaving a heavy sigh of disgust, she spoke.

"Now this is enough, Mr. Gerhardt." That got his attention, she noticed wryly as he brought his head up, casting her a questioning look from his dark brown eyes. "You'd better have a damned good explanation for this, ' she continued brusquely. "I haven't seen you for two whole weeks. In fact, I've had no earthly idea when I would see you again—and then you simply appear with no warning, in a very rude manner. For some reason, I don't know exactly why, I would have thought you a little more sensitive."

He cocked one dark eyebrow. "Exactly what I would have said about you."

"And what is that supposed to imply?" she asked dryly.

"It doesn't seem a very sensitive thing—sensible, I should say—to leave a stable full of horses—one highly valuable one at that—alone for an entire night."

Marla scowled, her eyes narrowing as she came back at him. "That's the most ridiculous thing I've ever heard. I haven't been out all night, and even if I had, what business is—"

Stefan glanced pointedly at his watch. "Since seven o'clock, I believe."

"What have you been doing—spying on me?"

"Spying was hardly necessary. I called several times, and when you didn't answer, I began to worry. I thought perhaps there was something wrong."

A plausible explanation, Marla thought, but her anger and resentment ebbed only slightly.

"I'm sorry, but you'll have to do better than that. It seems rather odd to me that after two weeks of not having the slightest knowledge of my whereabouts, you would suddenly become so concerned."

"But that is precisely it. I left one of the finest horses I own in your hands and—"

"As we agreed upon," Marla interjected.

Stefan conceded the point. "Of course. And we agreed you would train and care for my horse properly, which I fail to see how you can do by staying out until all hours of the night—with one of your . . . lovers."

Marla's fury finally boiled over. What incredible gall! If she had known all this earlier, his request that she train Rudi would certainly have had a different result. Her arms dropped to her sides, as rigid as her posture as she glowered into the deep brown eyes assessing her so coolly.

"All right, this whole ridiculous scene has gone far enough. I want you to get out—now. And if you think my life-style interferes with our agreement for me to train Rudi, then we'll simply call it off."

Stefan calmly bent forward to place his near empty glass of Scotch on the coffee table, keeping his arm draped across the back of the couch, then leaned back again. His gaze, which had taken in the intensity of emotion on her face, now glided slowly downward across the soft lavender cowl of her knitted sweater, coming to rest on the swell of her breasts, rising and falling in rhythm with the increased tempo of her breathing.

Marla flinched under the visual undressing. Instinctively she sucked in her breath, and he lifted his eyes to her mouth, aware of her physical response. Her eyes seemed locked into place under that intense scrutiny. Languidly his gaze broke with hers, drifting farther down the front of her sweater. She resented his invasion of the privacy of her home, but she absolutely despised him for what he was doing to her now. The burning look in his eyes, a naked hunger both frightening yet somehow incredibly exciting, told her she could just as easily have been standing before him totally naked. Her insides felt warm, the sensation spreading throughout her body, her legs rapidly weakening so that she wondered if they would support her.

Determined to somehow break the spell he'd cast on her, Marla finally propelled herself into motion, moving toward the coffee table and bending forward to pick up his glass and take it into the kitchen. Her fingers had barely wrapped around it, though, when Stefan sat forward with lightning swiftness and grabbed her wrist. Her fingers slid off the glass, and his hand tightened even more securely around hers. She was in a half-bent position, and as her head came up, her widened blue eyes met his in unmistakable warning.

But Stefan ignored whatever it was she would

have warned him against. He stood up, stepping lithely around the coffee table to stand next to her. Marla took a step backward, but his grip tightened almost painfully, and his other hand came up and around her lower back to pull her roughly toward him.

"Stefan...I said...." Her voice quavered, and she swallowed, unable to go on.

"I heard very well what you said." He was looking down at her; a pulse beat erratically in her throat. "The agreement stands. I have no desire to change things." The dark brooding look in his eyes shone, strangely, with an intensity that caused a shiver to shoot down the length of her spine. "You didn't deny he was your lover." His tone was low, determined.

Marla pressed both hands against his hard broad chest, but the effort was useless. "Who—" The realization hit her full force then. He was actually jealous of Scotty!

"And how is he as a lover?" the low voice persisted. Marla found her eyes riveted then to the wide rigid line of his mouth; she couldn't bear the simmering heat of his gaze a moment longer. She had no answer to his ridiculous question. To admit she had come home that night with her lover would be an outright lie. She and Scotty were friends—had always been only that. Yet to deny what he was implying would be to dignify a question that had no business being asked in the first place. But it was more than the unfairness, the absolute absurdity of the question that kept her silent. . . .

His hand, which had been resting lightly on her back, now pressed against her spine, pushing her even closer to him, so that the only barrier separating them was the slender width of her hands wedged between his abdomen and her breasts. Every cell in her body was stimulated, as though an electric current were traversing her nervous system.

"Does he please you?" Stefan asked gruffly, his head lowered to her forehead, the faint smell of Scotch fanning across her face. Still she could say nothing. She was caught up completely in the game he was playing, and the anger she had felt, her only defense against her own powerful response to him, was rapidly dissipating beneath the shock of sheer physical awareness.

Marla gulped as his thumb began caressing one corner of her mouth, persisting until her lips parted. "Does he please you when he kisses you. . .like this?"

Marla felt her head being tilted backward, her lips raised to meet Stefan's. But her closed eyelids were the first to receive their warm feather-light touch before they drifted downward across the edge of her jaw, across her chin to press finally against the flesh of her parted expectant lips.

The kiss was soul shaking, like none she had ever experienced. Marla became lost within a whirling funnel of overwhelming physical hunger. She was long past the point of collecting her wits and pulling away from him. She wanted this. Every atom of her being cried out for the fulfillment of a need she had only become aware of since... since she had first laid eyes on him.

How long they were locked within that passionate embrace Marla couldn't have said. When he finally did pull away, the shock of it was as great as a slap in the face. Her eyes blinked open, and the expression on his rugged handsome countenance was like none she had ever seen. There was no mistaking the intent of that look, and suddenly Marla panicked, reacting like a terrified doe, sensing the precise aim of the hunter's rifle. She pushed hard with both hands against him. He released her.

She stepped back and turned away, drawing in a ragged breath as she schooled her emotions. Her voice, when she at last found it, was surprisingly controlled, despite the turmoil churning inside her.

"It really is none of your business, Stefan. I don't know why I'm even telling you this, but Scotty Hamlinson, the man I had supper with tonight, is a business associate and an old friend—a very dear one. And that's all.''

Silence hung between them for a long moment before he spoke. "And the others?''

Marla whirled around to face him. "This is ridiculous! Just because you're my landlord gives you no right to question me like—like some Gestapo agent!'' She had meant the slur to sound as vicious as possible. Stefan's reaction, though was altogether disconcerting.

His face, darkly rigid, began crinkling into a smile. Apparently he was amused by her accusation. She couldn't begin to fathom yet another of this man's unpredictable moods, but she was nevertheless grateful that at least something—anything—had broken the nerve-racking tension between them.

"Perhaps you are right,'' he said quietly, smiling oddly at her. "Perhaps we have pursued this topic for too long.''

We, Marla wanted to scream. She'd had nothing to do with it. She was sure she had never seen such a display of pure unadulterated arrogance in one man. Nevertheless, if he wanted to drop the subject, she was more than willing to oblige.

"That's one way to put it,'' Marla replied dryly. She lifted a hand, looping back her curtain of blond hair behind one ear, the gesture revealing the sudden weariness that had washed over her. "Stefan, it's very late. There's a lot we need to discuss...about Rudi. Can we talk about it later?"

Stefan had been standing with one thumb hooked inside a belt loop, the other shoved in the front pocket of his pants. He was incredibly overwhelmingly masculine, and for more reasons than her weariness Marla wanted him to leave.

"As you wish," he agreed with a nod. "I will come by later in the morning."

Without another word he walked through the dining room and kitchen to the back porch. Nik was sleeping soundly and did not awaken as Marla followed him, watching as he let himself out the back screen door. Turning, he spoke quietly, his tone unrecognizable from the accusing fearful one of only a few minutes earlier.

"Good night, Marla."

She shivered and heard herself mutter some inane sort of farewell as he strode across the gravel drive to his car. The shivering continued unabated for several minutes, but Marla knew it had nothing to do with the coldness of the early-morning air.

Woodenly she turned and made her way back through the house to her bedroom. The anxiety she had experienced earlier, knowing she might have to leave Morning Meadows because of the new owner, invaded her mind again now, though with far greater intensity. Something very significant, some inexplicable change, had occurred that night, had penetrated the carefully erected protective shell around her psyche. She was instantly on guard against the threat of a challenge she'd so painstakingly and successfully avoided till now.

Instinctively Marla knew she must tread carefully from now on. . . very carefully.

CHAPTER SEVEN

MORRIS RELEASED the crossties from Rudi's halter and led him from the washstand into the aisleway. Slipping the bridle onto the gelding's head, he led him around in a circle to face Marla, who hoisted her lightweight jumping-and-dressage saddle onto his back and threw the girth on top of it. As Morris fastened it from his side, he asked, "Will Mr. Gerhardt be here today?"

"Probably," Marla answered, pulling the buckle up a few notches, leaving it loose, to be tightened further after she led Rudi outside.

"He's really keeping a close eye on his horse," Morris commented.

"Mmm-hmm." That was certainly the truth, Marla thought wryly. Ever since he'd got back from Germany he'd driven up to her stable on a daily basis, ostensibly to observe the progress his prize horse was making.

Marla couldn't blame him. Rudi was improving dramatically with each workout. Any intelligent observer's interest would be understandable; the horse's owner's was to be expected.

There was something else, however, a far subtler reason for the unrelenting regularity of Stefan's visits, and Marla was all too uncomfortably aware of it. Her suspicions had been growing daily—ever since that last night at her house—that Stefan's interest in her exceeded the boundaries of their business relationship.

Yet he was a difficult man for her to comprehend. A quiet private individual, he nevertheless had to be the most determined, single-minded—yes, stubborn—man she had ever encountered, traits whose sheer extremism should have put her off. Yet oddly she found herself attracted to them. Some sensitive chord within her responded to the attention he focused on her. Day by day, bit by bit, her resistance was slowly being eroded. The simple fact of their being together so often created an atmosphere of familiarity that was gradually becoming acceptable, despite her well-intended, preplanned precautions.

The hard fact of the matter demanded admission: what had begun as an undeniably significant physical attraction was rapidly expanding into mutual friendship and something more. . . .

Unlike so many of the other men with whom she was acquainted, Stefan Gerhardt seemed to know instinctively what he wanted out of life.

Indeed, he had set out early on a predetermined course, working hard to provide the wherewithal to enjoy himself in later years. He had not said as much in so many words—yet Marla was somehow sure of it. Knowing this increased her respect for him, making it difficult to summon up an antagonism that would have come in nicely handy to ward off her growing emotional bond with him.

She was mulling all this over as she led Rudi into the arena. Expelling a sigh, she reached under the saddle flap to tighten the girth, then pulled down the stirrup and swung up onto the horse. Winter would come early this year; there was no doubt of it, she thought as she pulled the collar of her jacket up around the back of her neck. She shivered slightly in spite of the thick, down-lined parka and double-thick woolen hat she wore. But the discomfort would disappear, she knew, as soon as she and Rudi began their exercise.

Stefan appeared just as she started working Rudi over the fences, watching silently from his post at the end of the arena. Her concentration did not allow for distractions of any sort, especially when she was jumping, but she was aware of his presence as he kept his gaze focused on her. Strange how the fathomless onyx eyes affected her, as though he were communicating some sort of message to her while she rode, a message of confidence that she could feel expanding inside her, improving her riding and handling of Rudi, eliciting even more cooperation from the horse than was expected.

Afterward Stefan opened the gate for her, and she rode Rudi through it at a walk. "Very good today," he said, slapping the horse's gleaming rump.

Marla reached down to pat the side of Rudi's neck approvingly. "Yes, he was the best," she said, smiling.

"Are you hungry?" Stefan asked.

"Mmm-hmm. I could do with something warm on a day like this." The exercise had warmed her up quite a lot, but a stiff wind had picked up, and once more she was beginning to feel the effects of the cold weather.

"Then you must come to the house with me. Eileen was preparing a stew this morning. It should be ready by now."

They had reached the stable, and Marla dismounted lightly, flipping the reins over Rudi's head as Morris came up to them. "Can you take him, Morris?"

"Sure," the older man replied, taking the reins from her. "I'll be leaving pretty soon, though."

"Oh, that's right. I guess I forgot." She

turned to Stefan. "I'm sorry, but I can't go now. It's about time for Morris to leave, and I've got too many things to catch up on here."

Stefan pressed his lips firmly together. He was standing, feet planted wide apart, hands on hips, and Marla found her gaze resting on the solid breadth of his chest as he looked away for a moment, considering. "Then I will return to the house and have Eileen pack us something. I will bring it back here."

"Oh, no, you don't have to...."

Her objection went unheeded. There seemed to be no way of overriding the stubbornness Stefan possessed in abundant supply. He was already walking toward his car, and as she watched him, she smiled and shook her head. *Well, why not take advantage of it,* she thought. She *was* hungry, and if he insisted.... It would probably be a far cry better than anything she could have whipped up herself.

Stefan returned half an hour later. Marla had just waved goodbye to Morris, who was due at another farm for the afternoon. The hearty aroma of beef stew preceded her host as he walked into the stable carrying a hamper on one arm.

"Mmm, that smells divine," Marla commented as she stepped out of Rudi's stall. He had cooled down by now, and she had just put him up as Stefan drove up. "Here, let's take it into the tack room."

The beef-carrot-and-potato stew was mouth-wateringly delicious, and Stefan's housekeeper had also packed a loaf of crusty warmed French bread and a plastic pitcher full of iced tea. Marla was certain she had never relished a meal as much as this one, and from the looks of it Stefan's appetite was not lagging in the least, either.

They sat in the two straight-backed chairs on opposite sides of the small square wooden table, and for several minutes the silence went unbroken as they consumed the meal. Eileen had even included two generous slices of apple pie, but Marla had to decline as she watched Stefan delve into his.

"You can tell your housekeeper her cooking is excellent," Marla said, taking a sip of her tea. "Is she German, also?"

Stefan shook his head. "No, she's American—a native Virginian even. But you're right. Her cooking is superior. One would think she was German."

"Oh, ho," Marla chided him. "Another of your prejudices."

Stefan was chewing on the last forkful of his pie, and he merely raised his eyebrows questioningly.

"It sounds awfully familiar, something like the comment you made about American equestrianism. I've rather proven you mistaken on that one, haven't I?"

Stefan smiled and leaned back in his chair, balancing it on the back legs as he stretched. "You've shown me a lot, but as yet nothing to prove my horse is champion quality."

"But I will—you just wait." Marla glanced down at her empty paper plate. Suddenly a question arose in her mind; it begged an answer. She lifted her eyes to meet his. "Stefan, why did you have to go to Germany?"

He said nothing for a moment, and she wondered if he was going to answer. "Why do you want to know?"

If it had been anyone else, Marla would have taken immediate offense, inferring from his tone that she was prying into a matter that was none of her business. But she had got rather used to Stefan's blunt manner during the past couple of weeks. He was a man of few words, yet those he spoke were never minced. And if something was on his mind he said so—a habit Marla definitely found refreshing.

"I'm simply curious," Marla went on in her own forthright manner. "You haven't mentioned a word of it since your return. Roy said you had business to take care of. Was it your family business?''

"Actually, it was more family than business," Stefan stated. His eyes, which had met hers squarely, slanted to stare unseeingly at some distant point.

Marla sensed then that she had intruded on some area that was perhaps best left undiscovered. That glazed faraway look in his eyes confirmed her hunch, and she hesitated, wondering if she should drop the subject before they really got into it. But curiosity got the better of her, and she persisted. "Is it just your parents whom you visited? What about the other members of the family?''

Stefan hesitated for a fraction of a second before answering. "Just my parents—them and my brother's daughter, Anne-Marie. She was ten at the time he was killed. My parents have been raising her ever since.''

"I see," Marla said softly. "I'm sorry.''

Stefan's blank gaze confronted her suddenly. "For what?''

Marla frowned. "For your loss," she explained, hearing the defensive tone in her voice.

"It happened a long time ago. There is nothing to be sorry about now.''

Marla remained silent, suddenly wishing she hadn't decided to bring the subject up. It had revealed very little more than she already knew about his trip. But then, Stefan had shown yet another darker side of his personality, one more piece to fit the puzzle.

"And you," Stefan's voice cut into the silence between them. "I know very little about your family."

Marla raised her eyebrows. She cupped the almost empty glass of iced tea in one hand, her thumb tracing the flowered raised pattern on its surface. "Yes, I suppose that's true. What would you like to know?"

"Who they are, where they live, what your father does for a living."

"There's not much to tell about that last one. I have no idea what my father does for a living. My parents were divorced when I graduated from high school. My mother lives alone now. She has a job in upstate New York. I have an older sister who is married, living in Canada, but we see very little of each other." Shrugging, she lifted the glass of iced tea and drained it.

"And why have you never married?"

Marla placed the glass back down on the table and grinned ruefully. "You are incredible, do you know that? Why do you keep bringing up the subject of my single status? I know you haven't lived such a sheltered life that you are unaware there are millions of women like me who are perfectly happy living alone and supporting themselves."

Stefan's dark eyes steadily held her own. "You are very reluctant to give a straight answer to my question. Why is that?"

"And why are you so damned stubborn?" Realizing she had raised her voice, Marla sighed shallowly. "Look, I've answered you often enough. I *like* living alone. I *enjoy* my independence. Whether you want to believe it is your problem, not mine." She paused, seeing that her words hadn't made a dent in his composure. "But why are you so interested in me? I could ask you the same thing. Why have you never married?"

She wondered if she'd lost him there for a moment. He was still staring at her, but now he seemed to be looking straight through her. Slowly his eyes focused and met hers unwaveringly. "It was not important to me before."

"Oh?" Marla cocked an eyebrow. "And it is now?"

"Yes."

Marla leaned back, crossed her arms over her chest and regarded him for a moment with genuine interest. "And why is it important now when it wasn't before?"

Absently Stefan reached up and with the third finger of his hand massaged behind one ear. His answer, as she had come to expect from him, was to the point. "It is time now for me to settle down; time to raise a family—children who will carry on my name."

Ah, that, Marla thought, experiencing a certain twinge of bitterness at his admission. *I should have guessed that much about him.* "And families are important to you, I presume?"

His surprise was evident in his expression. "But of course. Aren't they to you?"

"Not really," Marla said offhandedly. She stood up then and began tidying the table, throwing away the paper plates and placing their empty glasses back in the hamper. "Some people do better without them."

Unexpectedly Stefan reached out to grab one of her wrists, bringing her to a halt. She looked at him, frowning slightly. "Was your parents' separation that bad for you?" he asked in a low tone.

Marla glanced down at the hair-darkened hand clasping her wrist, then back at the remains of their dinner still lying on the table. "For a while, I guess. But that was a long time ago. Please. We need to get this mess cleaned up."

Still his hand held her tightly, and finally she turned to confront him. "Stefan, there really is no point in discussing this any further." She smiled halfheartedly. "All right?"

He continued to stare at her for a long while. Then, giving a barely perceptible nod, he released her hand. Relieved, Marla finished cleaning up the table and picked up the hamper as she walked with Stefan into the aisleway.

"I will call you later tonight," Stefan said as they continued on to his car.

Besides his daily visits to see Rudi, Stefan had taken to phoning her in the evenings—something she probably should have discouraged. After their discussion just now she felt even more doubtful about the growing relationship between them. What good could come of it? There was nothing other than her expertise as a trainer that she could give him...or any man.

Ah, that again. Unexpectedly a sickening sadness seized her, wrapping its ugly talons around her heart. God, how she hated that emotion, one she had tried so hard to put behind her— had almost believed she had.

But if Marla had developed anything during the past couple of years it was a certain mental toughness, a fierce protective armor against that sometimes devilish emotion that swept over her. And besides, she reflected, perhaps she was making far too much of the whole issue at this point.

Yet it was difficult to deny she had developed a certain dependence, however slight, on the constant increasing attention Stefan bestowed on her. Then again, perhaps there was another reason for her response. This was the time of the year when most of her acquaintances and friends were gone, showing on the indoor circuit up north. Perhaps she was simply lonelier than usual, and Stefan filled that empty space in her life right now.

Waiting as he got inside the Mercedes, she caught sight of a slender shaft of sunlight as it glinted off his dark brown hair; a sudden thrill caught her.

"All right," she answered him, hearing the eagerness in her tone, wondering wistfully if it would always be this way. Would she ever experience genuine anticipation without the inevitable inner word of caution that accompanied it?

Stefan smiled back at her as he started up the motor, then drove off slowly toward his own stable. Automatically Marla smiled back at him. Despite all her negative thoughts, despite the deeply rooted suspicion she was getting in way over her head with this man, she was essentially powerless to fight the ever-present, ever-growing need that drew her closer to him day by day.

CHAPTER EIGHT

MARLA SHIVERED and clapped her half-numb hands together. Even with gloves on they felt frozen. The wooden barn was insulated, but the night was bitterly cold, rendering the special precautions she'd taken—long underwear, woolen hat and heavy sweater beneath the down parka—practically useless. The late-autumn night was the coldest Marla could remember experiencing since she'd moved here.

She'd have given anything to retreat to the warmth of the house, light a fire and settle down in front of it, all wrapped up in one of her knitted afghans. But what was happening now took priority over any physical discomfort of her own.

Marla checked her watch once more. She'd been leading Badger up and down the aisleway in this same monotonous pattern for the past forty-five minutes. For a few hopeful minutes he'd appeared to be responding, but now his head was drooping ominously, his body sagging

weightily, forcing her to cluck and tug and ca-
jole in a constant attempt to keep him moving.
Twice in two months, she thought, remembering back to the first time the gelding had displayed similar symptoms of ill health. That was
the first time she'd met Stefan. . . .

Shaking aside the inconsequential reflection,
Marla reviewed that night's developments, re-
calling how, shortly after Morris had left following feeding time, she noticed that Badger
wasn't the least interested in his grain—certainly
an alarming factor, considering that the gelding
usually attacked each meal as if it were the first
after a month-long starvation period. Thinking
back to Stefan's earlier admonishment that she
was too hasty with the needle, Marla had reluctantly delayed medicating Badger, opting instead to try walking the horse in the hope that he
would respond to the exercise. Obviously this
time it wasn't working.

Discouraged by the lack of progress, Marla
stepped into the tack room, holding the lead
rope in one hand while she flipped on the light
switch and searched the medicine cabinet. Locating the amber vial and a syringe, she drew
out the prescribed dosage and walked back into
the aisleway.

"Here you go, boy. This ought to fix you
up." She rubbed the V-necked section of neck

muscle with the palm of her hand after injecting the painkiller, then began leading the horse up and down the aisleway once more.

After a while Badger began exhibiting barely perceptible signs of improvement, but Marla continued with the tiresome walking, her hands and feet as stiff and numb as rock. When she finally thought the horse had recovered sufficiently, she led him back into his stall, stepping inside to remove his grain bucket but leaving the hay, hoping to see his appetite return.

She returned to the tack room, picked up the syringe and broke off the needle, then threw them both in the trash can. She busied herself for a few more minutes, straightening up the tack items she had used during the day. More than eager to get back to the warmth of her house, she walked back to Badger's stall, wanting to check to make sure he was going to be all right.

One look inside told her the night had not yet ended. Badger was showing not the least bit of interest in the hay, and he stood with head hung low, his labored breathing punctuated by deep, unnatural-sounding groans.

"Damn," Marla muttered aloud, knowing she'd have to call her veterinarian now. There was nothing further she could do. The important thing was to get the horse out of the potentially dangerous situation without delay

Hurrying back down the aisleway and into the tack room, she picked up the phone and began dialing. Midway through she realized there wasn't even a dial tone, and she hung up in agitation.

"Of all times!" she exclaimed, punching repeatedly on the button. But it was no use. Apparently the line was out. Hurriedly she left the barn, taking one last look at Badger as she left. He was no worse, she could see. but neither was he any better. Her footsteps quickened as she stepped out into the cold night, ignoring the faint drizzle of freezing rain, the first relenting of the stubborn dark clouds that had shrouded the sky with their ominous presence.

Inside the cottage Marla found the relative warmth comforting, albeit only a short respite. The long grueling day—and night—were far from over yet.

Her stomach was growling, craving the lunch and supper she'd not as yet had time for, but the immediacy of the situation overcame the temptation to stop and have a bite of something. She snatched up the telephone receiver in the kitchen, only to be stunned by the discovery that it, too, was not working. *Great,* she thought heatedly. *Of all times for my line to be out of order!* Dropping the receiver onto its cradle, she stood for a moment next to the kitchen sink, nervously tapping her middle finger on the countertop as she mulled over her next step.

Dr. Warren lived in Charlottesville, a good fifteen minutes from here—certainly not an excessive drive had it been any other time. But she hated to leave Badger for the half hour it would take her to get there and back. And with the threat of rain, possibly even flashflooding, according to the weather reports that day, she was even less inclined to make the trip. Still, she had to do something.

Of course, she thought suddenly, then walked over to the brass key holder near the door and removed the set of keys to the truck. Stefan should be home from his stable by now. And even if he wasn't, she could drive on over to Roy's place, one of the houses that had been vacated by a former tenant, in the hope of finding Stefan there.

The rain had begun in earnest as Marla pulled into the driveway leading up to the main estate house, Stefan's home. Lights were visible, though from what rooms in the rambling house Marla had no idea. Although she saw the house practically every time she drove down the main road to the connecting highway, she had never been up close to it, let alone inside. She pulled the hood of her raincoat over her head before jumping out, then dodged across the pea-graveled, curving driveway and onto the sidewalk leading up to the front entrance of the house.

Even beneath the awning the rain pelted against her, slicing through the night air in almost horizontal sheets. After ringing the doorbell several times in succession she heard a voice calling out from inside, "Coming, coming," and the simultaneous sounds of locks being released. The door creaked as it opened.

A round, generously lined face peered out from behind the half-opened door at the dripping figure on the front porch. "Yes?"

Marla's teeth were chattering audibly now, and her voice, when she spoke, quavered. "Hello. I—I'm Marla Faraday. I don't think we've ever met before, but I live just—"

"Faraday...." A comprehending light shone in the older woman's eyes. "Oh! Yes, come in, come in." Marla stepped in, still shaking from the penetrating cold. She remained just inside the door, afraid to move in case she scattered the entire area with the water off her slicker.

"Mr. Gerhardt has told me about you," the woman was saying, her friendly tone matching her warm hazel eyes, set in a plump face. She held out one hand toward Marla. "Here, let me have your slicker. You'll freeze to death standing there in that thing."

"Thanks," Marla said, pushing back the hood before slipping her arms out of the sleeves and handing it to the woman. "But it's awfully wet."

"Doesn't matter. The floor is marble. It can stand a little water." Suddenly the woman smiled at her. "I'm sorry. I haven't introduced myself. I'm Eileen Hagers, Mr. Gerhardt's housekeeper."

"Nice to meet you," Marla said, smiling as she pushed a damp lock of hair behind one ear.

The housekeeper hung Marla's raincoat on the coat rack, then turned to her. "Come on in. I'll just go and get—"

"Oh, no, really." Marla held up her hand. "I only came by to see if I might use your telephone. One of my horses is quite ill, and my line is out of order."

"Well, for goodness' sake, of course, of course," Mrs. Hager gushed, her forehead creased in concern. "Just step in here, honey. There's a telephone just inside—"

"What is it, Eileen?" Stefan's deep tones broke in on them, and he stopped in his tracks as he looked past his housekeeper, clearly surprised to see Marla standing behind her. "Marla. What are you doing here? I've been trying to reach you for the past couple of hours, but I kept getting a busy signal."

Despite her worried state Marla was instantly affected by Stefan's presence, the familiar sound of his voice somehow soothing, reassuring.

"My line's been out," she explained. "I didn't know about it until I tried to call the veterinarian."

Stefan frowned. "What happened?"

"It's Badger again. He's colicky. I walked him for more than an hour and then finally gave him something for pain, but he still hasn't improved. I hated to leave him, but I had to get to a telephone."

From her position in the foyer Marla could see beyond the doorway into what appeared to be the den. An enormous room, its high, vaulted ceiling was accented every ten feet or so with massive oak beams. A floor-to-ceiling flagstone fireplace covered an entire corner and a good portion of the adjacent wall. Heavy Persian rugs were strewn at random across the polished wooden floor. Contemporary furnishings—a cleverly integrated assortment of couch, love seat and various leather-upholstered chairs—mingled with an impressive assortment of antique appointments. A comfortable personalized room, Marla thought appreciatively, in stark contrast to the uninviting storm raging outside. And she dreaded to think what awaited her back at the stable....

Stefan moved quickly across the room to a walnut rolltop desk in one corner, picked up a pad and pen and returned to Marla. Mrs. Hager had disappeared for a minute, after extracting a promise from Marla not to leave before she returned.

"All right," Stefan said. "Give me your veterinarian's number. I'll call while you drive back. Then I'll drive over."

"Oh, but you don't—"

Stefan's direct glance stopped the words in her throat. She knew his stubborn nature far too well by now to attempt an argument. Anyway, she wouldn't mind the help—or the company.

"Well, all right," she agreed. She gave him the name and number, then turned to remove her slicker from the rack. Stefan was already back at the telephone and dialing when the housekeeper appeared, a large mug of hot chocolate in one hand.

"Here you go, honey," she said. "I'm sure you could use this."

Marla opened her mouth to protest, but the aroma was far too enticing to refuse, especially in her famished condition.

"I know you're in a hurry, but it's not that hot. Go on and drink it." Eileen proffered the mug, and Marla accepted it, immediately relishing the warm sweet chocolate.

"Thank you very much," she said, handing the empty mug back.

"Oh, you're very welcome.' Mrs. Hager opened the door for Marla and waited as the younger woman stepped out onto the porch. "Now drive carefully."

"Thanks again," Marla said, raising her voice to be heard above the din of driving rain.

Mrs. Hager's caution to drive carefully, however, was truly unnecessary. Visibility by now was so poor that she was forced to put the truck into a virtual crawl as she inched her way back to the barn.

Her fears that Badger's condition might worsen were immediately confirmed as she hurried inside to the gelding's stall. The horse was lying on his side now, his head turned toward his stomach—the classical picture of advanced colic.

Several minutes later Marla had managed to get the horse up on his legs, although not without a tremendous amount of effort and coaxing. She was walking him up and down the aisleway again, by now so accustomed to the cold in her hands and feet she was barely aware of the discomfort. The hot chocolate had provided some measure of nourishment, at least a minimal amount of energy to keep her going for what was bound to be half the night

Stefan arrived minutes before the veterinarian, dressed appropriately for the night in jeans, knee-high rubber boots and a hooded rain slicker over his parka. Marla, weary beyond words, looked on as Stefan held the lead rope attached to the horse's halter while the veterinarian proceeded to transfer mineral oil to the horse through a gastric tube.

It was past midnight by the time Badger had improved sufficiently for Marla to feel in the least comfortable about leaving him alone. His eyes were brighter, he stood and walked without any outward signs of discomfort and he began snatching almost greedily at his hay as soon as Marla put him in his stall.

Stefan stood beside her as she watched the horse, concentrating more on her exhausted features than on Badger. He dropped an arm around her shoulders, and she looked up, smiling faintly. "I think he'll be all right, don't you?" she asked.

"I think so," Stefan answered, then smiled wryly. "I'm not so sure about you."

Marla frowned. "Now what does that mean?"

"It means it's time for you to go back to the house. You will be sicker than Badger if you stay out here any longer."

Marla took one last look at the gelding, then

turned away and said, "All right. I am about ready to drop."

Stefan held her hand, pulling her close to his side as they half ran, half walked to the cottage, sidestepping mushy puddles that had formed along the way. The back door slammed behind them as they hurried up the steps and onto the back porch. Nik was awake, of course, and came scampering across to sniff and whine in delight at Marla's presence. Tired as she was, she crouched down to cuddle the puppy, only then realizing that he, too, must be hungry. What with the turmoil Badger's illness had created, she hadn't had a chance to feed Nik his evening meal.

"Here you go, Nikiroo," she cooed, filling the dog's bowl with a ration of puppy chow and laughing as he attacked it voraciously.

Stefan was shaking out his slicker and looking around for somewhere to put it.

"Here," Marla said, reaching out to take it from him, "there's a hook over here." She hung up his slicker, then her own.

"Come on, let's go inside." Her teeth were beginning to chatter again, and she hurried as Stefan held the door open for her.

The house, however, was not much warmer. She hadn't bothered to turn on the radiator all day long; she'd been tied up at the barn.

"Brr! It's freezing in here," she said, her teeth still chattering audibly.

"I'll get a fire going," Stefan said, moving around the tiny house with easy familiarity.

"Good," Marla replied, rubbing her hands briskly up and down her arms. "I'm frozen."

"Where's your firewood?"

"There should be a couple of logs next to the grate—others out on the back porch."

Stefan removed his gloves and placed them on the kitchen counter. As Marla went around opening all the radiator taps, he busied himself coaxing a fire out of two medium-sized logs. Later Marla was to reflect on how naturally the events of the rest of the night had fallen into place. Not once had she stopped to consider the rightness or wrongness of Stefan's coming inside when he could just as easily have seen her to the door and gone back to his own home.

He simply belonged there, and it seemed that it had always been that way, as though she had known him and trusted him for a very long time.

Marla's hunger pains would not be ignored a moment longer, however, and she began to prepare the quickest meal she could. The two of them sat down to consume an enormous cheese omelet, which she had cooked in the largest skillet she owned and which, miraculously, turned out absolutely beautifully. She had baked bread the previous day, the one culinary talent that she was proud of, and they finished every last morsel of it, along with a perfectly ripened wedge of Brie and some apricot jam.

It was Stefan who found the bottle of wine lying on its side on the bottom shelf of the refrigerator. Marla had forgotten it was there. The perfect accompaniment to the meal, it, too, was polished off once their ravenous appetites were satisfied.

The house had warmed up considerably by that time, and the snapping and crackling of the blazing fire in the living room beckoned them with even greater warmth.

"Ah," Marla said, sighing as she slid down to a sitting position on the shag carpet between the couch and fireplace, resting her arm across the cushion as she leaned her head back and reveled in the feel of the heat licking across her neck and down the front of her sweater. "I thought this day would never end," she groaned, closing her eyes and stretching her legs out in front of her.

"Neither did I," Stefan said, and she heard a plopping sound as he removed the two cushions from the couch and propped them up against it. 'Here. Lean forward."

Marla did so, and he slid one of the cushions

behind her. She leaned back again and said, "Thanks. That's perfect."

A companionable silence ensued then, but Marla sensed a certain communication between them that had no need for words. Perhaps it was the sharing of the evening's experience or the rain, steadily pelting in a lulling soothing pattern against the roof and windows. It could have been any number of things that produced an almost palpable feeling of closeness between them.

At what point Stefan placed an arm around her shoulders Marla was unaware; somehow it felt as though it had been there all evening. When his fingers gently cupped her chin and turned her head toward his face, her eyes drifted slowly upward across the firm line of his jaw, the gentle hollows of his cheeks. Her gaze met his evenly, the dark brown pools mirroring the flickering blaze from the fire that cloaked them now in its warming blanket.

Stefan's hand slid to the side of her neck, his fingers gliding through the tresses of her hair, glinting like sparkling trapped droplets of liquid gold spilling around her shoulders. Slowly, carefully, he lowered his head, placing his lips, so firm yet soft and moist, upon her own. Marla opened her mouth willingly to them, eagerly tasting and returning the sweetness of his probing exploring tongue. Like the match that had ignited that first tiny spark of the full blaze now before them, their kiss touched off the kindling of passion within them both, firing it into a leaping flame of desire that rapidly consumed them.

Marla felt her arms, which had been wrapped around Stefan's back, being gently removed as he shifted slightly back and away from her. The question in her eyes was quickly answered as he slid his hands beneath her sweater, pushing it upward. Marla raised her arms, and the wool top was pulled up and over her head, her hair cascading down around her bare neck in shimmering highlights. Stefan's eyes were like bits of coal, glowing with undisguised passion and longing.

He undressed her unhurriedly, and as each part of her body was bared before him, the golden firelight bathed her smooth satiny skin in a buttered-honey glow. He moved the pillows from behind them farther back on the rug, then laid her down gently, her hair now covering the rug in a glistening corona.

Then Stefan stood up, his eyes moving slowly, hungrily, up and down the length of her body as he began to undress himself. Marla's heart began to pound in wondrous confusion at the tumult of physical responses inside her. She felt hot and cold simultaneously, excitement and anticipation leaping across every synapse of her nervous system.

She gazed at Stefan in fascination; he was truly the most exquisite man she'd ever laid eyes upon. He moved to stand directly above her, and she shivered visibly as her eyes raked slowly down the magnificent length of him. His wide shoulders were hard and sinewy, his broad chest tapering down to a narrow flat waist, his torso covered with a matting of soft dark hair. His hips were lean and muscular, his legs those of an athlete, with powerfully developed thighs and calves, long and straight.

Marla's breath caught in her throat as he lowered himself then, resting on his side next to her. His arm slipped around her waist, pulling her close to him, and the feel of his hard potent form merging with her soft willing body was almost too much to endure.

"Oh, God," she moaned softly as his mouth met hers once more. Gently, softly, in feather-light touches, his hands began to caress her, seeking and discovering every sensitive point of her body, his searching kiss burrowing deeper and deeper all the while, driving her wild with a burning need she had never dreamed she possessed. He rolled onto his back, pulling her on top of him, his hands cupping and pressing the flesh of her buttocks as he traced her lips with his tongue, muttering harshly against her mouth, "I want you. My God, I have wanted you from the very first."

Marla moaned, her fingers sliding roughly through his hair, then grasping tightly against the nape of his neck. "Stefan," she half cried, almost mad with melting yearning. "Stefan—" Her voice broke sharply, and she whispered, "Love me."

Stefan's arms moved up to wrap around her back, a protective embrace as he rolled onto his side, their entwined bodies reversing position as he lay above her now. Her hands slid down his back, caressing the rock-hard musculature, her thumbs tracing the ridge of his spinal column. Then, both hands resting on the smooth flesh of his buttocks, she pressed in. Stefan felt the urgency of her desire and Marla's demands were soon satisfied, his actions filling her entire body, her soul, with ecstatic pleasure.

The sounds of their lovemaking blended in passionate harmony with the crackling hissing fire, the ceaseless patter of rain. It was a sweet music, nature's melody in its most exquisite rendition. Marla lost herself within the liquid desire that flooded her being, responding with an intensity that both shocked and delighted her.

A peculiar sense of déjà vu swept over her.

Surely they had known each other before...
some other place, some other time. Stefan's lips
and fingers discovered, or rediscovered, the
most intimate responsive parts of her, bringing
her gradually, lovingly, to the brink of ecstasy.
And she, too, seemed to possess an intimate
knowledge of what could distill sheer gripping
pleasure from his driving masculine need.

When at last they reached the pinnacle of physical fulfillment, Marla moaned into Stefan's
shoulder, her fingers digging into the flesh of his
back as he shuddered violently, the sweet delicious consummation of their passion washing
over them both in wave after joyous wave....

MARLA MOVED SLIGHTLY, and Stefan turned his
head, which lay on her outstretched arm. His
hair fell across his brow, as he peered at her
from beneath half-closed lids. The intensity of
his dark penetrating eyes held her own blue ones
for a very long moment. Marla was seized by
some nameless riveting emotion that stirred her
to the very depths of her being.

Oh, God, she sighed, shuddering inwardly,
please don't let me have fallen in love with him.
The very possibility of it was both frightening
and exciting. She closed her eyes, terrified of the
treacherous vulnerability that consumed her.
She mustn't even consider such a thing.

Stefan rolled onto his side and pulled her over to lie against him, her head resting in the curve of his arm between shoulder and chest. The fire was beginning to ebb now, as had the heat of their passion, and as he stroked Marla's arm, he found it covered with goose bumps. Twisting slightly, he reached up behind them for the multicolored afghan that lay folded on one end of the couch.

He threw it over both of them, and as Marla nestled comfortably next to him, she was sure she'd never felt so absolutely relaxed and at ease with anyone in her life. Stefan's hand slowly, caressingly, massaged her shoulder, the side of her neck, and Marla sighed in sweet perfect contentment.

"You must admit I was right, you know," Stefan said, his chin gently nudging the crown of her head, her fragrant hair tickling his face and neck.

"Hmm?" Marla murmured lazily. "About what?" Oh, but she never wanted to move.

"About not always being able to cope by yourself. You needed someone else tonight."

"Mmm, I guess that's true," she conceded.

"Of course it's true," Stefan insisted. "Things might have turned out quite differently had you tried to take care of Badger all alone."

Marla clucked her tongue and expelled her

breath softly. "You're not going to start in on that again, are you?"

"No." Stefan pressed his lips lightly against her forehead, then moved downward, planting butterfly kisses all the way to the tip of her chin. "Just as long as I know that I've finally got through to you."

Marla's silence brought his head up sharply, and he pulled away from her almost roughly. "Well?" he insisted, his gaze holding her own firmly. "Have I?"

A tiny smile curled Marla's lips, and she slowly nodded her head. "Yes, Mr. Gerhardt. You have finally made your point."

He studied her thoughtfully for a moment, his eyes narrowing slightly as if to discern whether she was telling the truth. Satisfied at last, he lay back down, pulling Marla close to him and tucking the afghan in securely around them.

Marla's nostrils flared slightly as she breathed in his distinctive masculine scent. Resolutely ignoring the tiny inevitable voice of warning inside her, she closed her eyes, giving in to the impetuous impulse to simply take all that was being offered her, here and now.

With no questions asked.

CHAPTER NINE

As much as Marla would have liked to convince herself to the contrary, Stefan was rapidly making definite inroads into the major portion of her life. His presence alone would have been enough, she supposed, to do so, but of course now there were far more personal matters between them that drew them together. "Bound" would perhaps have been a more apt term, Marla reflected on several occasions, for indeed far more of her heart was being roped into this relationship than her mind could condone.

Yet there seemed to be nothing she could do about it at that point—and she would definitely have to do something at some point. As yet there was no real reason to cut things off between them, she reasoned, especially considering that their lives were so entwined on a business level.

And then there was the matter of their living so close to each other. Even if she had wanted to end the relationship then, it would have been difficult, seeing each other so frequently as they were bound to do.

Truthfully, though, Marla could think of nothing she would rather *not* do than stop seeing Stefan. He was still the same stubborn person, determined to see to it that she came around to his antiquated perception of the roles of men and women. Yet she genuinely liked the man, and if he was pigheaded about a few matters, well, that was to be expected. She would never agree with those particular opinions—and would continue to tell him so—but by now Marla had few illusions concerning most relationships. She had yet to meet the male fantasy of perfect good looks, intelligence, charm and total understanding all wrapped up in one human package, and she was certain she never would.

Yes, Stefan had his faults, there was no doubt about that. Yet Marla could not deny, anymore than she could claim that the sun was purple, that he affected her more than any fantasy figure she could have conjured up. The sound of his voice, deep and resonant, incredibly persuasive, the swirling dark irises that seemed to follow her whether she was with him or not, the driving virile maleness that thrilled her so completely and brought her to the heights of physical ecstasy—all were almost more than she could bear at times. He had effectively undermined her normally rational organized way of thinking, interrupted as it was these days by an unending onslaught of thoughts about him. She should at least have tried to do something about that almost overwhelming hold he had on her emotions, but what could she do? She didn't want to do anything and besides, would it really hurt if she let things continue for a while longer just the way they were?

And things were absolutely fantastic. November, for Marla, had always been a dreary dreadful month, cold and damp and gray. But this November had a magic to it, a romanticism due to one undeniable force in Marla's life: Stefan. It seemed nowadays that she lived not just on her own farm, but on two. She had become, in the three weeks since the night they had first become lovers, even more involved in Stefan's horse business than the training of Rudi entailed. The weather had slowed down workouts with the gelding considerably. Although occasionally she and Stefan and Morris would trailer over to a nearby indoor arena to exercise him and some of her other horses, all too often the rain, which was plentiful that year, prevented them from riding outdoors.

Most of Stefan's broodmares were kept inside now instead of being left out to pasture to graze.

On days when the weather was bearable, she and Stefan and Roy would each saddle up one of the mothers-to-be, then take them out for a walk along the grassy banks of the private road that wound through the three-hundred-fifty-acre estate. Most of the mares were due to foal in the spring and so were not yet showing their pregnant states. But Marla looked forward to the foaling season. She was considering breeding as an extension of her own business someday, though such an undertaking was definitely out of the question at present. Being around Stefan's operation would provide the satisfaction, at least for now, of that particular experience.

December was upon them before Marla was even aware of it. The necessity of shopping for Christmas presents for her mother and her sister's family was at the back of her mind, but it wasn't until the second weekend into the month that she decided she most definitely should take action. She offhandedly mentioned the subject to Stefan, and he suggested they drive to Richmond to take advantage of the larger selection of stores and shops. Marla thought it a marvelous idea, and they set out early one Saturday morning, arriving in Richmond around midmorning. After shopping for three hours, they stopped for lunch. Then each went his and her separate way for an nour before meeting again to leave. By the time they got home that evening Marla was exhausted but satisfied she'd got everything she needed.

After supper, one of Eileen's delicious creations, Stefan drove Marla back home. She was drooping with weariness, so Stefan told her he wouldn't come in but would call her in the morning. Marla agreed, and as Stefan watched from the car, she let herself in the back-porch door. After greeting Nik, she played with him for a while, then fed him. In her room she hastily undressed and fell into bed, drifting off immediately into a deep restoring slumber.

STEFAN STOOD before the enormous picture window in the den. It was dark now. Yet he could see clearly across the moonlit landscape as if sunlight spilled over everything: spreading oaks and maples, now bare and soon to be covered with snow; the natural, mirror-surfaced pond nestled between the gentle rise of the rolling hills.

Footsteps sounded on the parquet floor behind him, and he turned to see Eileen bustling around the couch and coffee table. She fluffed up a couple of throw pillows, then straightened to face him. "I think I'll go on to my room now," she said. "Is there anything else I can get you?"

Stefan shook his head and lifted the glass he was holding to his lips. The Scotch was smooth, and he downed the remainder of it. "No. I'll be going to bed soon myself."

"All right, then," Eileen said, untying her apron as she left the room. "Have a good night's rest."

Stefan bade her good-night, then resumed his perusal of the scene outside. Sometimes it seemed incredible that all this was really his. As far back as he could remember, this was exactly what he had always wanted—his own land, acres of it, with plenty of room to raise all the horses he could afford. His homeland of Bavaria was certainly one of the world's most beautiful jewels; he would always treasure the memories of his youth spent there. But it was a tiny land not simply for the taking—or the buying. After spending his college years in the United States, he had come to realize that here was the only place he would be able to see his dream come to fruition.

And so here he was now, with everything he had ever wanted, all of it within his control. But a cynical inner voice chided him for the arrogant assumption. Material things—yes, he possessed them in abundance. And so what, the taunting voice badgered him. So what if he had all of that? What of his more personal emotional needs, the part for which he'd had very little time? Until now...until Marla.

He simply could not think of all this that surrounded him, all that was now his life, without thinking of her. For she was very much a part of it, a very central part of it and of his satisfaction with it all. Independence had been of primary importance to him for most of his adult life, and of course it still was in regard to how he conducted that life and on what terms. But he'd had his share, more than his share really, of the carefree existence that had been his mainstay.

This picture of perfection and complacency was only that—a mere picture, as yet incomplete, awaiting the last few strokes of the artist's brush to give it the finishing touch. And Marla was that finishing touch he wanted, needed in his life now.

Turning abruptly, Stefan walked toward the built-in bar in the corner opposite the fireplace. He set the glass down in the stainless steel sink, then walked back through the den, turning out the lights as he went. The day's outing had been tiring; he looked forward to a sleep that would come easily tonight. His thoughts reverted briefly to the image of his life as an incomplete picture, and he found himself smiling in the secure knowledge that it would not remain that way for much longer.

MARLA HAD ALL HER PACKAGES wrapped and ready to be mailed by the following Saturday. She felt guilty about not getting them off until such a late date and vowed, as she did every year, that next year she'd be more organized. Stefan had just telephoned to say he would be in Charlottesville for most of the morning but he would come by that afternoon. She had just dressed and was putting on her coat, ready to make the trip to the post office to mail the gifts, when the telephone rang. For a moment she didn't recognize her mother's voice on the line.

"Mom! What a surprise," Marla said, setting the packages down on the counter and pulling out a chair at the kitchen table.

"Well, we haven't spoken in so long," Jillian Faraday replied with a light laugh. "I didn't want to wait until Christmas day to call."

"So how is everything going? How's Albany?"

"Albany is Albany," her mother responded dryly. "My job is going fine. I just got a promotion."

"Congratulations." Marla enthused. She knew how much her mother's banking position meant to her. Since her divorce she had made her work the primary factor in her life. "Are you off already for the holidays?" It seemed hard to believe that next Friday was Christmas.

"Yes. That's what I'm calling about. I was planning on flying up to see your sister in Toronto, but she and Dennis made last-minute plans to go skiing over the holidays. I thought if you were free, you could come up to visit me here."

"Hmm," Marla murmured hesitantly. Her mind was whirling with thoughts of how she might respond. She and her mother saw very little of each other during the year, and the thought of her spending Christmas alone was certainly not a comforting one. Yet Marla hated to leave just then. She'd had every intention of spending the holidays with Stefan. And of course it would be hard for her to leave the horses, if only for a weekend.

"Mom, why don't you come down here? You've never seen my place. It would be great if you could."

"Oh, sweetheart, that's a lovely idea, and I would love to. But . . . ."

"But what, mom?"

"Well, you see there's someone I've been seeing and . . . well, we planned on spending the holidays together—with you included, of course."

"Oh, mom, that's fantastic! Who is he? Tell me all about him!"

Jillian laughed at her daughter's enthusiasm, but she was obviously pleased and launched easily into a detailed description of the new man in her life. Marla hadn't heard such good news in a long time. It was about time her mother found someone, and judging by her tone, the relationship appeared to be a lasting one.

"All right, then, mom, why don't I call you in a couple of days? I'll see how things are coming along here, and that will still give me enough time to make arrangements to come up."

"All right, sweetheart. Talk to you soon."

"Bye, mom." Marla hung up, a nice warm feeling glowing inside her. She really didn't want to change her plans for spending the holidays with Stefan, but she'd promised to think about it. Whatever her decision, though, her mother certainly sounded happy enough. Her own appearance would merely be a bit of icing on the cake.

STEFAN ARRIVED LATE THAT AFTERNOON just as Marla was walking back from the barn. He let himself in and was in the kitchen, busy unloading two large grocery bags onto the counter, by the time she got to the house.

The screen door slammed behind her, and Nik

barked his usual greeting as he scampered excitedly around her. She tossed him a few doggie biscuits and went on into the kitchen.

Stefan stood with his back to her, and Marla's gaze roamed appreciatively over his jeans-and-sweater-clad figure. "Hey, what's going on here? Who's invading my kitchen?" Shrugging out of her parka, she hung it on a peg next to the door, then sauntered over to slip her arms around Stefan from behind, nuzzling her face in the bulky wool of his sweater. Taking her hands in his, he caressed both palms lingeringly, tenderly with his lips before turning to place a warm kiss at the corner of her mouth.

"Where do you keep these?" he breathed against her lips. Stefan had emptied and folded both bags and now picked them up with a look of inquiry.

Marla raised an eyebrow teasingly. "You mean you haven't found that out yet? You've been over here a million times and you don't know where I store the grocery bags?"

Stefan shot her a disparaging look, and she shook her head and smiled wryly. "Underneath the sink," she informed him. Picking up a large, plastic-wrapped package of thick red meat, she commented, "Mmm, this looks yummy. When did you go shopping?" From the looks of things he'd spent a small fortune.

"Just now," Stefan said, opening a cupboard and searching inside it. "Do you have a large plate or something?"

"I have lots of somethings," Marla said, starting to clear off the counter. "Look in the one to your left."

As Stefan hauled out a large platter, she picked up one of the two bottles of wine, and her eyes grew round as she read the label. "Stefan! How much did you pay for this?"

Stefan shrugged unconcernedly as he unwrapped the steak and placed it on the platter to be marinated. "I don't remember. Why? Don't you like white wine?"

"This is not just white wine, and you know it. Bernkasteler Spatlese 1979 costs an arm and a leg. Even I know that." She set the bottle on the counter and turned, her eyes narrowing as she observed him with a sidelong glance.

"What's all this about, Stefan Gerhardt? Is this some famous day in history? Your birthday? Your mother's birthday?"

Stefan chuckled. "Does it have to be a special occasion to enjoy a bottle of fine wine and a good meal?"

Marla crossed her arms over her chest and sighed dramatically. "I'm not going to get this out of you, I can tell already."

"Mmm-hmm." Stefan turned the steak over

and stabbed the tender beef with a long-pronged fork, then poured a prepared marinade over it.

Marla was getting none of his attention at the moment—that was certain. "All right, then. If you're not going to tell me why you're going to all this trouble, then I'm not going to help you."

"Fine."

"Oh!" Marla scowled at him, then moved away from the counter and placed her hands on her hips in an exaggerated gesture of exasperation. "Well, I'm going to take a bath."

"Take your time. Everything should be ready in about an hour."

"Fine," she called back airily over her shoulder.

Her impatience was all pretense of course. It pleased her immensely that someone else, and especially Stefan, was waiting on her. Never in her own home had she eaten a meal prepared by anyone other than herself. As she lounged in the bathtub, she stretched luxuriously, thinking how wonderful all this was. Being doted on by one's lover was perhaps the most exhilarating experience in life, she mused. Her eyes, which had been closed, suddenly popped open, and her hands, which had been lightly skimming the cloud of bubbles floating above the surface of the water, clutched at them.

What on earth had she just thought? Lover? What did that imply? Certainly not that she was in love with Stefan, she assured herself. That was the last state of mind she could afford to indulge in. Well, so what did it mean, then, that elusive term, *lover*? That they made love? Yes, that was true. Even now a slow warmth spread through her at the thought of the nights they had shared. She inhaled a deep shuddering breath. Yes, of course, that was all there was to it. They were lovers—period.

After her bath she dried off and slipped into a wine-red silk caftan, her most luxurious item for mere around-the-house wear. She pulled the pins out of her hair then unwound her braid, brushing vigorously until the golden mane fanned out around her head in wavy, almost kinky locks. Whatever Stefan was concocting in the kitchen smelled absolutely divine, and her stomach rumbled expectantly. Just as she left the bathroom Stefan called out to her, "Are you finished yet?"

"Yes. How about you?"

"All set."

"Be there in just a minute."

Sliding her feet into a pair of slippers, she walked back through the house to the kitchen. Stefan had just completed the finishing touches of the meal and had switched off the ceiling light. The only illumination was a single candle in the middle of the table. Marla would have never dreamed that her inexpensive tiny maple dinette could look so elegant. Even her ordinary pottery dishes and everyday stainless approached a sort of stylish sophistication.

Stefan held out her chair, and she sat down, smiling broadly as she surveyed the fruits of his labor.

"I hope you're hungry," he remarked, rubbing his hands together.

"Actually," Marla said emphatically, "I can't stand it another minute. This looks fantastic."

And it was, all of it—the perfectly broiled steak, the asparagus vinaigrette, the steaming baked potatoes brimming with all the trimmings, the fresh hot French rolls. They consumed every bit of it, including both bottles of wine. Marla was stuffed by the end of the meal; it was all she could do to get up and clear the table. She washed the dishes while Stefan dried and helped put them away, and by the time they were finished she was starting to feel a little more human.

"Come," Stefan said, taking her by the hand and leading her into the living room, "let's sit in front of the fire."

She followed him willingly and waited until

he slid down to a sitting position in front of the couch, his legs bent at the knees and spread apart just enough for her to slip in between them. Reaching up, she gathered her hair and pulled it over one shoulder, then leaned back, resting her head against his chest, the soft wool of his sweater tickling the nape of her neck.

Stefan's arms encircled her, and he pressed his lips against the side of her neck. Marla closed her eyes, reveling in the pure sweet luxury of the moment. A small unbidden sigh escaped her throat, and Stefan asked in a low tone, "Feel good?"

"Mmm-hmm," Marla responded, a tiny smile tugging at the corners of her mouth. "You know," she said softly, "I would never have guessed that you had such a domestic streak."

"Is that what it's called?"

"Yeah. You're pretty good to have around the house, y'know."

"Uh-huh. I take it you like my presence, then."

"Sure do. Keep it up." Marla opened her eyes slightly, and her smile widened as she tried to look up at him. His chin was resting on the top of her head, however, and all she could glimpse from her position was a lock of his dark hair which had fallen onto his brow.

She felt his chin grinding softly into her scalp

as he shook his head. "Don't get too used to it," he teased. "After we're married I expect my wife to act like a wife. I don't intend to spoil her."

His tone was light, almost playful. Yet Marla felt a lump of anxiety suddenly ball up inside her. He hadn't been entirely joking. She had no idea, wasn't prepared to handle the unexpected comment.

"Oh?" Marla finally responded nonchalantly. "Then I feel sorry for your wife, whoever she may be. Most women nowadays aren't too turned on by such a chauvinistic attitude."

She could feel his chin, which had been making slow circles on her scalp, come to a stop. Stefan loosened his arms, which held her inside the arc of his body, and leaned to the side. Marla, her balance thrown off, leaned to the right, and suddenly they were facing each other. Stefan's dark eyes searched her blue ones, moved down the length of her nose, across her lips, then back up to her eyes once more.

"I'm not concerned about most women," he said evenly.

Marla swallowed and nervously ran her tongue over her lower lip. The anxiety inside suddenly welled to overwhelming proportions. Dear Lord, what was he saying? And why was she reacting this way? Her heart burned to hear the words that would have made a younger, more innocent version of herself leap for absolute joy. Yet her mind waited in frozen awareness of the possible consequences of what he was saying. She knew instinctively that there was no turning back. The subject, she supposed, was bound to have come up sometime. There was no point—or possibility, she imagined—in putting it off any longer.

"What are you saying, Stefan?"

He stared hard into her eyes then, puzzled by the strange withdrawal that had suddenly shadowed their azure warmth. Or perhaps it was something besides withdrawal. Had he waited too long for this moment? His gaze softened, and he lifted one hand to her face, tracing his knuckles along the contours of her cheeks, then downward to the proud squarish chin that had been raised defiantly toward him so many times.

"I am saying," he said quietly, "that you are the woman I will not spoil by cooking her supper every night. You are the woman I want as my wife."

Marla met the tenderness in his eyes for a moment. Then, blinking rapidly, she looked away, the flickering flames of the fireplace reflected all too clearly in her eyes, a mirror of the torment seething inside her.

"Oh, Stefan," she whispered brokenly. Swallowing hard, she dropped her gaze to study the hair-roughened hand that had lowered from caressing her face to take her own hand. His nearness was agonizing. What she wouldn't have given just then to simply lie down beside him, feel the warm firm length of him cover her own willing aching body, fill her with the passion each had learned from and taught the other so thoroughly, so...lovingly. She winced as if in physical pain. "I wish you hadn't said that."

Stefan's thumb, which had been softly massaging the top of her wrist, stopped suddenly, and though she was not looking at him, Marla could sense his entire posture go rigid.

"Why not?" he asked, his own deliberately normal tone of voice curiously disturbing. It caused her to glance up quickly at him, his dark expression sending a knife of anxiety through her. He was not going to take this well—not at all. If only there were some easier way, she thought helplessly.

"I...." She met his somber gaze for a mere second before looking away, unable to bear its demanding scrutiny. Reaching up with one hand, she wiped away the dampness that had formed on her upper lip. "It's just...."

"What? Tell me, Marla," he insisted. "Why is it that you wish I hadn't asked you to marry me?"

"Be-because I can't." Her voice sounded faraway, as if it belonged to someone else.

"That is not an answer." Stefan stared at her profile, completely nonplussed by her unexpected reaction. A muscle along the ridge of his jaw twitched testily.

"I don't care to play word games about this, Marla," he said with thinly disguised impatience.

They were no longer touching each other. Marla had straightened, moved a little closer to the fireplace and drawn her knees up to her chest, wrapping her arms around them securely. Stefan still sat with his back to the couch, one leg extended, the other bent, his elbow resting on his knee.

"I'm not playing word games," Marla replied pensively. She felt sick inside. Why couldn't he just drop it? It had been such a beautiful evening. Why did he have to bring this up tonight?

"Then, dammit to hell, get to the point!" His voice thundered through the quiet room, and Marla jumped, shaken by the intensity of his reaction.

Her head swiveled to meet the angry storm brewing behind those dark irises. "What do you want me to say?" she retorted. "I told you before—on many occasions—that I want to live my life alone. I enjoy my independence."

Stefan snorted disgustedly. "Come on, Marla! Your independence! Don't tell *me* about independence. I know you too well now. I know that you realize, as I do, that one can be independent and still need other people. You wouldn't be completely happy living alone for the rest of your life."

Marla didn't respond immediately, and when she did, her voice was surprisingly steady.

"Stefan, we come from such entirely different backgrounds. It would never work "

Stefan frowned as he observed her closely. "And in what way are our backgrounds so different?"

Marla shifted uncomfortably. "It's obvious. We were brought up within entirely different cultures, taught different emphasis on important matters."

"Such as?"

She could say it now, get it over and done with, yet...yet she couldn't—not now, not again. Slowly she lifted her head, her eyes meeting his boldly. "You seem to be basing your reasons for wanting to marry me on merely practical concerns, Stefan."

"And what's the problem in being practical about getting married?"

"There's a hell of a lot more to it than that!" Her voice rose, and she flushed, embarrassed to hear herself letting her emotions fly so easily. Stefan said nothing, and Marla knew he was waiting for her to continue. When she spoke, her voice was barely above a whisper. "Love, for instance."

She dropped her forehead to her knees, and the silence that ensued became a tangible thing, a lead weight tugging on her heart until she was sure it would cease beating altogether. Suddenly she was aware of his strong hands prying her fingers away from her legs, and she lifted her head to see him standing before her. He tugged gently on her hands and helped her to stand. Firelight played on his features, softening the granite hardness as he looked down into her moist eyes, his arms snaking around her back to pull her closer to him.

"And you don't think I speak of love when I speak of marriage?" he asked quietly. "Don't you *know* that I love you?"

Marla's heart pounded ecstatically as his words touched her very soul. Oh, God, why couldn't she accept them? Accept him, accept the offer he was making, which should have filled her with supreme joy instead of this sick sinking sensation—the sensation of a drowning victim just within reach of a saving lifeline yet unable to grasp it.

"Stefan....." She spoke his name in a trembling voice, her eyes brimming with shining droplets that threatened to spill over. "I. . . ." She cleared her throat, aching now with a burning constriction.

Stefan frowned bemusedly, still unable to interpret her curious reaction. Then, with dawning awareness, he realized her tears were not tears of happiness. He lifted her chin, forcing her to look up at him. "Tell me, Marla," he said insistently.

Marla drew in a deep breath and held it in as she spoke "There's something you should know—a reason why you would not want me as your wife."

He waited, his expression blank, and for a brief moment Marla felt a surge of hope that it really wouldn't make any difference to Stefan. After all, he and Carl were two entirely different men. Surely this wouldn't happen to her twice in a lifetime. . . . The hope was a fleeting one, though, for as she spoke the words, "I can't have children," she saw the change in his eyes, recognized the disbelieving look plastered across his features.

"What do you mean?" He was looking at her as if surely there was some other meaning to what she was saying. Marla felt herself grow cold with panic, that same feeling of déjà vu invading her senses, transporting her to another place, another time...another hurt.

"I can't have children," she repeated into the dead silence between them. The cold within solidified to icy composure as she felt his arms loosen from around her waist, then drop to his sides.

"How do you know this?" Stefan's expression was steadily inquiring, his tone direct, almost clinical.

"I began having problems about two years ago, and while I was being treated, the doctors found out. I was born with a malformation of the fallopian tubes. There's nothing they—or I—can do about it."

His gaze dropped abruptly, then shifted to the dwindling fire. Marla watched in misery as she recognized the same reaction, the same disappointment registering on his face. Disgust surged through her—disgust with herself, for letting their relationship get so out of control that it had come to this, and disgust for Stefan, the one man she had believed, deep in her heart, to be different from all the rest.

She shouldn't have expected it. Of course he wasn't—that was painfully obvious. Her stomach churned as she recalled his words of love only a few moments earlier. And now...his total silence, a silence that erased them all completely. Her chest heaved as she laughed inward-

ly, a bitter laugh at the naive trusting vulnerability of her own nature.

"So," she said with false lightness, "now you
see what I mean." He looked at her then, and it
seemed to Marla as if he were seeing another
woman, as if she herself had already faded from
his conscious mind. And still he said nothing.
The constriction in Marla's throat burned like
smoldering embers now. What else was there for
him to say? It was so very very obvious, an old
bittersweet song that she refused to listen to this
time.

She lifted her chin proudly as she said, "Yes,
I can see you do." Abruptly she laughed, a
harsh almost inhuman sound. "Love. What a
hypocrite you are. Just like all the rest."

She paused, then drew in a shuddering breath.
"Well, I—" Suddenly she choked on the words,
her composure threatening to crumble, a humiliation she could not, *would* not, allow in his
presence. "Goodbye, Stefan," she whispered
rawly, then turned and fled the room, closing
the bedroom door behind her, leaning with her
back to it, her body shaking violently.

She stood that way, in darkness, for an inde-
terminate length of time. Her heart, it seemed,
had almost ceased its beating. Yet somewhere
within the crazy montage of thoughts whirling
around in her brain, the creaking sound of

floorboards registered. The ridiculous hope that perhaps he was standing outside her door, about to come inside and tell her that his reaction was not what she thought it to be, vanished into the chilly air. The footsteps she had imagined, for that split second of flickering hope, might be leading to her room were gone. As he was.

As she had always known he would be.

CHAPTER TEN

MARLA RUBBED HER MIDDLE FINGER against her forehead and shifted in the front seat of her mother's car. The weary gesture didn't escape the older woman's notice. Jillian glanced quickly at her daughter, then returned her gaze to the slick icy stretch of freeway.

"I was really surprised when you called to say you were coming, honey. You didn't sound like there was much chance you would when I called before."

Marla was gazing out the window. The frozen landscape beyond seemed to mirror the frigid terrain of her heart. Yet she answered her mother in a normal composed tone. "At the time I wasn't sure if Morris would be available. At the last minute he said he would be, so I took the opportunity. I had a hard time making reservations, though. The airlines were almost completely booked with the holiday traffic."

The lightness in her daughter's tone did not

ring true, but Jillian shrugged it aside for the time being.

"You look really tired, dear," she commented as she exited from the freeway.

Marla sighed. "I suppose I am. I didn't get much sleep last night, and then I had to leave at four-thirty to get to Richmond in time for the flight."

"Well, we're almost there. And as soon as we get your things inside you can take a nap. Gordon won't be over until seven, so you can take a long one."

It was Marla's turn to eye her mother. The tone she used when speaking her fiancé's name suggested she was truly happy. And it was about time, Marla thought to herself. If anyone deserved happiness it was her mother. She had spent far too much time alone with only occasional visits from her children to erase the painful void created when Marla's father left them.

Jillian pulled into the driveway that led to the back entrance of her townhouse, and soon they were out of the car, their boots crunching in the fresh-fallen snow as they removed Marla's luggage from the trunk of the car and carried it inside.

On those occasions when Marla had found time to visit her mother she had always enjoyed the small but comfortable two-story townhouse.

Simply yet tastefully furnished, it possessed the warm atmosphere of home. Already Marla felt an ebbing of the tension and nervousness that had gripped her unceasingly during the past couple of days.

"Would you like a cup of coffee, dear?" her mother asked as she walked into the kitchen and switched on the light "Chocolate-chip cookies?"

The tantalizing aroma of her mother's toll-house recipe permeated the air, and Marla's mouth watered in automatic response. She was bone tired, however, and in this instance the thought of the firm mattress and down-filled pillows awaiting in the guest room upstairs was more alluring.

"Actually, mom, I'm about to drop. I'd love some when I get up, though."

"All right. Let's take your things upstairs, then."

Marla visited the bathroom to wash her face, while her mother unpacked her suitcase and placed her clothing in various dresser drawers. Returning to the bedroom, Marla unsuccessful ly stifled a yawn, and her mother, folding down the covers on the bed, turned and smiled at her. "You really are tired," she said, trying to keep the concern out of her voice.

"Mmm, I am. You might have to wake me

up. I'm afraid I might sleep for twenty-four hours.''

"Well, don't you worry about a thing. You just get as much rest as you need.'' Jillian kissed her daughter lightly on the cheek and smoothed her hair. "It feels good to have you here, sweetheart. Maybe later we can have a good heart-to-heart talk, just like we used to.''

A lump formed in Marla's throat, and impulsively she hugged her mother tightly. "Oh, mom, I'm so glad I came.'' She swallowed and managed a smile as her mother released her and walked to the door, speaking softly just before she shut it behind her. "Sleep tight.''

Marla sat down on the edge of the bed, staring for a long moment at the pale blue wall opposite. Slowly, mechanically, her hands came up to unfasten the coil of hair at the nape of her neck. It cascaded down around her shoulders as she unbuttoned then removed her blouse, standing up to place it across the back of a wing-back chair next to the dresser. Removing the rest of her clothes, she put on a long, front-zippered lounging gown before slipping under the bed covers.

She stared into space for a long, long while, wondering if her body would finally give her respite from the overwhelming weariness she felt. It weighed heavily on her, and she longed desperately for even the slightest measure of peace of mind.

She'd had none of it those past couple of days. Fortunately the effort involved in making arrangements to take up her mother's offer to spend Christmas with her had managed to relieve her mind somewhat of the shock of what had occurred between her and Stefan. Shock, Marla thought ironically, her eyes narrowing slightly. How contrary to what should have been her reaction to Stefan's reception of the news that she couldn't have children.

Why, she berated herself mentally for the millionth time. Why had she allowed that tiny glimmer, the hope that perhaps things would turn out differently this time, to flourish and build during the months they'd spent together? Why hadn't she put a stop to the relationship in the very beginning, as she had known she eventually must? What had been the point in letting it develop to that wretchedly painful inevitable end?

She exhaled a slow unsteady breath, unaware until then that she'd been holding it in. She closed her eyes, a vain attempt to obliterate the screen on which she saw projected images of Stefan, bittersweet memories that washed her soul with a longing so intense that the pain of it was a physical thing, gripping her fiercely.

In agony she brought her hands up to cover her face, rolling over onto her side and bringing her knees up. "God, why can't I just forget!" she muttered aloud, swallowing deeply to force back the throbbing in the back of her throat that threatened to find release in tears.

But she couldn't forget it—couldn't forget that the hard-earned independence she'd cherished, had won so proudly, did nothing now to assuage the pain shrouding her heart, her soul. Here, alone with her thoughts, the anguish, all the emotions she'd held back those past couple of years, rushed back to haunt her. The empty feeling was there again, in her spirit as well as her body. She felt like a broken-down toy that someone had just discarded—broken and irreparable, not worth someone's attention any longer. And that hurt unbearably.

After a while she drew in a deep somewhat calming breath. Control. The most important facet of her personality that had stood her in good stead, had enabled her to achieve where others would have been stricken down long before. It was the only thing really that she had left. It wouldn't—couldn't fail her now.

Gradually, inexorably, the bitter sadness of rejection was replaced by a burning mounting anger, anger she should have felt from the beginning toward Stefan. Damn his chauvinis-

tic, totally selfish attitude that qualified his
love, his very respect for her, on the basis of a
physical incapacity for which no one could be
blamed. If that was all it amounted to—and of
course now she saw very clearly that it was
exactly that—sne wanted no part of any such
relationship.

The tightness that had clutched at her chest
like some steel vise mercifully relented, and
Marla sensed her muscles beginning to relax at
last. It was a hard thing to do, but it *was* possible, she realized. She would forgive herself for
making the very mistake she had vowed to
avoid. And with that forgiveness would eventually come a way of forgetting. She would
make it. She *would*.

EILEEN REMOVED the barely touched plate of
food from the table, noting that the only part of
the meal Stefan had consumed was the wine—
and more than just one or two glassfuls of the
heady Burgundy. He had drained four of them
as he read the evening paper, hardly bothering
even to pick at the beef Stroganoff and salad in
front of him. And still he sat there, his nose
buried in the pages of newspaper, occasionally
lifting the long-stemmed glass to sip at yet the
fifth glassful.

Eileen shook her head and clucked loudly,

then returned to the kitchen to turn on the automatic dishwasher.

Her bags were packed and waiting by the front door, where she had placed them earlier; her flight would be leaving in a little while. Roy would be by shortly to pick her up and drive her to the airport in Richmond. She glanced around the kitchen, then walked over to the refrigerator, opening it to survey its contents and make sure she had left enough prepared meals for Stefan.

The newspaper still hid his face as Eileen walked back into the dining room. She cleared her throat ''Is there anything else you'll be needing tonight, Stefan?''

The newspaper rustled, then lowered as Stefan peered over the top of it, looking at her as if aware for the first time that evening of his housekeeper's presence. There were deep shadows beneath the dark brooding eyes, eyes that only a week ago had sparkled with vivacity and warmth His expressior could only be described as blank an impenetrable unreadable void.

''I'm sorry, what did you say?'' Stefan asked politely.

''Did you need anything else tonight—anything before I leave?''

A slight frown appeared on his brow, a slow

dawning comprehension making him appear more alert. It was obvious that until that moment he had completely forgotten about her departure that evening.

"No. No, that's all right, Eileen." He let the newspaper fall into his lap and reached up to massage the back of his neck. "When does your flight leave?"

"At nine-fifteen." Eileen studied the weary man before her, her concern apparent. "There's still enough time, though, if you want—"

The honk of a car horn interrupted her, and she looked down at the heavy black purse she held between both hands. "Well, I guess there's not now. That must be Roy."

The rigid line of Stefan's mouth eased as he attempted a grin. Standing up, he followed Eileen through the living room and den into the foyer. He bent to lift her suitcase, but Eileen grasped the handle first, and she lifted it handily.

"Oh, don't bother," she said, smiling. "It's not heavy, and you don't have a coat on anyway." She stood uncertainly for a moment, then added, "You won't have to worry about food. I've cooked up most of your favorite dishes. They're all in the refrigerator. All you need to do—"

"I know, Eileen," Stefan interrupted her with

a gentle smile. "You've told me already." He managed a self-deprecating chuckle. "I doubt if I'm in any danger of starving to death."

Eileen smiled back at him, and the honking sounded again. "Well, all right." Squeezing her purse tightly under one arm as she picked up her suitcase, she walked through the door as Stefan opened it for her. She turned as she stepped out onto the porch. "Have a Merry Christmas, Stefan—and a Happy New Year, of course. I'll be back on the third."

"Yes, I remember. Merry Christmas to you, too."

Eileen nodded and smiled again at her employer, then turned and hurried through the cold night air to the Bronco awaiting her in the circular driveway.

Stefan closed the door and secured the lock that was connected to an alarm system. Sighing, he ran one hand through his hair as he walked slowly back to the dining room. He picked up the discarded newspaper and dispassionately eyed the half-filled glass of red wine. He was thirsty, but not for any more of that.

Taking the sports section with him, he walked into the den and stepped behind the bar, pulling open a cabinet door and extracting a squat dark flask of brandy—some of his best. He filled a snifter full and left the bar, setting the broad glass down on the coffee table in front of the couch.

Sighing heavily once more, he sank down onto the velvet upholstery, leaning back to stare blankly in front of him. He sat that way for some time, finally snapping back to reality as his eyes flickered and spotted the amber liquid, as yet untouched. Picking up the snifter, he brought it to his lips, the liquor's heady vapors sharply invading his nostrils. He grimaced as he sipped the fiery liquid, as much from the realization that he really had no desire for the stuff as from the potent tang of it on his tongue. He studied the glass in his hand for a moment, then stood up, walked to the bar and emptied the contents into the small sink. The alcohol he had consumed in excessive proportions had failed miserably to improve his state of mind. He seriously doubted if anything could make a difference that night.

Barely aware of his actions, he made his way toward the coat closet in the foyer. It wasn't simply Eileen's departure that had lent the house a lonely air he was in no mood to tolerate. His own mental turmoil was simply too much to contain in such a stifling atmosphere. He needed to move around, breathe a little fresh air, despite the razor-sharp bite of the cold late December night.

Dressing swiftly in parka, hat and gloves, Stefan left the house, following the circular, pea-graveled driveway to the road, the briskness of his step belying his earlier display of weariness. But his physical state was the least of his concerns. The mental debate waging within him now was far more detrimental. His very happiness was at stake.

In the days since he'd last seen her Stefan had dwelled on little else but Marla. He was totally, overwhelmingly confused by a situation he had thought to be simply and unquestionably under his control. Few matters in his life thus far had gone askew, and those that had, he had usually decided, were of minor significance in the greater scheme of his life's plans. The confrontation with Marla had provided the first exception to his principal maxim: once he knew what he wanted, he had only to go after it. That hadn't worked this time, and the anger he'd initially experienced at her revelation had by now been further analyzed and redirected—toward himself.

Her accusation ate at him constantly—the one—the only—thing she could have said to truly gouge into the wall of pride he had spent years building up around him.

To be accused of being a hypocrite sorely rankled. He had always abhorred that trait in others. Had it been anyone else, he would have scoffed immediately, shrugged aside the criticism. But to think that *she* thought of him that way cut his self-assurance to the quick.

The frigid air snapped at him like the yapping jaws of some angry cur. Stefan's stride lengthened, and he was soon within a few yards of the long, night-darkened stable. Clouds drifted across the moon in kaleidoscopic patterns, then raced away, a stream of white moonlight illuminating the building with crisp clarity. Stefan stood still before it, his shoulders hunched, his hands shoved deep into the pockets of his parka. He hardly noticed the biting cold as he studied the solid structure for a long contemplative moment. Then his gaze traveled to the shadowy outlines of the distant pastures and paddocks, their boundaries marked by continuous rectangular lines of split-rail, creosote-stained fencing.

This was all his—all of it. A muscle in his jaw worked involuntarily as the thought voiced itself in his brain, as if reminding him of something he had forgotten. But of course he hadn't. He had lapsed on occasion into self-indulgent, self-satisfied reviews of his life to date, a life that he had every reason to be proud of. He had struggled hard to attain this dream. Yet a sense of dissatisfaction accompanied it all, tainting his accomplishment with bitter disappointment.

The reason for that disappointment was not beyond his grasp. He saw his mistake all too clearly now with the aid of invaluable hindsight. All of this before him, the material aspect, had been the simple, relatively easily attainable part of the dream. Stefan well knew the extent of his intelligence, had developed and utilized it to its fullest. As a result, major accomplishments had more or less fallen into place for him.

The human factor was still the failure. He thought he'd learned a valuable lesson about emotional needs, and had sought to satisfy his by proposing to Marla. But how, the question nagged at him, how could he have ignored one of the basic tenets of life itself—that human relationships did not necessarily, in fact rarely did, fall into any predictable pattern.

The warmth of the stable beckoned, but he held himself back. He would not indulge himself now, would not delay a moment longer this reckoning of what should have been dealt with long ago. Turning, he started back up the slight incline of the gravel road, ducking his chin inside the zippered front of his parka and retracing his steps at a slower pace toward his house.

So all right, she had been right. He had been a hypocrite. He had claimed he loved her, then qualified that love on the basis of her not being able to carry his child. He dwelled on this thought heavily, for it was the crux of all that was wrong, the issue he had vainly tried to ignore these past few days. But like some infected blister it had only festered, its persistent throb demanding treatment.

Marla's image, clear and fully detailed, emerged in his mind's eye: soft unfettered strands of honey-gold hair falling back from her sun-kissed forehead; features small and delicate; slender tapered fingers that had touched, explored, teased, soothed and tormented him with insouciant abandon, satiating his every physical desire. His hands clenched reflexively as her warm smile beckoned him, but it was her eyes, deep pools of crystal-clear cerulean blue, that drew him most.

He had been captivated by their disarming frankness from the very beginning, and as their relationship had grown, as he'd come to know her better, he'd come to cherish that rare quality in her—total honesty. In his anger he had tried to convince himself that such had not been the case, that she had lied to him because she had withheld the information about her infertility from him. With the dissolution of that anger had come the acknowledgment of his own stupidity, his presumptuousness. It was her own business, and after all his ridiculous carrying on about how important it was to him to raise an heir, his own offspring, it was no wonder she never volunteered the information.

He looked up as the road began to bend where it met the circular driveway in front of the house. His steps slowed considerably, despite the increasing wind that substantially lowered the already icy temperature. Somehow he knew he could not enter that door looming ahead of him without having come to terms with this whole situation. He must decide there and then what he wanted, what was most important to him.

He drew in a deep breath, the sting of it burning his lungs yet helping him to think clearly. "Marla...." He whispered the name aloud, the sound of it seeming to float in front of him within the swirling vapor of his breath on the air. Such a beautiful name...a beautiful wonderful person. Oh, she could be frustrating at times, so damned headstrong, so much his opposite.

In that regard there were times when he was almost envious of her. Words, expressions came easily to her, whereas he, having always been a man of few words, found it disconcerting that another could so readily verbalize what he must struggle with. His upbringing had never stressed admitting to one's emotions, let alone expressing them. There were times when it was necessary to do so, though, and this was hard for him. But their different natures worked together in so many ways, ways he'd become used to, dependent on.

Combined with his logical pragmatic consideration of this woman was his deep emotional response to her, emanating from a source other than his ever-rationalizing brain. His very soul held the want of her, the need of her. He admitted to himself that he would be no more than a fool even to think he could deny such an integral part of himself. With the acceptance of this irrefutable fact, the recognition of a love that must realize only one end, a restorative peace washed over Stefan's troubled mind.

Just then he reached the house, his step almost jaunty in its quickness and eager determination.

CHAPTER ELEVEN

MARLA PUSHED BACK a wisp of hair from her face, the wind blowing through the open car window fingering and lifting the unbound tresses in willful abandon. Despite the cold she left the window cracked open a bit, the fresh air a welcome change from the stuffiness of the airplane. The journey from Richmond to Keswick was almost over now. Yet she felt no particular enthusiasm for getting back home. The visit with her mother and her fiancé, Gordon, had turned out to be quite enjoyable, and although she had never completely succeeded in putting Stefan out of her mind, there had been moments when she felt a merciful easing of the pain.

In a way she wished she could have stayed longer in Albany. As the scenery rushed past, her anxiety mounted with the ever-increasing awareness of what waited at home. The prospect grew bleaker and more depressing with each mile.

Even the untracked glinting white snow that

blanketed the rolling hills and hung heavily from cascading branches of trees could not dispel the underlying sense of sadness that threatened to overwhelm her as she came within a few miles of Keswick. Try as she would, she could not rid herself of the thought that things had changed—everything had changed.

Marla blinked rapidly, the tears that suddenly appeared in her eyes caused by more than the freezing wind blowing through the window. Her hands gripped the steering wheel tightly, her spine unconsciously stiffening from the tension that had been building up ever since she'd left Albany. Her mouth twisted lopsidedly as she chewed nervously on the inside corner of her mouth.

This is ridiculous, she chided herself for the hundredth time in the past five days. *Surely I have better control over my emotions than this.*

Yet despite her efforts, one particular thought continued to nag at her; Carl's rejection, not Stefan's, should have affected her this deeply. Her relationship with him had lasted far longer. Logically, he was the one who should have accepted her medical problem without a question, should have stuck by her all the way. His withdrawal should have caused her all this anguish, this heartbreak. Should have. Should have....

How sick and tired she was of that phrase!

She chided herself for the naiveté of such an assumption. Nothing ever worked out the way it should. One could only arrange one's life to a certain extent. There were some things that could not be changed, ever.

It would take time to get over her breakup with Stefan, as it had taken time to get over her broken engagement to Carl. Over and over that thought repeated itself in her brain, a chant that seemed to keep pace with the steady drumming of her tires over the seams in the highway. At length she was lulled into a dull acceptance, the bittersweet memories that popped up eventually shoved safely, if only temporarily, from her conscious mind.

The scenery along the drive down the winding estate road went unnoticed as Marla maneuvered the car up the crest of the hill toward the cottage. The bitingly cold weather was tempered by a bright blue sky, the sun's rays glinting off everything they touched with a golden clarity. Yet she was oblivious to it all. As if she were afflicted with tunnel vision, her gaze took in only what was directly in front of her; the peripheral images of Stefan's property merely a blur as she insistently blocked them out.

Replacing the depressing thoughts about Stefan was another, equally sobering realization, a distinct awareness that she was only going through the motions. What lay before her now, the work, the catching up after her short holiday, held none of the appeal it would have just a week earlier. It seemed incredible that her life—indeed her entire outlook on it—should have changed in such a short period of time. But it had. Irrevocably.

Forcing the thought aside, Marla headed the car up the driveway and around the back of the house. Morris's truck was parked outside the stable, and she could hear Nik's bark as soon as she got out of the car. Really, she should check with Morris to see how things had gone while she was away. But the weariness that had plagued her throughout the drive home felt like a leaden weight, now that she was here. At the very least she could allow herself a few minutes to go inside and freshen up before she greeted the groom.

Nik yapped delightedly as she entered the back porch. Marla set her suitcase and tote bag down on the wooden floor before stooping to nuzzle and pet the excited puppy.

"I missed you, too, Nikky," she crooned softly, her fingers massaging his furry head. For the moment there was only the two of them as they reveled in the pleasure of being together again. A tiny smile curved Marla's lips as she held up Nik's still floppy ears with her fingers. "Just wait till your ears stand up, Nik. You're gonna be real handsome.'' As if on cue, Nik barked his agreement, and her grin widened.

It faded quickly, though, as Marla let herself into the kitchen, an almost overwhelming sense of loneliness invading her senses, coloring her memories of what had occurred there before. Vanished was the satisfaction she had cherished before Stefan had come into her life. Was that the way her life would be defined from now on—before Stefan, after Stefan?

Time, she thought. She would require a lifetime to recover from what she had lost. Flipping on the light switches as she went through the hallway and into the bedroom, Marla set her luggage down on the bedroom floor, her gaze slowly, almost painfully coming to rest on the patchwork-quilt-covered bed. She stared at it, unable to move as a flood of other, far more disturbing memories washed over her: images of arms, corded and sinewy, snugly wrapped around her; knowing hands exploring, eliciting murmurs of rapturous delight from her, playing the most sensitive chords of her achingly stimulated body with exquisite awareness, evoking responses she had never known she was capable of.

Stop it! Marla's disciplined inner voice brought her up short. Abruptly she walked into the bathroom, stopping as she caught sight of herself in the mirror above the sink. A sense of unreality seized her at that moment, a frightening conviction that it wasn't herself that she saw in the mirror. It seemed as though the real Marla existed on some other plane and she was merely looking down at the physical form of her being. The sensation was unshakable, and for the first time since she'd been living there she felt truly afraid.

What was happening to her? Had Stefan damaged her that much—taken away her independence, the fundamental self-confidence she had come to depend on? She was angry to think that after all the effort, all the self-growth that had led to such a peaceful state of being, she should experience this sort of anxiety in her own home.

Jerkily she turned away from the mirror and bent over to start the water for her bath. Determined to dispel the pall that had descended on her, she set about unpacking, the routine nature of her actions somehow reassuringly ordinary.

The bath felt wonderful, and Marla was refreshed afterward. She slipped into a pair of old comfortable jeans and tugged a woolen rust orange sweater on over her head. Braiding her hair quickly, she pulled the long plait up on top of her head and secured it in a tight coil. There was nothing unusual now about her appearance in the mirror, and her chin tilted slightly, as if defying that earlier image. Things were back to normal, she told herself firmly, ignoring the mutinous lurch in her chest as she walked out of the bedroom toward the kitchen.

She lit a burner on the gas range and set the kettle of water on to boil. Morris would probably appreciate a cup of coffee about now. She'd make them both a cup, then take them out to the stable, where they could chat for a while about what had happened since she'd been away.

As she walked into the dining room to get two mugs from the hutch, the flash of red that flickered at the periphery of her vision didn't register as she searched through the maple cupboard. But as she straightened, one gaily painted ironstone mug in each hand, she found herself facing the living room, the sight awaiting her causing her to gape in astonishment.

Centered in the middle of the coffee table was the most elaborately arranged bouquet of scarlet roses she had ever seen. She was unaware of placing the mugs on the dining-room table. Slowly, disbelievingly, she approached the table and the magnificent, richly scented bouquet.

A small white envelope sat conspicuously among the blooms, and Marla reached out carefully to pick it up. Her heart was thumping wildly in her chest; her hands shook visibly as she fumbled to open the card. A glimmering wetness shone in her eyes as she read the simple inscription: "shall we start from the beginning?"

Absently one hand came up to the smooth golden column of her throat as she read the note over and over again, the spark of hope that had lingered deep within her all this time now burning bright. Could this really be true? Her breath caught as she reached down and lightly touched a silky scarlet petal. Her first impulse was to run to the telephone, to experience the joy of hearing his voice again, expectation sending shivers down her spine. But what did he mean, her rational side asked. What did he mean by "start from the beginning?" There was only one way the relationship could possibly end, and she would be nothing short of a fool to—

The jangle of the telephone startled her so that she jumped. Rational thinking took a back seat now. The card fluttered down to rest on the coffee table next to the vase as she turned and walked quickly toward the phone.

"Hello?" she asked breathlessly, gripping the receiver so tightly that her knuckles visibly whitened.

"When did you get back?" Stefan's voice was warm. wonderfully inviting. Marla felt every ounce of resolve melting at the sound of it.

"Just a little while ago." Her voice was strained, almost faltering.

"I've been calling you all morning. Morris told me you were getting in today, but he didn't know what time."

"Yes. .well, I wasn't sure which flight ..." Why were they doing this, she wondered wildly, chewing her bottom lip fiercely, unaware of the pain.

"Do you like them?" Stefan asked quietly.

"Oh, Stefan," Marla whispered, swallowing as her voice caught. "Yes, of course. I've never received roses before in my life. Thank you."

Silence yawned between them, and finally Stefan broke it. "And what is your answer, Marla? Are you willing to start from the beginning?"

Marla closed her eyes tightly and drew in a deep silent breath, praying fervently that she would not live to regret her answer. "Yes."

Her voice was so soft, barely above a whisper, that Stefan wasn't sure he'd heard her correctly. "Are you sure?"

"Mmm-hmm."

She sounded so subdued, so unlike the self-assured, vivacious woman he knew. Suddenly the absurdity of discussing all this over the telephone hit him.

"I'm coming over now," he said abruptly.

"All right," Marla replied softly. "Just give me a few minutes to take care of things with Morris."

"Half an hour," Stefan said, wondering if he could actually wait that long.

"Okay." The line clicked at the other end and Marla replaced the receiver. Walking back into the living room, she picked up the vase of roses, breathed in the sweet pungent scent. A marvelous feeling of well-being flooded through her, and she wondered only for an instant if it was too good to be true. A tiny giggle bubbled up in the back of her throat, and she almost laughed aloud from the sheer delight of knowing that it was true—very true indeed!

THE DISCUSSION WITH MORRIS had taken longer than she expected, and by the time she left the stable to walk back to the house Stefan's car was parked in the driveway.

Her heartbeat, which had finally returned to normal, picked up at a furious pace, her legs going rubbery as she headed for the back of the house. *This is ridiculous,* she chided herself. She was acting as if she'd never met the man before. But then, perhaps she hadn't. They were going to start from the beginning again, right?

She reached the back porch, let herself inside and then greeted Nik briefly before she opened the kitchen door. She took one step inside and stopped, her pulse pounding in her throat as she looked up to see Stefan standing there. The entire room seemed to have been brought alive by his presence. She stared at him mutely. Even if she had known what to say, her lips couldn't have formed the words.

Stefan stood with his back resting against one of the tile-covered countertops, his arms crossed over a forest-green chambray shirt that hugged his broad torso, his beige corduroys seemingly molded to his long muscular legs. His stance was casual, one foot crossed over the ankle of the other. Yet his gaze was anything but.

His dark brown eyes seemed to smolder as they slowly traveled the length of her, sending ripples of sheer desire along her spine. Finally his gaze lifted to meet hers, and they stared at each other for a long, soul-searing moment. His eyelids narrowed revealingly, and Marla, too, experienced a powerful sense of relief at rediscovering something she had feared lost forever. She felt herself moving toward him, propelled by the sheer force of her emotions.

She was overwhelmed with joy when his arms encircled her, pulling her close as he uncrossed his legs and positioned her between his thighs. Through the material of their shirts, she could feel the pounding of his heart against her own.

Tentatively she reached up to touch his face, her slender fingers tracing the heavily shadowed ridge of his jawline, the tender pad of her thumb smoothing the darkened hollows beneath his eyes. Her heart swelled with the dawning knowledge that he, too, had suffered as she had. Bittersweet tears brimmed over as she wondered how two people so in love could manage to inflict such pain on each other.

Marla closed her eyes and swallowed deeply, warm salty tears trickling down the sides of her face to the corners of her mouth. "Oh, Stefan," she whispered shakily, "I'm sorry. I'm really sorry."

He grasped her chin with the fingers of one hand and tilted her face up to him. "You have nothing to be sorry for," he stated quietly.

"Yes. Yes, I do. I should have told you from the beginning. I knew it meant so much to you. I had no idea you wanted to marry me."

"You owed me no explanations," Stefan said firmly. "It was my mistake for making assumptions where I had no business making them."

Marla's eyes widened slightly at the thought that slashed through her then like a knife. Too terrified to ask, she could only speculate on the possible meaning of all he was saying. What really lay behind those words, "start from the beginning"? Of course that was impossible—

they both knew it now. Had he simply come to terms with her infertility and decided to keep the relationship going the way it was?

Which was exactly the way Marla had wanted it before. Before, she mused, her eyes shifting painfully away from his. It was she who now wanted more from their relationship. Having once been asked, she could never ignore the fact that he would have married her if—

"What is it, Marla?" Stefan wanted to know, instantly recognizing the fear that had suddenly altered her previously animated expression.

Marla shrugged. Yet the fact that she would not—could not—look at him betrayed her real feelings.

"You must tell me," Stefan insisted. "What did I say? What is it?"

Marla's chin jutted out slightly as she slowly lifted her eyes to meet his, summoning all her inner strength to ask what should have been made clear from the very first.

"Does this. . . this new beginning. . . . Does it mean you still want to marry me?"

Stefan was thunderstruck. A deep vertical furrow grooved his forehead, and his eyes narrowed as he slowly shook his head in disbelief.

"How can you even ask that? Did you think I would—"

"I didn't know what to think," Marla interjected. "You didn't say. All you said was that we could begin again. I have no idea whether that includes marriage."

Stefan was silent for a moment, his dark eyes searching Marla's face intently as though discovering parts of her for the first time. He gave a low ironic laugh and said, "We have a long way to go, don't we? We know each other very little, really."

His arms slid up her back, and his hands grasped her shoulders solidly, surely. "I was an ass, Marla. I hope you can forgive me. The news that you couldn't have a child—well, I was stunned. I suppose I was angry, too, but I had no right to such feelings. *You* are the reason I want to get married, Marla—not for some pompous egotistical desire for sons and heirs. That doesn't matter—not when we have each other. We're all we'll ever need."

Marla's eyes glistened with tears as her mouth curved upward in a quivering smile. "I love you, Stefan," she whispered, the words hovering between them as his lips lowered to hers.

Marla's tongue met his with matching fervor, a passionate spark igniting within them both as Stefan's hands moved down her spine, his thumbs caressing the gentle outward curve of her hips in a drugging methodical massage. A muffled moan escaped her, all Stefan needed to

take her by the hand, words unnecessary between them as they walked side by side to
Marla's bedroom.

THEIR LOVEMAKING was sweet bliss, the gentle
rhythmical rocking of their bodies against each
other satisfying Marla so completely that she
could only pray their love, day to day, could
rival it even in some small way. As they lay
quietly within each other's arms afterward,
Stefan's words drifted back through Marla's
sleepy brain, making her instantly more alert.
Would their togetherness be all they would ever
need, as he had said?

She lay very still, afraid that Stefan might
sense the sudden apprehension that gripped her.
Gradually it faded, replaced by hope and a fer-
vent plea that he would be right—that their love
for each other would be enough. Always.

CHAPTER TWELVE

FROM HER POSITION on the wide front porch, Marla watched Stefan and Roy unload the last of her belongings, which had been moved over from the cottage that day. She brought her arms up and hugged herself, contentment swelling inside her at the thought that from then on, this was her home. She smiled to herself, happier than she'd ever been in her life.

"Now look, you guys," she called out, "I can help unload some more of that stuff." As she took a step toward them, Stefan straightened from the bent position he'd assumed to set a large carton on the ground and scowled fiercely at her.

"You're not going to do anything, and I'm not going to tell you one more time. The next thing I'll be doing is taking you to the hospital."

Marla sighed resignedly and stuck out her tongue. Roy, catching sight of her gesture, laughed out loud.

"You two make the weirdest newlyweds I've

ever seen," he commented, walking past Marla, arms laden with a variety of small boxes.

"Just because I dropped something on my foot doesn't mean I'll do it again," Marla insisted stubbornly.

Stefan grunted as he hoisted a heavy box from the back of the pickup. "You could have broken your foot. And I wish you'd go inside the house. It's too cold for you to just stand around watching us. There's plenty of unpacking to be done, you know."

"Yes, I know." Marla dragged out the last word, and rolling her eyes dramatically, she turned and limped back inside the house.

Despite the pain along the top of her foot and Stefan's insistence that she might have excellent coordination on a horse's back but was abominably clumsy on foot, Marla was lighthearted. There *was* plenty to do, mostly unpacking all the boxes Stefan and Roy were bringing inside. She wasn't, however, in the frame of mind for such tedium, so she continued down the wide hallway toward the kitchen, beckoned by the enticing aromas of Eileen's baking.

The housekeeper was on the telephone, placing a rather lengthy order with the butcher she frequented in Charlottesville. She waved toward a pot of freshly made coffee, and Marla nodded, finding herself a mug and pouring out some of the steaming brew. Snitching a couple of still warm gingersnaps from a plate on the counter, she pulled out a barstool and placed her snack on the bar. She bit into one moist cookie and chewed appreciatively. It tasted heavenly, as did the cup of coffee, a brand she had been drinking for several years but which now seemed to have acquired a most extraordinary flavor.

Was that what marriage did to you, she wondered, sighing contentedly as she bit into the second cookie. Was everyone affected the way she'd been ever since hers and Stefan's wedding two weeks earlier? The answer, of course, was up for grabs, and truthfully she couldn't have cared less anyway. All that mattered was that the doubts and pressures she had enforced on herself so strenuously those past couple of years were now insignificant. She was deliriously, wondrously happy, and *nothing* could put her in a negative frame of mind.

Eileen hung up the telephone at last and shook her head as she turned to walk back over to the sink. "That man," she said, clucking in exasperation. "He's really the dearest person, but Lord, he can't get anything straight the first time. I have to repeat everything at least three times before he gets it right."

"These are scrumptious, Eileen," Marla said,

swallowing the last bite and sipping her coffee. "And I don't know what you do to get your coffee to turn out like this, but it's marvelous."

"Mmm-hmm. Scrumptious, marvelous." Eileen grinned broadly at the golden-haired young woman, whose brilliant blue eyes were sparkling with mischief. "Next thing I know you'll be saying I'm beautiful."

"And you are," Marla said, smiling in genuine fondness.

Eileen waved a damp hand, then glanced down at herself as she began chopping a head of cabbage with practiced precision.

"I think, my dear, that your brain has been permanently affected by that Hawaiian sun you and Stefan soaked up."

Marla raised both arms over her head and stretched luxuriously. "Mmm...now that could be." Dropping her arms to her sides, she exclaimed enthusiastically, "Oh, Eileen, I wish you could have seen it! Maui was simply perfect for a honeymoon, unbelievably romantic.... I wonder if the pictures have come back yet."

"Tomorrow. I called just a little while ago."

"Oh, good," Marla said, getting up and limping over to the sink to deposit her cup and saucer

"Now what happened to you?" Eileen said, frowning in concern.

"Oh, I was coming up the driveway with a box in my arms and stumbled over something—a pebble I think it was." She rubbed her hands briskly under the running faucet and dried them on a kitchen towel. "It doesn't hurt really, but Stefan has forbidden me to help with the rest of the moving."

Finished with the cabbage, Eileen's nimble fingers snapped off the end of a long green bean and tossed it into the colander. The smile that played on her lips transformed her plump face as she shook her head slowly in silent contemplation.

"Is it my imagination, Eileen, or are you laughing at me?" Marla asked in mock offense. "I know I must look like a goose, padding around like this, but that's not fair, you know. I—"

Eileen waved a bean in the air as she inserted, "I'm not in the least laughing at you, dear. I was just thinking how radically things have changed around here since you and Stefan got back."

"Oh?" Impulsively Marla snatched another cookie, the texture crunchy by now as she bit into it. "What do you mean?"

"Well—" Eileen eyed the younger woman thoughtfully "—this place resembled a mausoleum in the days before you left for your

Christmas vacation. I've never seen a man so gloomy and depressing to be around." She moved the colander to the sink and began rinsing the vegetables. "Then when you got back, and for the next two weeks until you got married, all I could do was hope I made it until the wedding. That man drove me crazy, running around like a chicken with his head cut off."

Marla felt a giggle gurgling up in the back of her throat. She raised her eyebrows quizzically as she asked, "Now this is interesting. That's certainly not the picture Stefan presented to me. He was so calm you would have never guessed he was getting married. But then, I suppose that's the way a lot of men are about tying the knot. His mother wrote me a letter to that effect, full of well-meaning advice—and warnings!"

"I certainly wouldn't lump Stefan Gerhardt with a 'lot of men,'" Eileen stated knowingly. "He's about as different a man as they come." Her tone indicated that the comment was purely complimentary.

Marla eyed the heaping plate of cookies hungrily. Her appetite certainly wasn't suffering. She restrained the impulse to take another one, though, lifting her cup of coffee to her lips instead and draining it.

"So you're finally sitting down," Stefan's deep voice came from behind.

Marla turned to find him standing in the doorway, one fisted hand on his hip as he stood there, frowning slightly. Her heart lurched as she smiled back at him; she wondered if she'd ever get used to the sight of the man. His dark hair was windblown, and the crisp cool air had pinkened his cheeks above the evening's growth of beard. The plaid flannel shirt he wore was coming loose at the waistband of his jeans, and unconsciously she rubbed the palms of her hands against her corduroy slacks. Propriety demanded that she control herself, so she stood up and walked casually to the sink to deposit her cup. Had it been merely the two of them, she'd have wasted not one second in placing her itchy fingers just where she wanted to.

"Are you satisfied?" she asked coyly.

"Hmm," Stefan grunted in reply, brushing past her to wash his hands in the sink.

"Coffee, Stefan?" Eileen asked.

"Juice would be better," Stefan answered, opening the refrigerator to see what was inside. "Or milk."

"Here, let me get it for you," Eileen insisted. "Have one of these cookies. They're freshly baked."

"And delicious," Marla added, picking one

up and holding it to her husband's mouth. Stefan bit into the cookie, playfully nipping her finger as he did so.

"Ouch!" Marla exclaimed, snapping her hand behind her back. "Get your own cookie next time, you old goat."

Stefan chewed thoroughly, then swallowed, cocking his eyebrow as he rested one hand on the bar, his body pinning Marla back against it as he leaned over her threateningly. "Old, eh? Is that what you think of me? Middle-aged, yes. But old?"

Marla laughed, slightly embarrassed at the silliness they were displaying in front of Eileen. But the housekeeper merely shook her head and smiled as she turned back to her preparations for dinner.

"Dinner will be ready in about an hour," she informed them.

"All right," Stefan said, moving away from Marla to drink the rest of his milk. "Roy should be back from the stable by then."

"Then you two go on upstairs and make yourselves more presentable," Eileen ordered. Pulling open a drawer, she began removing the linens for the dining-room table. "Go on, scoot, out of here. You're getting in my way."

"Here, give me that," Marla said to Stefan, taking his empty glass from him and placing it in the sink. "This lady is getting tired of our company," she added with a sly grin at the housekeeper, "so we'd best do as she says."

"Mmm-hmm," Eileen mumbled, bustling past them to the dining room.

Stefan followed behind Marla as she led the way toward the east wing of the large rambling house, his eyes feasting hungrily on the gentle unaffected sway of her firm hips. As she stopped outside their bedroom door, his hands grasped the underside of her buttocks, eliciting a squeal from Marla.

"Stefan!" she objected with a laugh. Then, realizing how loud she was, she dropped her voice to a whisper. "What are you doing? We're supposed to be getting dressed for—"

"Hush," Stefan commanded in a husky tone, closing the door behind him with the heel of his boot and pulling Marla roughly to him.

Marla felt as if a rush of electricity were coursing throughout her nervous system as his hands slid up her back, thrusting her against the hard length of him, his lips grazing the sweet perfume of her soft hair. Unable to wait a moment longer, Stefan picked her up, strode across the room to the king-size bed and, spreading his arms wide, dropped her suddenly into the middle of it. Marla's slender frame took a single bounce, then rolled from side to side as Stefan's heavier weight came down beside her.

Her delighted laugh belied the admonishing frown on her face. "What's all this Neanderthal behavior? Where is your club?"

"I don't think one is needed," Stefan pointed out. "This time." A provocative smile tilted one corner of his mouth as his gaze rested on Marla's chest. She cast a glance in the same direction. Beneath her knitted sweater even her bra couldn't hide the hardened tips of her breasts—evidence enough of her reaction to Stefan's stimulating presence. His unsteady breathing and trembling fingers were proof of his own arousal.

Her eyelids fell heavily as Stefan pushed the sweater up over her head. Then, swiftly removing both it and her bra, he flung them to the edge of the bed. An uncontrollable groan escaped Marla's throat as his lips pressed wetly against the smooth column of her throat, leisurely gliding downward, tasting the slight saltiness of the skin along her collarbone, drifting farther toward the valley between her full stimulated breasts. His tongue was warm and moist as it seared concentric paths around one firm globe, teasing the already taut nipple to a bursting burning ripeness.

Marla's hands reached down to grasp the

back of Stefan's head, her fingers shoving carelessly into the thick mass of dark hair, lifting
his head and moving it to the other breast. Instinctively her hips rose, slowly undulating in
anticipated fulfillment. Her arms snaked
around the broad chest that covered her own,
hands stroking the powerful muscles of his
back, sliding down to slip inside the waistband
of his jeans. Marla's head was thrown back, her
mouth parted as ragged breaths escaped her.
She grasped the smooth firm buttocks, her
hands caressing, kneading them in slow sure
strokes.

A thrill of pleasure shot through her at the
low fevered groan that came from Stefan. The
knowledge that she could excite this normally
unshakable, superficially unemotional man so
profoundly infused her with an incredible sense
of wonder.

Stefan pulled back abruptly and stood at the
foot of the bed, his dark brown eyes glowing
like fired nuggets of coal as he swiftly removed
his clothes. Marla's hands fumbled with the
snap on her corduroys, drawing his intense gaze
as she unzipped them, lifted her hips and shim-
mied them down her legs along with her panties.
Stefan grabbed them as they reached her ankles,
tossing them onto an adjacent daybed.

"Come here," he commanded in a low voice,

lying on his side and pulling Marla into the depression created by his heavier weight.

Marla was tingling from head to toe, and her clear blue eyes shone with desire as she slid into his hold, giggling softly as Stefan rolled onto his back and pulled her on top of him.

"We're supposed to be getting dressed, you know," she whispered, delighting in the sensation of his crisp curling hair against her breasts.

"You said that already," Stefan murmured, his strong hands beneath her armpits lifting her slightly off him as he positioned her more comfortably.

Conversation was not exactly what he had in mind at the moment, and as his hands began their sensitive fondling of her body, which he had come to know so intimately, Marla didn't need to be told.

"Yes, I guess I did," she muttered, planting moist tantalizing kisses along the outer contours of his ears, playfully darting her tongue inside the inner recesses. Stefan reacted explosively, the heat of his passion igniting her own.

Hungrily he rolled her over, pushing his body upward with the palms of his hands, which rested along either side of her head. His weather-browned features were flushed, and Marla's exploring hands became slick with the fine mist of sweat dampening his body.

"You talk too much," he said throatily, not wasting another moment in joining his body with hers. Marla gasped audibly and wrapped her legs around him, thrusting against him as the flame of their union grew to sweltering intensity.

They had introduced each other to a wellspring of sexual pleasure. Yet each and every time they were together seemed to reveal some undiscovered harmonious response. Their lovemaking now was swift, impetuous, yet every bit as fulfilling as the tender, more patient moments they had enjoyed.

Together their bodies moved in a perfectly synchronized tempo, rocking in a steadily rising crescendo of sensual delight. Stefan's control at last exploded in a shuddering release, the surge of his passion triggering an instantaneous response in Marla. She clung to him, her body rigid yet shaking as the sweet rapture overwhelmed her, then finally dissipated in a warming afterglow....

STEFAN LAY ON HIS BACK, one arm over his eyes, the other curled snugly around Marla's shoulders as she lay on her side, the tip of her chin resting on the edge of his wide, still damp chest. Slowly she raised herself up slightly, peering through the curtain of hair that had fallen across her face to read the illuminated numbers on the bedside clock radio.

Very little time remained before they were due for dinner. Yet Marla was loath to make the first move to get up. She lowered her head, resting it on his shoulder, the intermingling scent of their glistening bodies filling her nostrils like some heady drugging perfume. All she wanted to do was remain here, beside her husband, drinking in the supreme luxury she had known for the past two glorious weeks of her marriage, the privilege of being loved and needed, the joy of knowing those same emotions were returned with equal intensity.

Could this state of blissful peace, a peace she'd never known until this point in her life, be expected to last even half their lifetime together? Reason, of course, denied the possibility. Yet somehow she couldn't help believing that a mere fraction of that serenity would provide more than enough happiness for one lifetime.

A tiny smile blossomed at the corners of her mouth as Marla considered the irony of it all. Had she known marriage could be like this, so wonderful in its rewards, making any sacrifice well worth the effort, she doubted she would have held out so long, adopting such a defensive attitude since her broken engagement to Carl.

The speculation was purely academic, though. If the truth be told, even if she had been inclined to get married, none of the men in her life before him could have held a candle to Stefan. None of them, she was certain, would have or could have loved her so easily, so selflessly, could have accepted her for what she was, not merely on the basis of what she could or could not offer them.

She stretched luxuriously, feeling wondrously, beautifully alive—in every sense of the word.

"What are you trying to do—make us miss Eileen's meal altogether?"

Marla, her arms still stretched upward, turned her head to find her husband's eyes smoldering as they caressed her slender length. His glance alone was enough to make her go hot and tingly inside, and she suppressed the coy answer she longed to give. She was playing with fire already, and though a part of her yearned for the blazing heat of it, her saner self prevailed. With a muffled groan she rolled over and slid to her feet at the edge of her bed.

"I won't be but a second in the shower," she said over her shoulder as she walked into the adjoining bathroom. There was no need to turn her head to know that Stefan's gaze followed her like a shaft of light, its illumination tracing down the length of her nude back until she rounded the corner of the door and was out of his line of vision.

The cool spray of water was exactly what her overheated stimulated body needed. In spite of her promise to Stefan, Marla's turn in the shower took longer than she'd expected, so she dressed quickly as Stefan gathered his things to take his turn. He was just toweling off when she left him to meet Eileen and Roy in the den.

THE EVENING MEAL was a relaxing affair and a convenient opportunity for Stefan, Marla and Roy to discuss specifics of Morning Meadows's ever-increasing business.

Marla's work would continue in much the same way as it had before she'd moved into her new home, though with a few changes. She intended to continue a steady training program with her own horses, who were now boarded, along with Rudi, in the main stable near the house. It was a far better situation than before, in that she could devote herself to riding and training now that the time-consuming chores she'd had to deal with on a daily basis would be taken care of by others. Besides the stable hands already working for him, Marla had convinced Stefan to hire Morris part-time.

Much of Stefan's time from now until late spring would be taken up with the rather unexpected number of bookings he'd acquired for Donavwind, the Trakehner stud he'd added to his stock last fall.

After the meal, while Eileen cleaned up in the kitchen, the three of them retired to the den, discussing details of the business over liqueurs.

Roy left at nine o'clock, and Marla gave in to the fatigue that she'd been trying to hide for the past hour. The delicious meal and the liqueur had made her quite sleepy, and she was more than ready to call it a day. She was just about to announce her intention to do so, when Eileen walked into the den, a pale blue envelope in one hand as she approached Stefan.

"I knew there was something I forgot to give you, Stefan," she said, handing the envelope to him. "My hands were full when I got this out of the mailbox this morning, and I stuffed it in my apron. It fell out when I took it off a few minutes ago."

"Thank you, Eileen." Stefan crossed the room to the rolltop desk and picked up a silver-plated letter opener. He sliced through the top of the envelope and withdrew the folded stationery inside.

"Whew," Eileen exclaimed, wiping the back of her hand across her brow, "I've about had it for the day. Is there anything else you both need before I turn in?"

Stefan's attention was focused on the letter he was briskly scanning, and he didn't answer. Apparently he hadn't even heard the housekeeper, and Marla watched curiously as the slight frown etching his brow developed into a deep furrow.

"No...no, thanks, Eileen," she answered. "We're going to call it a night in a few minutes. The supper was absolutely divine," she added, smiling at the older woman.

"Oh, go on," Eileen chuckled, waving a hand dismissingly yet obviously pleased by the sincere compliment. "It wasn't exactly a Julia Child specialty, but if you liked it, then that makes me happy."

"It was better than Julia Child," Marla insisted. "Good night. See you in the morning."

"Good night, dear," Eileen said as she walked out of the room.

Marla turned her attention back to her husband, but he was obviously concentrating on the letter ne was still reading. She'd caught a quick glimpse of it and recognized the air-mail envelope. She presumed it was a letter from someone in Germany, his family probably.

"Stefan?" Marla said, but still he seemed oblivious to her. "Stefan?" she repeated in a louder tone.

"Hmm?" Stefan flipped over one of the pages and continued to read.

"Who is it from?"

"Hmm?" Pulling his eyes away finally, Stefan glanced up and acknowledged his wife's presence. "What did you say?"

"I asked you who the letter's from," Marla repeated. "You look like something is wrong."

Stefan shook his head once. "No, nothing's wrong—just a letter from my parents."

Marla crossed the room to stand beside him, reaching up casually to remove a piece of lint from his shirt.

"So what do they say?" she insisted with elaborate patience.

"Nothing much," Stefan muttered, scowling again even as he said it.

Marla chewed on one corner of her lip thoughtfully. Well, if he didn't want to talk about whatever was in the letter right now, she wasn't going to push. It probably had something to do with their small family export business, which admittedly didn't interest her all that much anyway.

"Well, I'm going to bed now, all right?"

"Hmm?"

"I said, I'm going to bed. Is that okay?" Placing both hands on her hips, she frowned now herself. Whatever it was must be *awfully* interesting.

"Sure," Stefan said, barely glancing up as he

began to reread the letter. "I'll be there in a few minutes."

Marla didn't bother to answer; no doubt she'd just have to repeat herself anyway. Yawning uninhibitedly, she left the room, hoping that whatever it was Stefan was reading didn't keep him up much longer. She much preferred to be awake when her husband joined her in bed. If he was much later, though, she doubted she'd respond to anything.

CHAPTER THIRTEEN

HER FACE HALF BURIED in the fluffy, down-filled pillow, Marla awakened slowly, a sprinkle of sunshine dancing across her one exposed eyelid. She opened it and blinked, then turned onto her back, unwilling to abandon the sleepiness that still enveloped her.

Flinging one arm outward, she found the space beside her empty. Stefan, as usual, was up early, she thought, smiling to herself at that particular trait she had discovered about her husband from the very start. At least one of them was an early bird. She had been too, of course, for years, but only out of sheer necessity. Though it wasn't in her nature to sleep unnecessarily late, either, she was more than happy with the less demanding schedule that allowed her to indulge herself a bit more.

Marla had no idea what time Stefan had come to bed last night; she'd fallen asleep as soon as she'd climbed into bed and turned out the light, awakening only when he slid beneath the covers next to her. She had snuggled next to him before drifting off to sleep once more, secure in the knowledge that he was there beside her.

Stretching in luxurious contentment, Marla yawned and opened her eyes to the new day. Despite that substantial meal last night her stomach had awakened, also—with hunger pains. She sat up suddenly and swung her feet over the side of the bed. Eileen's hearty breakfast would be just the thing to satisfy her appetite this morning—

The thought was abruptly cut off as Marla stood up and glanced over to the adjacent sitting room. A large suitcase lay open on the bamboo-printed love seat, a smaller one and an attaché case next to it. The bedroom door opened just then and Stefan walked in, placing a manila folder inside the attaché case before turning to see Marla standing there.

"Good morning," she said, her gaze shifting back and forth from the luggage to her husband.

"Morning," he returned the greeting, pausing only briefly before snapping shut the brief-case.

"What's going on? Why are you packing?" Marla's eyes followed every move he made around the bedroom, narrowing as he pulled open a dresser drawer and began extracting various items of clothing.

"I'm leaving at noon," he answered. "I'm flying out of Richmond to New York, and from there to Germany."

Marla stared at him in dismay. "Today? You're kidding."

Stefan stopped what he was doing and turned to her, shoving one hand through his hair. "No, I'm not. My parents are having some problems, and I think it's best that I fly over and help them."

Marla sat down on the velvet-cushioned stool in front of her dressing table and crossed her arms. "What kind of problems, Stefan?" Then suddenly she understood. "Was that what the letter was all about—the one you received last night?"

Stefan nodded. "Yes." He began sorting through the items he'd already packed, checking to see what he'd left out.

Marla was annoyed by his laconic replies. Yet she hesitated to push him at the moment. "Is it serious? I mean, they're not sick, are they?"

Stefan shook his head as he stepped back, bending down to snap shut the fasteners on both pieces of luggage and set them next to the attaché case.

"Stefan?"

"Hmm?"

"Stefan, talk to me," she insisted, moving

swiftly to stand beside him. "You haven't told me a thing," she went on. "Only that no one is sick. What could be so important that you have to leave less than twenty-four hours after receiving a letter from them?"

Marla's gaze focused unrelentingly on her husband, until finally he sighed and answered her. "My parents are having problems with my niece."

"Anne-Marie?"

Stefan nodded but said nothing else. Marla frowned in confusion. Why was he being this way with her? Why couldn't he just tell her about the problem—whatever it was—without her having to harp at him until she got it out of him?

Marshaling her reserves of patience, which by now were running low, Marla said, "But why do you have to go so soon? Is the problem that bad that you have to leave immediately?"

Stefan hesitated as if ready to say something, but the expression on his face changed as he bent to pick up the luggage. "My parents are getting old. Neither of them is in the best of health. They've been taking care of the child for too many years already. The problem with Anne-Marie is just too much for them to handle at this point."

Marla waited for him to continue, but when

he didn't, she lowered her eyes, refusing to allow her pride to be trampled any further. She would meet him halfway—no, three-quarters of the way—but she wouldn't beg.

She looked up again as Stefan reached the bedroom door and set one of the suitcases down to free one hand to open it. "How long will you be gone?"

Stefan looked at her then, his eyes focusing on her as though seeing her for the first time since they'd begun talking.

"A week or so. No more than ten days."

Marla bit her upper lip and nodded slightly. The lump that had formed in her throat seemed suddenly to grow to ominous proportions, and she swallowed hard to be rid of it. Still, there was a film of tears over her eyes, and she blinked rapidly and swallowed again.

Stefan's form was a blurry haze as she watched him move back toward her. Resting his hands on her upper arms, his thumbs tenderly massaged the joints of her shoulders. "The next time we will go together," he said softly.

What was the matter with this time, Marla wanted to ask. What had happened to sharing the bad times as well as the good? Her pleading gaze melted under the warm loving glow of his, and as his lips pressed against her own, Marla felt the familiar surge of love well up within her for this man, her husband.

How naive she still was. how foolish really, to think that in a mere two weeks of marriage she would know everything about him. Decisively she pulled away and cast him a bright-eyed look.

"Let me hurry up and get dressed, and I'll take you to the airport."

"No, that's all right. I've already spoken to Roy. He's going to drive me into Richmond."

Marla tilted her head to one side. "What time is he supposed to be here?"

Stefan glanced at his watch. "I told him we should leave by ten-thirty. It's nine forty-five now. I imagine he'll be here in a little while. He's usually early."

Stefan was still speaking as Marla walked away from him to the small desk in the sitting room. She'd already picked up the telephone receiver and begun dialing.

"Who are you calling?"

"Roy. I— Hi, Roy. It's Marla. Listen, I'll be taking Stefan to Richmond, so you don't have to bother. Right. Sure. I'll be back sometime this afternoon." She paused, then went on, "I think so. The weather looks pretty nice, so we can give him a short workout." She grinned, then laughed lightly. "Of course I'm ready for it. It hasn't been that long since I've ridden. All right, see you then.''

Stefan was studying her intently as she turned around and faced him guilelessly.

''That wasn't necessary,'' he said, frowning perplexedly. There were a few things about his wife that two weeks of marriage hadn't made clear to Stefan, either.

''I don't care if you consider it necessary or not,'' Marla said, shrugging as she crossed the room to the dresser and pulled out a drawer. She extracted fresh lingerie before she turned briskly and walked into the bathroom.

''I won't be but a minute,'' she called out over her shoulder. ''I'll meet you downstairs. We'll have time for coffee before we leave.''

The sound of the water as she turned on the taps full blast drowned out any reply Stefan might have been making, but for her part Marla didn't want to hear one. Coping with the news of Stefan's departure was enough; she was determined to exercise at least some control over the situation.

''THANKS FOR THE BREAKFAST, Eileen,'' Marla said as she helped carry the dishes from the breakfast nook into the kitchen.

''Don't bother with those, honey,'' the housekeeper said, pausing to wipe her hands on a dish cloth. She was standing on the opposite side of the counter in the kitchen, her hands now laden with the thickened dough of bread she had been kneading while they ate a meager breakfast.

"No, I'll take care of it," Marla said, quickly clearing off the rest of the table before the older woman could object again.

Stefan, who had left a few minutes earlier to start up the Mercedes and put the luggage inside, returned, his nose reddened from the sting of morning air. He rubbed his hands together briskly and asked, "Are you ready? We'd better get going."

"Okay," Marla answered, pulling on her sheepskin jacket and slipping into a pair of dark brown leather boots.

Eileen walked with them to the front door. "Stefan, I hope everything is all right with your family."

Stefan nodded, but his expression remained as stolid as it had all morning. "Thank you, Eileen."

"Take care—and don't worry about Marla. I'll see to it that she doesn't get into any trouble."

Stefan smiled slightly as his eyes rested on his wife's face for a moment. "I'd appreciate that," he said, and Marla noted with pleasure the sincerity in his tone.

They left then. Ten minutes later they were on the freeway to Richmond.

KEEPING ONE HAND on the wheel, Marla fumbled with the other inside her purse, squeezed between the console and the driver's seat. Finally she found what she had been searching for—a tissue. Drawing in a ragged breath, she held the tissue to her nose and blew, then grabbed for another to wipe the telltale moisture from beneath her eyes.

The turnoff for Keswick was only a few more miles—and it seemed like a hundred. Had she been driving all day long? She glanced into the rearview mirror, the black-and-silver cab of an eighteen-wheeler a dangerous few yards behind. Tensing, she pressed down on the accelerator, hoping a slight increase in speed would satisfy the anxious driver. Suddenly the semi pulled out beside her, the narrow two-lane highway providing little room for such a maneuver. Marla grabbed the steering wheel with both hands, her stomach curled into a knot of fear as the Mercedes swerved, caught up in the draft of the larger vehicle.

"You idiot!" she shouted, followed by a particularly acrimonious and definitely unladylike curse. The sound of her voice reverberated within the confines of the car, and Marla shook her head, not knowing whether to laugh or cry.

Slowly she drew in a breath and let it out unevenly. She had to get hold of herself. True, the stupid ignoramus of a truck driver had frightened her practically senseless, but what could she do about it now? He was gone. She couldn't very well catch him and have it out with him on the spot.

She heaved a sigh. No. He was gone, just as Stefan was gone and would be gone for the next ten days. Why was she being so immature about it? She'd held back the tears while seeing him off, but as soon as he'd turned to walk onto the airplane, she'd broken down, fleeing from the parting scene as if she were on fire.

She couldn't ever remember having been this emotional about anything in her life. The tears just wouldn't stop flowing. Why did he have to go now, the childish question kept repeating itself. They'd been married only two weeks, and everything had been so wonderful, just like all the fairy tales she'd secretly never quit believing in.

But just as she got caught up on the merry-go-round of emotional turmoil, the saner part of her brain would assert itself, bringing her back to the reality of the situation. It wasn't as though he was leaving her forever. And there *was* a genuine reason for his leaving. She felt a little better at that thought.

It all made sense, and she was behaving like a juvenile, crying and going to pieces like this. Yet she couldn't forget her dream—her assumption—that she would be taking her first trip to Europe with Stefan—a romantic wonderful fairy-tale holiday far better than any tourist-guide itinerary. And now he was going alone, and regardless of the reason for it, Marla found it difficult to suppress a large degree of resentment and envy.

Inwardly, however, she acknowledged a more significant cause for her state of near depression over the whole thing. It wasn't simply Stefan's going and subsequent absence that bothered her. Her repeated attempts to gain his confidence had given her little more information than he'd already revealed about the problems his family was having. The drive to the airport would have been stifling had Marla not finally relented and focused the conversation on other topics. But it had hurt, just as it did now, knowing that Stefan couldn't trust her enough to open up and confide in her.

Husband and wife were supposed to share this sort of thing, weren't they? That was one basic tenet of marriage in which she truly believed. She'd assumed he did, also.

Oh, it's useless, Marla told herself, gulping back the last of her tears as she braked and turned the car into Morning Meadows's private lane. Some of the horses had been turned out into the paddocks closest to the stable, and somehow the mere sight of them lifted her spirits. At least there would be plenty to do while Stefan was away. Perhaps the time would fly from now until he returned.

By the time she'd parked the car in the garage Marla was beginning to feel more like her old independent self. Hadn't she learned anything during all the time that she'd devoted to living alone? Most definitely, she reminded herself firmly, stepping lightly out of the car and slamming the door shut.

She had coped with far less tenable circumstances at other times in her life. The experience would surely stand her in good stead.

CHAPTER FOURTEEN

MARLA CHECKED HER WATCH for what was surely the tenth time in the past hour. What was
keeping them, she wondered worriedly. Stefan's
plane was supposed to be on time; she had
called earlier to make sure. She'd agreed to let
Roy pick them up at the airport in spite of her
eagerness to see her husband. She wanted to
take care of all the arrangements before they arrived, and by being there, in her own home, she
could summon up at least a semblance of the
calm she didn't feel.

Perched on the edge of the couch in the living
room, she sat nervously inspecting her finger-
nails. Absently she patted the smooth coil at the
nape of her neck, then reached for the decanter
of brandy on the low walnut-and-glass coffee
table in front of her—another sure indication of
her intractable state of anxiety.

Taking another healthy swallow, she winced
as the fiery liquid burned its way down her
throat. She was being totally ridiculous about

this whole thing, but dammit, it couldn't be helped. Ever since Stefan had called two days earlier and informed her he would be bringing Anne-Marie back with him, Marla had been beside herself.

The news had been a total surprise, and Stefan had remained just as tight-lipped about this turn of events as he had about his reasons for going to Germany in the first place. All he'd said was that his niece would be coming back with him for a visit. Since he hadn't mentioned how long she'd be staying, Marla could only assume it would be for an indefinite period.

Her surprise had eventually changed to worried confusion. More than anything, she looked forward to being with her husband again. Although she'd kept busy enough during his absence, the time had dragged by, especially the nights without him next to her. Her love had grown to aching proportions, and she longed for his presence to fill the yearning void his absence created within her.

In a very large sense his mere return was enough, and she was glad of the opportunity to meet another member of his family. But a more selfish part of her wanted him solely to herself. She wanted nothing more than to lock him in the bedroom with her and remain there until they were both satiated—a state she sincerely doubted would ever be accomplished in this life-time.

But it was silly to let her fantasies run in that direction, since that was all they could ever be anyway. She would have to adjust to some amount of sharing of her husband with a new member of the household for a while at least, and with others on a day-to-day basis.

The ring of the telephone in the study jolted Marla out of her preoccupied state, and she stood up abruptly, walking swiftly across the room and into the hallway connecting the two rooms.

She was staring at the floor, and Eileen's sudden appearance in the doorway turned into a near collision.

"Oh!" Marla exclaimed, her hand going reflexively to the hollow of her throat, "I'm sorry. I didn't see you coming. I was just about to answer the—" She started to take a few steps as Eileen placed a hand on her arm and stopped her.

"I answered it for you," she said. Marla frowned. She hadn't even heard it stop ringing.

"It was Roy," Eileen continued. "He—"

"What happened?" Marla broke in, eyes widened in alarm.

Eileen smiled reprovingly. "Nothing happened, Marla. Good Lord, child, you've been as nervous as a ninny around here. He was calling from a phone booth at a gasoline station. They had to stop to fill up. Stefan's flight was about a half hour delayed,'' she added.

"Great," Marla muttered in annoyance, turning and walking back into the den. She sat back down on the couch and sighed heavily as she glanced at the grandfather clock on the far wall.

Eileen studied the younger woman for several minutes, then came into the room and absently began fluffing up the pillows. "Honey, you shouldn't be so nervous about their coming," she said soothingly. "I'm sure everything will work out just fine."

"Oh, I know, Eileen," Marla said, sighing forlornly. "I just hope we get along. You know, Stefan said Anne-Marie was the cause of the problem with his parents. He didn't tell me any details, but it must have been pretty severe for him to rush over and bring her back."

"Well, I can't say you don't have a point," Eileen agreed, adding brightly, "It'll all work out, though. We'll make it."

Marla smiled back affectionately, fervently hoping Eileen was right. "Well, at least we don't have to worry about a language barrier. Stefan said she speaks fairly good English."

"See, there. You've already found something positive in the situation."

Mollified somewhat, Marla got up and followed Eileen into the kitchen, eager to find something to do until they arrived.

A LOUD THUMP at the front of the house caught Marla's attention, and her head snapped up from her task. Hurriedly she placed the silverware on the table and removed the apron covering her dress. The doorbell chimed as she ran through the den and down the hallway to the front door.

"I'll get it, Eileen," she called out over her shoulder.

But the door flew open even before she could place her hand on the knob. Roy burst inside, his cheeks flushed from both the cold and the effort of carrying the heavy suitcases he brought in with him.

"Hi, there," he greeted her cheerily, setting the luggage down with a resounding thud on the marble floor.

"Hi, Roy," Marla said, hoping the tremulous note in her voice went unnoticed by him. "Where are—"

Stefan stepped inside just then, his ebony hair tossed carelessly by the wind, his ruddy face burnished, as was Roy's, by the frigid weather, though to a much deeper hue.

Marla's throat constricted at the sight of him.

She was standing almost behind the open door and at first he didn't see her. A familiar frown etched his brow as his gaze swept the entry hall searchingly, and Marla's own eyes smarted as she softly spoke his name. "Stefan?"

He turned, a smile slowly transforming his features as he set down the attaché case he was holding and took a step toward her. The warmth in his eyes matched her own, and instantly Marla's world was complete as she felt his arms wrap around her, pulling her close against him. The cold still lingering on his dark gray twill overcoat penetrated the wool of her dress. Yet Marla was oblivious to it as the whole of her responded to his warming nearness.

They kissed, a brief formal kiss for propriety's sake, yet one that served to fire the passionate response she longed to show. Later, Marla reminded herself more than a little reluctantly.

Stefan slid one hand lingeringly down her back before removing it, and as he turned, he kept the other arm firmly secured around her waist. Marla compressed her lips and looked away for a moment, suddenly aware that Roy had witnessed their display of affection and was a trifle embarrassed by it.

Roy grinned playfully at them both, before his glance shifted to another person standing next to the front door, now closed. Marla blinked in surprise. In her absorption, she had completely forgotten her expected guest. She opened her mouth as if to say something. Yet she hadn't the slightest idea *what* to say. Mercifully Stefan relieved her of the burden.

"Marla, this is Anne-Marie, my niece. Anne-Marie, my wife, Marla."

Marla held out her hand to the young, dark-haired girl standing tensely in front of them, nervously biting her upper lip. Anne-Marie had been staring at the floor, but with Stefan's introduction she slowly lifted her head.

The girl's slight figure was hidden by a voluminous gray maxilength coat, but her head was uncovered. Her straight, thick, chocolate brown hair was parted in the middle and hung in a blunt cut to just below her chin. It was a full-bodied mane; with the slightest movement of her head it swung with a natural bounce. She hadn't a trace of makeup on her narrow face, and Marla noted that her unblemished complexion hadn't reacted to the cold. It was pale, too pale for a young girl, and the dark crescents drooping beneath her large brooding eyes, almost the exact color of Stefan's, told their own story. In that one brief moment of assessment Marla became convinced that whatever other problem Stefan had stepped in to solve, the teenager was definitely not in the best of health.

"I'm very pleased to meet you, Anne-Marie," Marla said, smiling at the girl. "Here, let me take your coat." She reached out to help her take it off and was taken aback when Anne-Marie instantly shook her head.

"Thank you, but...no," the girl replied—a little too quickly. Marla was puzzled by the furtive glance she cast in Stefan's direction, who merely stared back at her with an expression that could only be described as stern.

"I am still a little cold, if you don't mind."

Marla smiled graciously at her again. "Of course I understand." Anne-Marie's accent was stronger than Stefan's who had lost most of his through years of studying and living in the States. Her soft voice and delicate demeanor touched Marla deeply, and her own nervousness was rapidly overshadowed by the more obvious, even painful discomfort Anne-Marie was suffering.

Eileen joined them then, and after initial greetings all around she urged them all into the den. Supper would be ready in a little more than an hour, which would give everyone time to freshen up and relax over aperitifs beforehand.

"Come along, dear." Eileen smiled at Anne-Marie, placing her arm around the slender girl's shoulders and showing her the way to her room.

Roy, carrying Anne-Marie's luggage, followed behind, chatting amiably with the housekeeper.

Stefan and Marla watched them disappear around the corner before renewing their embrace. Stefan's kiss was deep and penetrating, and Marla responded in full to the ardor of the moment. His need for her was evident, and for one very tempting moment she was ready to throw propriety to the winds and let the company take care of itself while they adjourned to the bedroom.

Stefan placed both hands on her shoulders and, applying a firm pressure, pushed her away a bit. "I missed you," he said huskily, his dark brown eyes searching her face intimately.

"Oh, Stefan, I missed you, too," Marla whispered. "So much!" She cocked her head to one side and smiled thoughtfully. "I don't understand why you just didn't take me with you."

Stefan studied her hesitantly for a moment before answering. "The situation was too complicated. It was better that I was there to handle it alone."

Marla frowned and raised one shoulder in a slight shrug. "But what sort of complications? I don't—"

Stefan was staring blankly over Marla's head. "You will find that out soon enough. Come, let's join the others."

Roy was behind the bar when they entered the den, pouring himself a drink and relating some particularly humorous story to Eileen, who was finishing Marla's half-completed job of laying out silverware on the dining-room table.

"What would you two like?" Roy asked as Stefan and Marla walked in.

"Scotch would be fine," Stefan said, continuing on to the rolltop desk and picking up a stack of mail lying there for him.

"Sherry, please," Marla said, moving toward the bar and plopping down on the bar stool in front of it. "Where's Anne-Marie?"

"Eileen left her in her room so she could freshen up before supper."

"Oh." Marla took the glass of sherry and sipped at it. "By the way, Stef, there's more mail for you in the study. I picked it up this morning and put it there for you."

"Good," Stefan said, accepting his drink from Roy and walking over to the couch to sit down with it. "So why don't you two tell me about what happened in my absence?"

The conversation for the next several minutes centered on both Marla's and Roy's accounting of the general business and related problems that had cropped up during the past ten days.

Anne-Marie's entrance into the room was so unobtrusive that Marla was startled when she happened to glance over and notice the girl standing near a window at the opposite end of the room. She had her back to the three of them, and Marla studied her taut slender form curiously. The navy blue dress she was wearing seemed a little old-fashioned for Marla's taste, but she mentally dismissed the judgment, reasoning that she really had no idea what constituted current European—in particular, German—fashion anyway.

Stefan and Roy were engrossed in a discussion in which she had no particular interest or involvement at the moment, so Marla set her glass down on the bar and stood up. Obviously the girl was very much ill at ease—not really surprising, in Marla's opinion. Stefan was not without fault in that regard. He'd done nothing thus far to make his niece feel welcome other than to run through the necessary introductions.

As she walked around the sofa, Anne-Marie turned suddenly at the sound of Marla's heels clicking on the hardwood floor. The movement was so swift Marla was reminded of a startled doe. But the surprise on her own features in that one revealing moment far exceeded the teenager's.

In the second it took for Marla's eyes to move rapidly over the girl's figure she was suddenly aware of the reason for her unlikely attire. The navy blue dress was even more strictly fashioned than it had appeared from the back. A simple A-line cut, long-sleeved, its only departure from the monotonous was a frilly rounded collar. Her look would have been altogether nondescript if it hadn't been for the obvious swelling just below the bustline.

Marla's eyes lingered on the substantial protrusion and immediately surmised there could only be one reason for it. Anne-Marie was pregnant, around six months pregnant, from Marla's estimation.

Schooling her surprised features was an exercise in careful control, but Anne-Marie had seen the look on her face and immediately turned her back. Marla turned, too, to look at her husband, who was still talking to Roy. A surge of anger welled up inside her. Why hadn't he told her Anne-Marie was pregnant? He'd kept quite a few things from her, she'd discovered, but this was ridiculous! No wonder the girl was so distressed. It was enough to cope with such a situation at her age, but to be subjected to her uncle's insensitivity was not only unnecessary but downright cruel. Shelving her irritation with the intention of speaking to her husband later, Marla moved to stand beside Anne-Marie, who was now staring out the large picture window.

"May I get you something to drink, Anne-Marie?" she inquired pleasantly.

The girl shook her head, her dark brown hair swinging against her chin. "No, thank you," she muttered in a barely audible tone.

Marla studied the girl's profile for a moment, at a loss as to what else she should do or say. But there was something in the brooding profile that touched a deep compassionate chord within her. She had no inkling of the factors that had led to Anne-Marie's becoming pregnant, but the whys and wherefores were entirely irrelevant at that point.

Stefan's niece was so young, so fragile, so... yes, innocent-looking, despite her physical condition, that Marla felt she had to try to reach out to the forlorn young girl. "Did you find your room all right? If there's anything you need, just—"

"No. Thank you very much, but...everything is all right."

Marla sighed and stood indecisively with her hands clasped tightly together, revealing her tension. "Good. Good.... Listen, Stefan didn't mention anything about the flight. Was it all right? Were there any problems?" How ridiculously trite her attempts at conversation must sound, but she didn't know of any other way to get acquainted with her diffident guest.

"No, everything was good," Anne-Marie answered, her eyes slanting to Marla once, then returning to gaze out on the sloping meadows beyond the grounds of the house.

Marla was about to give the faltering conversation—if it could be termed that—one more try, when Eileen called out from the dining room that supper was ready.

Stefan and Roy kept up a constant flow of chatter during the meal, a continuation of their conversation about business-related matters. Marla and Eileen carried on another conversation at their end of the table, both attempting at times to include Anne-Marie. But the girl's answers were so curt and mostly monosyllabic that the women gradually abandoned the effort, deciding it was going to take a great deal of time and patience to win at least some of her confidence.

Over coffee, Marla gave Stefan a full account of what she had been doing with Rudi while he'd been away. She couldn't help but notice that for the first time that evening Anne-Marie was showing an interest in this particular turn of the conversation.

"Do you ride, Anne-Marie?" Marla asked, and at the girl's shy nod she smiled encouragingly. "Then you'll certainly have fun here. We have more than enough horses. You can have your pick."

The last remark drew Stefan's attention away from something Roy was saying. He was sitting on the sofa opposite them, and Marla looked away from Anne-Marie just in time to catch the odd shadow of a frown that flitted across his face. He was looking at her pointedly, but for the life of her she couldn't imagine what she could have said or done to elicit such an expression of obvious disapproval.

Marla's expression didn't change, but her eyes held a questioning look as she leaned forward to pick up her after-dinner drink. Stefan, however, had turned back to Roy, leaving Marla to contemplate what, if anything, had gone wrong.

The incident was forgotten by the time Roy took his leave, at which point Anne-Marie decided to go to bed. Eileen took over with the young girl, leading her to her room to make sure everything was all right.

Enormously relieved that the long day, indeed the long wait itself was over, Marla preceded Stefan to their room. Usually preferring a bath, tonight she opted for a quick shower. Stefan was unpacking a few items when she emerged from the bathroom, naked beneath her long velour bathrobe, her hair still fastened in a knot on top of her head.

"Why don't you let Eileen take care of that, Stefan?" Marla asked, standing just inside the doorway, one hand on her hip, the other reaching up to smooth back an escaped tendril.

Stefan looked up at her, his gaze soaking in the vision of softness she presented posed that way. She was even lovelier than he remembered. Suddenly he dropped the stack of handkerchiefs he'd been holding and strode across the room to stand in front of her.

He was still dressed in his charcoal wool slacks. A smattering of dark curling hair escaped the unbuttoned neckline of his shirt. His arms snaked around Marla's slender waist as her hands reached up to rest on his broad shoulders, her fingers massaging their hard muscular texture with long loving strokes.

"Mmm...you smell good," he said huskily, his chin grazing her forehead as he drew in an exaggerated deep breath.

"And you look good," Marla half whispered, slipping her hands across his collarbone, then downward as her fingertips plied loose, one by one, the buttons of his shirt. Languidly her hands slid inside his opened shirt, the feel of his skin provoking a low moan of desire.

Pressing her face against his chest, she said,

"Honey, I missed you so much. It seems like you were gone forever." She pulled back to glance up at him, her blue eyes searching, reflecting the question that demanded an answer.

"Why didn't you tell me about Anne-Marie?" she asked, her eyes pleading with him to include her this time.

"What do you mean?" Stefan pulled back a little and looked down at her. Her expression told him she would brook no evasion this time.

"I think, Stefan, that you know exactly what I mean," Marla said firmly, pulling out of her husband's embrace and walking to the bed, crossing her arms and plopping down on the end of it.

Momentary irritation surfaced on Stefan's face. Placing his hands on his hips in a familiar gesture of annoyance, he lifted one eyebrow as he regarded his wife curiously.

"I think it's time we talked, Stefan," Marla said, leaning back on her elbows and watching as Stefan sighed and walked back to his suitcase. She regretted spoiling the moment of passion between them, but the confusion she'd suffered during the past ten days surfaced again with persistence. She would not let another moment go by before obtaining at least a few answers to the questions that had plagued her.

"Don't ignore me again, Stefan. I want an answer or two."

Stefan, who had resumed his unpacking, shrugged noncommittally. "Such as?"

"Please, honey, don't be so distant about this. Why can't you just tell me what happened while you were in Germany? Why do I have to drag it out of you?"

"You don't have to drag anything out of me," Stefan stated quietly. "I fully intended to tell you about everything."

"You did?" Marla sat up a bit straighter. Frowning, she asked, "But why didn't you tell me Anne-Marie was pregnant? It might have helped if I'd gone with you. She's as scared as a lost rabbit. You may be her uncle, but you've certainly done nothing to put her at ease since she arrived."

Stefan turned abruptly on his heel and snorted with disgust. "As if she's done anything to deserve being put at ease." He paused, then added in a low voice, "Anne-Marie's foolish actions are responsible for putting my father in the hospital!"

Stefan's anger was apparent, and suddenly Marla was aware of how very little she knew of the situation. Obviously he was far more emotionally involved in whatever had happened than he'd let on. She would have to proceed cautiously to get the whole story out of him.

"Is he all right now—your father?"

"Yes—for now. There's no telling how much of a setback he suffered, though."

Stefan snapped shut the suitcase and slid it against the love seat, to be stored later. His own blood pressure probably wasn't faring too well at the moment. This wasn't exactly what he had in mind to talk about with his wife right then, when he hadn't seen her for almost two weeks

Marla began pulling the pins out of her hair. wishing for all the world that she hadn't brought the subject up in the first place. Yet it had in one sense been unexpectedly revealing. Never before had she seen her husband display such depth of emotion. That he should be so judgmental was not really surprising. She was coming to understand and accept, at least when applied to himself, the traditional values he adhered to so faithfully. But the anger that had banished his usual stoicism had been almost shocking.

Marla was coming to understand, too, how naive she really was about marriage itself. Stefan's behavior when he had decided to fly off to Germany without her had apparently merely indicated the tip of the iceberg. Undoubtedly he would do other unpredictable things. Undoubtedly, in time, she would begin to truly know

him...in time. Be that as it may, it was nevertheless pointless to spoil his first evening back
home.

Stefan had gone into the bathroom, and after
hearing him turn on the taps in the shower,
Marla switched out all the lights in the room but
one small bedside lamp. Removing her robe, she
then pulled back the covers on both sides of the
bed, sliding between the chilly sheets, hugging
herself with her arms and shivering until the
heat of her body became trapped under the
layers of covering. The shower stopped, and
after a few minutes Stefan emerged from the
bathroom, stopping just outside the door to rub
the towel he held in both hands against the nape
of his neck. Marla's head was barely visible
above the down comforter; he could feel more
than see her eyes upon him.

Suddenly the days of waiting were over, the
endless worry and arrangements behind him. As
he flung the towel across the back of a chair,
Marla's breath caught in her throat at the sight
of his hard potent form. His eyes never leaving
hers, he folded back the covers and slid inside
next to her.

And Marla breathed a sigh of relief and contentment that finally he was back beside her.
Nothing else mattered. Her world was complete.

CHAPTER FIFTEEN

GETTING STEFAN TO SIT DOWN and explain exactly what had happened while he was in Germany was not exactly an easily accomplished feat. Each and every time Marla broached the subject he reacted in a way that she found increasingly difficult to understand, emotional displays being a definite contrast to his normally forbearing nature.

Yet bit by bit the entire story did come out. Instead of giving Marla more insight into her husband's puzzling behavior, however, it only confused her more. From what she could gather, he still held a grudge against his niece for having disappointed his parents to such an extent that his father's heart condition had been exacerbated.

Marla could certainly understand his anxiety, even his anger. Yet she couldn't abide his stubborn refusal to consider the whole picture. Anne-Marie hadn't had an easy childhood by any means. That she had got in with the wrong crowd was not so incomprehensible, considering the fact that she'd been raised without parents. From all accounts, her grandparents had had a hard time of it, trying at their age to properly look after a young impulsive girl.

Yet as the days went by and Anne-Marie's presence in the household became more and more acceptable, Stefan's sternness gradually abated. Still, Anne-Marie remained, despite her uncle's changed attitude, quiet, almost withdrawn—except for those moments when Marla detected a gleam of defiance in the girl's eyes, defiance aimed not only at her uncle but at those around her. Marla could well imagine Anne-Marie's feelings of frustration at being plucked out of familiar surroundings, to be set down here in the midst of virtual strangers and a disapproving uncle.

Marla was reluctant to intrude too much on her niece's self-imposed isolation, however, reasoning that in time she would adjust. Pregnancy could be a traumatic state for any woman, not to mention an unmarried teenage girl away from her home, family and friends.

More than a week passed before Marla decided the girl had spent enough time alone. There was no point in brooding over her situation, and Marla was determined to see at least a shadow of a smile on the lonely young girl's face, regardless of what it took to produce one.

It was a Tuesday morning in early February, and in spite of the unrelenting cold that gripped the countryside Marla was determined to get Rudi outdoors for some long overdue exercise. The rain, which had fallen virtually nonstop throughout the month of January, finally let up for several days in a row. The sky was overcast, but Marla decided to take the horse out for at least a few minutes. A change of scenery would do them both a world of good.

Stefan had been at the stable since very early that morning. February and March were heavily booked months for Donauwind, and he was kept busy with the mountains of detail involved in that particular aspect of his breeding operation.

Marla, having just finished breakfast, was on her way to her room to dress for the day's outing. Passing through the living room, she almost missed Anne-Marie, who was seated inconspicuously in a leather wing-back chair next to the fireplace, thumbing through a fashion magazine.

"Good morning, Anne-Marie," she greeted her cheerily. "Did you just get up?"

"Yes, ma'am," Anne-Marie answered softly,

lifting her large brown eyes briefly, then dropping them back down to the magazine.

Marla took a few steps toward her, then stopped, shaking her head as she said, "Anne-Marie, I wish you'd just call me Marla. 'Ma'am' makes me feel so old."

The girl looked up and replied somewhat timorously, "All right."

Marla sighed. She wished Anne-Marie would respond in more than just monosyllables. "How are you feeling?"

Her niece shrugged slightly. "Fine."

"Well, you don't look so fine," Marla stated candidly. "Those shadows under your eyes aren't exactly the picture of health." She paused. "Are you remembering to take the vitamins Dr. Sloan prescribed?"

The girl nodded and turned another page.

Marla chewed on her lower lip thoughtfully for a moment. Glancing outside, she noticed gratefully that at last the sun was peeping through the clouds, though more than likely only a temporary state of affairs. An idea struck her, and she decided to act on it.

"How would you like to come with me today, Anne-Marie? I'm going to work Rudi over a few fences in the hunt field. Wouldn't you like to get out of the house for a couple of hours? Some fresh air should put a little color into your cheeks.''

A spark of interest showed in the dark brown eyes, tempered, though, with uncertainty. ''I don't know if Uncle Stefan would want me to....'' Her voice trailed off, but her gaze wandered longingly to the wide picture window.

''You let me worry about what Uncle Stefan thinks you should do,'' Marla said affectionately, gratified by her niece's apparent interest. ''Why don't you go to your room and get dressed? I'll be ready myself in a few minutes.''

Slowly Anne-Marie closed the magazine. ''Do you really think it will be all right? I mean....''

Marla chuckled lightly. ''Of course it will be all right—and besides, I could use your help. Morris is busy all the time, and Roy and Stefan are occupied with Donavwind's bookings all day. And,'' she added, ''I'd appreciate the company.''

Gradually a smile spread across Anne-Marie's face, and finally she set the magazine down on the coffee table and stood up. ''Okay.''

''Be sure and dress warm.''

''Yes, I will.''

''See you in a minute,'' Marla said, walking briskly out of the room, more than pleased she was finally making inroads into the girl's quiet subdued nature.

THE STABLE was a bustle of activity that morning, and Marla's and Anne-Marie's presence went virtually unnoticed as they moved the from tack room, to tend to Rudi.

As Marla attached the crossties to Rudi's halter, she noticed Anne-Marie watching her very intently. Encouraged by her obvious attentiveness, she turned to her and said, "Could you lend me a hand, Anne-Marie? I'd like to change the bit on his bridle. If you don't mind grooming him, that would speed things up quite a lot."

Anne-Marie bit into her lower lip shyly and nodded rapidly, walking over to where Marla stood. "Okay."

"Here are the grooming supplies," Marla said, indicating a small wooden cabinet on the wall. "Brushes, hoof pick...hoof dressing— whatever you need." She watched as Anne-Marie reached for a curry comb and brush before she moved away. "If you can't find anything, just yell. I'll be in the tack room."

Anne-Marie nodded, then turned her attention to the chestnut.

As Marla entered the tack room she glanced back surreptitiously; Anne-Marie was setting about the grooming task in a natural, obviously educated manner. She noted the definite eagerness in the girl's movements, the spark of interest that was truly heartwarming, and smiled to herself as she continued on her way. She should have thought of this sooner. Whatever Anne-Marie's problems had been back in Germany, she was still a young innocent girl in many ways. Marla could remember all too easily the awful growing pains associated with being sixteen years old.

When she emerged from the tack room several minutes later, Anne-Marie was squatting down, applying dressing with a paint brush to Rudi's hooves. There was no doubt about the girl's experience with horses. Rudi was a magnificent animal to begin with, but thanks to Anne-Marie's efforts every inch of him was positively gleaming, the beautiful picture he presented drawing Marla's appreciative comment.

"You did a fantastic job, Anne-Marie," she said, standing with the bridle draped over her shoulder as she waited for the girl to finish dressing Rudi's hooves. "He looks great."

Anne-Marie smiled as she placed the can of dressing, along with the brush, back inside the cabinet. "He's very easy to work around." Stepping closer to Rudi, she ran a hand down one side of his long gleaming neck.

"Yes, he is," Marla agreed. "Here, would you mind putting his bridle on while I get my saddle?"

"Sure." Anne-Marie took the bridle and, unhooking the crossties, removed Rudi's halter to slip the reins over his head.

Marla returned with her saddle, and a few minutes later Rudi stood fully tacked. "Well, ready to go," Marla said lightheartedly. "I'm going to hop on here. You can follow me out to the hunt field."

"Okay," Anne-Marie agreed, and something clicked inside Marla as she noticed the girl give the horse a pat on the rump as he and Marla stepped ahead of her. A younger version of herself, perhaps? Ah, well, it didn't really matter whether she was or not. Marla felt a growing sense of kinship with the young girl that she'd never expected. And she liked it. She really did.

STEFAN WAS SEATED at his desk in the sitting-room portion of their bedroom that evening as Marla emerged from the bathroom. Her bathrobe was tied loosely around her waist, and as she padded barefoot across the carpet, she patted her hair dry with a towel.

"It's about time you got home," she chided her husband playfully as she plopped down at her dressing table and plugged in the cord to the blow dryer. "Have you eaten yet?"

"Hmm?" Stefan mumbled, still preoccupied with a sheaf of papers in his hands.

"Stefan, I'm talking to you," Marla said, snaking her head. "Can't you put that away for tonight? You've been at it all day long." It was true. She hadn't seen him since early this morning, and he'd got home from the stable only a few minutes ago.

"I just want to look over these contracts. I'll be with you in a minute."

"'I'll be with you in a minute,'" Marla mimicked him. "I'm going to have to start making appointments with my own husband."

"Hmm?"

Marla clucked her tongue and sighed heavily. "Nothing," she murmured, switching on the blow dryer as she separated and lifted the wet strands of her hair. A definite disadvantage to long hair, Marla mused, was the time it took to dry. But when she'd finished, Stefan had finally turned off the desk lamp and was shucking off his heavy wool sweater.

Putting away the blow dryer, she went to her husband, sliding her arms around him and pressing her cheek against his cotton undershirt. "Aside from working, how was your day?"

"Productive, I think would be the proper term," Stefan said, pulling her closer to him and resting his chin on top of her head. "But actually, that's the last thing I'm in the mood to talk about."

"Then why don't we talk about mine?" Marla suggested, pulling back to look up at him, her wide blue eyes shining with her exuberance.

"Okay," Stefan agreed, releasing her and walking over to the leather low-boy. "You look rather pleased with yourself. What did you do today?"

Marla plopped down on the bed, fluffing up a few pillows behind her back and drawing her knees up to her chest. "Well, I gave Rudi a good workout. He really enjoyed the change of scenery."

"Good," Stefan said, removing the rest of his clothes and donning a maroon dressing gown.

"And Anne-Marie had a really nice time, I think. She certainly knows a lot about horses. She groomed him to absolute—"

"What are you talking about?" Stefan, heading for the bathroom, had stopped in his tracks. His chin came up.

Marla stared blankly at him. "Rudi. He looked really—"

"What were you saying about Anne-Marie?"

Marla shook her head and clucked her tongue. "Just like a man. You weren't listening to a word I—"

"Marla, what did you say about Anne-Marie?" At Stefan's stern impatient tone Marla's expression darkened.

"I said she had a good time. I took her with me while I worked Rudi today." Marla paused, confused by her husband's scowl. "She really knows her way around horses. I let her groom Rudi, and she did a really first-class job. But I guess that's to be expected. She said she had a couple of years' training in Germany."

Stefan shoved his hands into the pockets of his robe. "Whose idea was it that she visit the stable today?"

Marla shrugged. "Mine. What difference does that make?"

Stefan's wide mouth tightened into a grim line, and he strode to the foot of the bed.

"I can't understand why you would even think of such a thing. The girl is obviously in no shape to be standing around in the cold—and grooming horses, of all things."

Marla's mouth dropped open in astonishment, and she laughed shortly. "Stefan, come on! I can't believe you just said that."

Stefan regarded her seriously. "Well, I did— and I meant it."

Marla sat up, straightened her legs and slapped her palms angrily against her thighs. "Then it's the most ridiculous thing I've ever heard you come up with. What's your objection? Are you afraid she's going to suddenly keel over and die the minute she walks out the front door? Stefan, she can't—"

"She's pregnant," Stefan inserted dryly.

"So?"

"So she doesn't need to be exposing herself to all sorts of unnecessary hazards."

Marla sighed, striving for patience. "Honey, I don't think what Anne-Marie did today constituted an unnecessary hazard. Being outdoors did her a world of good. Do you know she even laughed for the first time since she's been here?"

Stefan turned and walked across the room to stand next to the long bay window. He gazed pensively into the moonlit acres that bordered that side of the house, and Marla took advantage of his momentary silence.

"Listen, Stefan, I realize you're concerned for her welfare—I think that's highly admirable of you—but the best thing for anyone is exercise, regardless of his or her physical condition. Are you saying you'd rather she stay cooped up inside this house all day long—every day? Why not let her enjoy herself as long as she's here?"

Stefan said nothing, and Marla frowned, suddenly realizing there was one subject that had yet to be discussed. In a lower tone she asked, "And by the way, how long is she staying?"

Stefan said nothing again, not for a long

while. Then he turned away from the window, lifting a hand to rub the back of his neck. He cast his wife a direct look. "Until she delivers."

At Marla's shocked exclamation he said, "I thought you'd assumed that much."

Marla bit her upper lip and raised her eyebrows briefly, then looked away. "Actually, no, I hadn't."

"Do you object?"

Marla shook her head. "Uh-huh." Gulping, she lifted her head slowly, her blue eyes shining with unconcealed hurt. "Why didn't you tell me before? There seem to be a lot of things you just wait until the last minute to tell me. I don't understand it."

"There's nothing to understand. I wasn't sure myself, so I never brought it up."

"Oh."

Stefan crossed the room and started to walk into the bathroom, hesitating just before he went in. "I don't mind Anne-Marie's getting a little fresh air. I just don't want her to overdo it."

Marla stared disbelievingly at her husband for a moment before answering. "Fine, Stefan. I wasn't planning on having her clean stalls and pitch hay."

Stefan ignored the sarcastic reply, saying only, "Well, I'm going to shower now."

Marla made no reply as he closed the bathroom door behind him, merely stared straight ahead as a replay of their conversation went through her mind. Slowly she brought her knees back up to her chest, wrapping her arms around them and resting her chin on her hands.

For the first time she began to worry about what was really going on in her husband's mind. She simply couldn't understand this over-concern on his part. It was as though he became a different person when he discussed his niece. Well, she could only try to make him see that Anne-Marie was, although pregnant, still a teenager, with all the normal needs and desires that went along with that particular age. Surely once he got used to the situation he'd adjust and abandon that ridiculous overprotective attitude

CHAPTER SIXTEEN

"RIGHT. GOOD. We'll see you then." Stefan replaced the receiver and propped one elbow on his desk, rubbing thumb and forefinger along the bridge of his nose. After a while he sat back and stretched his arms above his head, pulling the green plaid of his flannel shirt tautly across his chest.

Weariness permeated every pore of his body, and he closed his eyes and leaned his head back against the chair. It was a satisfying weariness, though. Despite the complications that might have led to sadder circumstances, he, Roy and Dr. Richardson had managed to see the first mare of the season foal. He'd just delivered the news of the strapping colt to the owners in upstate Virginia, who had immediate plans to come down and visit the newborn.

Stefan opened his eyes and raked a hand through his hair as his gaze slowly traveled around the paneled office, located a floor above the main stable. It was a comfortable yet functional room, furnished with a wide spacious desk, behind which stood two large steel-gray file cabinets and floor-to-ceiling bookcases spread the length of the room. A hunter-green corduroy couch and love seat were separated by a low walnut coffee table strewn with a variety of equestrian and breeding journals.

His gaze rested on several framed photographs of Donauwind, his Trakehner stud, whose bookings by now were completely filled for the rest of the breeding season. Standing, he shoved his hands inside the back pockets of his jeans and crossed the room to one of the windows beside his desk. Patches of snow spotted the distant pastures and paddocks, the rye grass beneath showing through here and there in vivid green shoots. His eye was arrested by a movement beneath him, to the far end of the stable. Marla, astride Rudi, was walking the horse down the gravel drive, heading him toward the pathway leading to the hunt field.

Stefan watched appreciatively as the pair made leisurely progress toward their destination. He was proud of what Marla had accomplished thus far in training Rudi. He didn't doubt that the gelding would make a fine show horse. As soon as the weather permitted, Marla intended to begin taking him to local schooling shows in preparation for his first season of competition.

He was about to turn away from the window when two other figures emerged from the stable, apparently following in the direction Marla and Rudi were taking. It was Anne-Marie, walking somewhat awkwardly beside Roy.

Stefan's lips tightened grimly at the sight of the couple. Anne-Marie's arms were crossed over her ever-growing abdomen, her dark brown hair swinging against either cheek as she moved along. Roy was saying something to her, and suddenly she threw her head back. Though Stefan couldn't hear her, he could see she was laughing delightedly.

His frown deepened, and he turned away from the window, walked back to his desk and picked up a silver-plated letter opener. Tapping the slender instrument repeatedly against the palm of one hand, he mulled over what he'd just observed.

Contrary to his own opinion, Marla had insisted that his niece would fare better by getting outdoors as much as she wanted to. Stefan had grudgingly relented, though he still disapproved to a large degree.

He was grateful, however, for the relationship between his wife and his niece. He would never have thought such closeness would have or even could have developed between the two of them. Anne-Marie was not the easiest person to get to know as it was. The girl's attitude was baffling. Though she had never said as much, the anger and resentment were there, surfacing occasionally in those large brown eyes. And all of it aimed at him, he recognized.

But who could blame her? It was *he* who had deserted her, to be raised by grandparents too old to deal with a young girl's needs and emotions. *He* who had snatched her up from what she was familiar with, setting her down in the midst of complete strangers. It was amazing that Anne-Marie was able to keep her feelings of frustration at bay.

He'd felt badly from the beginning about the entire situation. He hadn't wanted Marla to be a part of these family problems that had begun a long time ago, before she had ever even known him—problems, he admitted readily now, that had been in large part due to his own selfishness.

Even now, almost seven years later, the events preceding the death of his brother, Rolf, still burned within him like a brand. Cruel words, words never meant to be spoken, flooded back into his mind, and Stefan cringed inwardly at the unwanted memory. It was all in the past, he kept reminding himself often enough, only to have the haunting memory of that last conversation between them assault afresh.

The two brothers' sibling rivalry had followed them into adulthood, settling into a pattern of unceasing bickering. Their parents hadn't helped matters, always holding Stefan, the firstborn, up as an example for Rolf to follow. Rolf had resented this, and had often done just the opposite to spite his older brother. Their arguments were usually over petty matters, but the words were thick and accusing—never more so than during that last quarrel...the day before Rolf had been killed. All of it was imprinted on Stefan's brain, every stinging acrimonious word hurled at his brother, who'd simply stared back at him, but with a different look in his eyes this time, a look of hurt—deep, unforgiving hurt.

The overwhelming anguish Stefan suffered after Rolf's untimely death had been pushed to the back of his mind, however, because of the grief and suffering his parents were going through. Later, when time had healed at least some of the pain of loss, he had backed away more and more from the responsibility of caring for his only brother's offspring, leaving the duty of raising Anne-Marie to his parents.

They were getting older, had aged considerably with the death of their younger son. But busily pursuing a fast-paced life aimed at eventually realizing his career ambitions, Stefan had

conveniently shoved aside the occasional pangs
of conscience over the shirking of what he considered his family duty

He was paying for the mistake he'd made now
with an intensity of guilt he'd never thought
possible. His parents hadn't been able to contend with either day-to-day dilemmas or the
fundamental problems—drugs, sex—of a
modern teenage girl. Their love for her was
never in question, but their lack of guidance had
left Anne-Marie free to get involved with a
group of peers as lost and immature as she was,
eventually resulting in a relationship that had
led to her becoming pregnant. Oscar Gerhardt's
illness had been worsened by the entire situation, and Stefan couldn't forget or forgive
himself for that, either.

Enough harm had come to his family as a
result of his negligence, and he'd decided to
take over, as he should have when his brother
died. He'd be damned if he'd shirk his responsibility to his family again. No harm
would come to Anne-Marie or her baby. He
owed that much to the memory of Rolf and his
parents' peace of mind for the rest of their
lives.

Stefan let go of the letter opener, and it
bounced once on top of the leather-bound desk
pad. He walked around the desk and sat down

again, sliding a thick ledger toward him. After opening it, he sat staring at it blankly. His mind was no more geared to a hour's worth of bookwork than it had been before. He thought of the scene he'd just witnessed: Anne-Marie and Roy walking side by side. Roy had the type of personality that attracted friends, male and female alike, like moths to a flame. It was no wonder Anne-Marie had grown to like him so much. She was around him practically every day, now that she visited the stable on a regular basis with Marla.

He'd spoken to Marla about it, and expectedly she'd laughed aside the thought that anything other than friendship was developing between Roy and Anne-Marie. What was wrong with Anne-Marie's having someone she liked to talk to, she'd insisted? And, besides, didn't Stefan trust his manager?

Yes, he did trust Roy. He had no reason to do otherwise. Stefan heaved a sigh and brought a hand up to rub the back of his neck. Determinedly he picked up a pencil and flipped through a few pages in the ledger until he located the one he needed. He might as well get started. Although he'd been up half the night seeing to the foaling, the day was still young, with plenty that needed attending to before he was ready to call it quits.

"COME ON, BADGER, don't be such a stick-in-the mud. Don't you wanna go outside and have a little fun?"

Anne-Marie's laugh seemed to ripple like a silvery clear stream. She was watching as Marla tugged on the reins, urging the reluctant horse forward down the concrete aisleway toward the door.

"He does not like to be cold today," Anne-Marie said, patting the horse encouragingly on the rump. "Come, Badger, you will like it when you get there."

"Did you hear that, boy? If Anne-Marie says you'll like it, then you will—believe me."

Anne-Marie's laugh was echoed by Marla's as Badger stepped off as if on cue.

"See, what did I tell you?" Marla joked. "This horse understands English."

Anne-Marie laughed delightedly as she walked along the opposite side of the gelding. "He is certainly a smart horse—there is no doubt. I wonder if he could understand German, too?"

"I don't know. Why don't you give it a try?"

"*Wie geht es Ihnen,* Badger?" Again as if on cue, Badger jerked his head up and looked at Anne-Marie. Both women erupted into hysterics at the hilarity of Badger's timely response, their laughter reverberating throughout the long stable.

"Hey!" Roy's voice called out from the opposite end of the stable, "what are you two up to?" He was leading an obviously pregnant mare inside from her turn in one of the paddocks, smiling broadly at them as he stepped out of the mare's stall.

"We're just talking to Badger," Marla said, shrugging as if it was the most natural thing in the world.

Roy placed both hands on his slim hips and shook his head from side to side. "Women," he said in mock disparagement. "Be damned if I'll ever understand 'em."

Marla chuckled and called out teasingly over her shoulder as she and Anne-Marie led Badger outside, "They're too intelligent for you, that's why," adding, "We'll be in the arena if you need either of us."

"All right," Roy shouted back, returning to his chores.

MARLA SLOWED HER STEPS for a moment to accommodate Anne-Marie's pace. Her abdomen had grown tremendously, but for her eighth month of pregnancy she seemed to be faring quite well. Marla was gratified that not only had she remained in general good health but that her attitude had become decidedly more cheerful.

Marla's affection for the teenager had grown

into genuine love, the mutual reward being an invaluable bond of trust. Anne-Marie had by now opened up to her on more than one occasion, sharing confidences, and through the intimate talks Marla had learned a great deal about her husband's niece.

"You don't have to tell me about it, Anne-Marie," Marla had said one afternoon as they walked slowly down the lane to the house.

Anne-Marie shrugged. "It doesn't matter, not anymore." She hesitated, twisting a strand of hay in one hand. "I'm sorry I did. . .what I did. It was wrong, a bad mistake. But . . . ."

"But what?" Marla prompted.

Again she hesitated, her large eyes narrowing perceptibly. "I don't think I was as bad as Uncle Stefan thinks."

Marla glanced over at her then, surprised at the sharpness in her tone. "Anne-Marie, I don't think Stefan thinks that at all about you." Her tone was soft, reassuring.

Anne-Marie laughed gruffly. "Yes, he does. And he doesn't really want me here."

Marla stopped and grabbed Anne-Marie by the arm. "That's not true, Anne-Marie—not one bit. He *does* want you here."

A mixture of emotions—defiance, anger, hurt—shot through those dark brown eyes so much like her uncle's. "Only because he thinks I'm better off with him than with them.''

"Who?"

"*Oma* and *opa*.''

Marla sighed heavily, searching Anne-Marie's face. Something told her this outburst was simply that and nothing more. And who could blame the girl? She had been through so much for one so young.

"You know something, Anne-Marie? I think when all this is over—after you've had the baby—you'll feel a lot better about everything, even your Uncle Stefan.''

Anne-Marie said nothing as they continued on toward the house, but Marla noted a certain change in her, as if she might at least be giving the possibility some consideration.

But if that was the case, Stefan certainly wasn't giving his niece too much encouragement as far as Marla was concerned. He hadn't relented one inch in his belief that Anne-Marie was a frail, almost helpless creature. But at least Marla was able to get around him at times—like this afternoon.

"Come on, Nik, run! Get it!"

Marla put aside her reflections, turning to see Anne-Marie straighten from throwing a piece of wood. Nik raced after it, snatched it up between his ferocious-looking teeth and ran back to drop it at the girl's feet. The dog had grown by leaps

and bounds, too; the exercise he was now getting every day, roaming the larger spread of
the main estate of Morning Meadows, had
toned and firmed him up. He was almost fully
grown.

Anne-Marie reached down to pat the puppy
on the head, and Nik licked her hand affectionately.

"I'm going to get on now and hack around
for a while," Marla said, lowering the stirrups
on her saddle.

"All right," Anne-Marie said agreeably, tossing the stick again for Nik to fetch.

Marla smiled as she mounted Badger, more
than pleased that her beloved puppy had also
made a friend of the young girl.

Badger was lazy today, so much so that Marla
was obliged to apply more than the ordinary
amount of leg to even get him interested in the
day's workout. Nevertheless she put him
through his paces, and by the end of the session
the gelding had worked up a healthy lather.
Marla headed the horse in the direction of the
end gate. Anne-Marie was leaning against it, her
chin propped on her arms, which were folded
across the top rail.

There was a certain wistfulness reflected in
her eyes that touched Marla deeply. Swinging
down off the saddle, she asked cheerfully,

"Now what's that look all about, Anne-Marie? Are you tired? Bored?"

The girl straightened instantly. "Oh, no! I love to watch you ride." She started to say something else, then stopped, releasing a lengthy sigh instead.

"And you wish you were doing the same," Marla put the words in her mouth. She circled around the horse and stood beside the end gate, cocking her head to one side as she smiled at Anne-Marie.

"What do you mean?" Anne-Marie asked guilelessly.

"Oh, I think you know. I've been watching you for a long time now. You'd give anything to ride yourself, wouldn't you?"

Anne-Marie studied the ground for a moment, then glanced up shyly at Marla. She nodded demurely but shrugged one shoulder. "But I can't—not now at least."

Marla chewed on her low lip for a moment, her gaze slanting to Badger, who stood with his head down, thoroughly ready to call it quits for the day.

"Hmm. You know, I don't know why you couldn't ride right now," Marla said.

Anne-Marie's eyes widened in astonishment. "But—" her eyes lowered to her protruding stomach before she lifted them to look at Marla again. "—I cannot ride. Not *now*."

"Well, I didn't really mean ride," Marla amended. "I can't see any harm in your just sitting on him. He's so quiet today a bolt of lightning couldn't get a charge out of him."

Anne-Marie's gaze shifted to Badger, then back to Marla. Lifting one hand, she bit her forefinger gently, her brown eyes sparkling with growing enthusiasm for the unlikely suggestion. "Do you really think it would be all right?"

"Sure. Might do you some good to get it out of your system," Marla said encouragingly.

A smile broke across Anne-Marie's pretty features, and she clapped both hands together. "Okay," she said, nodding eagerly. "I want to do it." She stopped, frowning suddenly. "But how will I get on?"

Marla snapped her fingers and opened the end gate, leading Badger out and walking several feet to an old stone mounting block, rarely used.

"Come on, just climb up on this, and I'll lower the stirrup some," Marla instructed.

Anne-Marie took the two steps up to the top of the small platform and waited for Marla to lead Badger into a position perpendicular to it.

"Okay, ready?" Marla asked.

Anne-Marie nodded and took the reins, which Marla had thrown over Badger's head. Mounting proved to be relatively easy, and within seconds she was astride Badger, grinning from ear to ear.

"Feel all right?" Marla asked.

"Mmm-hmm."

"Let's adjust the stirrups," Marla suggested, and proceeded to take up the slack until the bottom of the stirrup was level with the girl's ankle.

Anne-Marie inserted her feet into the stirrups and took up the reins with obvious proficiency. She applied pressure with the calves of her legs, and Badger moved forward.

"Just walk him around in the ring until you feel like stopping " Marla said, pulling back the gate for them to ride through, then swinging herself to the upper plank of the fence.

She grinned as she watched Anne-Marie guide Badger around the ring. Despite her bulky form, her riding skills were apparent. She sat the horse well and even demonstrated a few successful dressage maneuvers.

Marla clapped loudly and called out, "Very nice. Let's see that again."

As Anne-Marie continued to ride Badger at a walk around the arena, Marla watched with growing appreciation. She could imagine how well her niece would perform without the restrictions imposed by pregnancy.

The sound of wheels throwing up gravel

didn't intrude on Marla's preoccupation with observing Anne-Marie. Only at the sound of a door slamming did she turn to see Stefan emerging from his car.

Waving at him, she called out, "Hi, honey. Come and watch what Anne-Marie is doing with Badger. She's even had him—" She stopped, perplexed by the thunderous expression she detected on her husband's face as he neared the arena.

"Stef—"

"What in God's name is going on here?" Stefan spoke in a low, barely controlled tone.

Marla frowned slightly and gestured toward the arena. "I thought it would be nice if Anne-Marie had a chance—"

"Nice!" Stefan seethed. "Are you out of your mind!"

Marla stared at him, shocked, as he strode away from her, flung open the gate and took a few steps into the arena.

"Anne-Marie!" he bellowed.

The girl turned her head, the smile on her face disappearing instantly as she recognized the expression of intense displeasure etched on her uncle's face. She turned Badger and walked him slowly toward Stefan, who stood with both hands on his hips, glowering more fiercely than Marla would have imagined him capable of.

He grabbed the reins near the bit as Badger came to a halt, then jerked his head upward as he asked tersely, "Do you think you can get down?"

"Of course she can," Marla inserted. She'd hurried into the arena behind him, hoping to prevent what looked to be developing into an unpleasant scene. "She didn't have any trouble getting on at all. We used the—"

"Swing your right leg over the front of the saddle, not the back," Stefan interrupted her. "Maria, hold the reins."

Marla did as he said and watched silently as he moved around to the horse's left side and held up his hands. Anne-Marie, still without uttering a word, bent down and, with her uncle's hands beneath her arms, slid gingerly from the horse. Stefan let go of her, saying, "Get in the car and I'll drive you back to the house."

As Anne-Marie started off, Marla flipped the reins down over Badger's head and stared angrily at her husband. "What are you doing, Stefan? How dare you make a fool out of me in front of her that way!"

Stefan glared steadily at her as he reached into the back pocket of his jeans and withdrew his set of car keys. "I don't need to 'make' a fool out of you. You obviously are one already."

Marla drew in her breath sharply, stung by

the viciousness of the accusation. "I don't know what's wrong with you, Stefan Gerhardt, but I won't stand here and let you insult me."

"No more than I'll stand by and let you break my niece's neck."

"*What* are you talking about!" Marla's voice rose shrilly. "Good heavens, Stefan, she was just sitting on him—at a walk. And that's all I intended for her to do. She wanted—"

"I don't give a damn what she wanted," Stefan inserted brusquely. "She's too young to have any idea of what's right or wrong for her in the state she's in. I would have thought my wife would have had a little more sense, though." Stefan's eyes narrowed slightly and his jaw tightened as he said, "What if Badger had spooked? Or bolted?"

"Come on! Don't you think you're dramatizing this just a little?" Marla shot back, crossing her arms over her chest. "And besides," she added, "the only reason I even thought it appropriate was because of Badger's condition today. I practically had to beat him every step of the way, and I worked him hard for thirty minutes. It was very unlikely he would pull anything funny."

Stefan was as unmoved by Marla's explanations as if she'd never spoken. "Anne-Marie is about to give birth. I don't *ever* want her on a horse again. Do I make myself clear?"

Marla stared mutely at her husband, her nostrils flaring slightly as she struggled to control the whirlwind of emotions she was experiencing: rage, confusion...and hurt. She gave a barely perceptible nod, then watched through blurred eyes as Stefan turned abruptly and stalked off.

As the car's engine gunned to life, she started, blinking rapidly and swallowing back tears of humiliation at her husband's words. What was wrong with him? Why was he so damned unreasonable when it came to anything—everything—concerning Anne-Marie?

Slowly, insidiously, with painful dawning awareness, Marla began to understand. She remained rooted to the spot in the middle of the riding arena, her stomach churning at the realization that perhaps she *was* a fool.

A naive gullible fool at that.

CHAPTER SEVENTEEN

BADGER SNORTED LOUDLY and pawed the ground, eager to get back to the warmth and security of his stall. The movement succeeded in getting Marla's attention, although she did nothing more than turn her head slightly to glance at the Thoroughbred.

She remained stock-still, unable, unwilling, to move, her brain refusing to deal with the shock of what had just happened. Stefan's rude abrupt departure still cut her to the quick, the doubts and suspicions unearthed from within her still too much for her wounded psyche to contend with.

This had certainly not been the first argument between them, and she was by no means laboring under the impression there would never be another. She could handle that—she could handle most arguments and disputes between them, for that matter. But this, this was something far more than a simple dispute over what was right or wrong for Anne-Marie

Hadn't it been there all along—the real reason behind Stefan's overprotective attitude toward the girl, his anxiety over just about every move she made? Marla swallowed painfully, the faintly nauseated feeling intensifying. How could she have been so blind that she hadn't seen this earlier? Or had she merely consciously ignored what her heart had recognized?

It made perfect sense, actually—all the pointless petty disagreements she and Stefan had had those past few months. With frightening clarity she could now put her husband's inflexible demands into perspective. The sad thing was that Stefan himself was probably unaware of the reasons for his behavior.

She had only herself to blame, however, for not having realized this would happen. Yet she shouldn't be too hard on herself. How, in fact, could she have known that Anne-Marie's pregnancy would have anything to do with a situation she had thought resolved between herself and Stefan?

For that was the crux of the problem—the only real problem—in their marriage. Anne-Marie's pregnancy had suggested, to his subconscious mind at least, the one very important thing Stefan had sacrificed by marrying Marla. It was a constant reminder of what he had wanted from the beginning: a child of his own.

Without actually expressing it, or indeed being aware of it, Stefan had transferred what would have been his own fatherly instincts into an overly concerned, paternal protectiveness toward his niece.

"Oh, God," Marla whispered, the constriction in her throat burning unbearably. It was there again—that sick aching void in the pit of her stomach, a void that seemed to echo her childless state, the emptiness that ruled her life and now ruled her husband's. And there was nothing she could do about it. Ever.

Her eyes smarted, and the corners of her mouth drew down in automatic response to the overwhelming urge to cry. Again Badger snorted impatiently and pawed the ground, and Marla looked through the gathering tears at the restless animal. Putting an arm around his long graceful neck, she leaned her head against him, her body jerking as she began to sob her heart out.

EILEEN LOOKED AT the barely touched tureen of thick homemade vegetable soup and shook her head. Most of the other food had hardly been touched, either, at that night's supper. Anne-Marie had excused herself early, having only toyed with a piece of her roll, spending most of her time at the table casting furtive glances in

Marla's and Stefan's direction. Without warning or comment to either of them, she had finally got up and gone to her room.

Marla had left soon after, declaring she wasn't hungry and would like to go to bed early. Stefan hadn't paid any attention to either of the women but had merely buried his face in the copy of *Die Zeit* he read regularly—but not before the housekeeper caught the scowl of discontent on his face.

The strange discord between the members of the household persisted as the days went by, even intensified. Anne-Marie, who had been in such high spirits in spite of the fact that she was in the final stages of her pregnancy, never left the house now, spending the days idly flipping through magazines or watching segment after segment of the television soap operas.

Though Marla and Stefan treated each other with politeness and respect, that was all there was between them. Gone was the playful affection that had often marked their time together. Stefan was all business these days, as was Marla, who spent more and more time with the horses. The month of March hinted that spring was eager to appear. Yet no one at Morning Meadows seemed to pay it much attention. Something was definitely amiss, and it hung like a pall over the house.

As THE DAYS PASSED, Marla's anger over the scene with Anne-Marie and Stefan subsided. Her depression, however, only increased, though she tried everything she could think of to overcome the self-punishing feeling. Yet try as she might, she simply couldn't shake the uneasy sentiment that her analysis of the situation was correct.

Hers and Stefan's public demeanor extended to their private lives. Marla was too hurt this time, too stunned, to ignore her feelings. Stefan remained aloof, and she assumed he still harbored anger over her supposed carelessness in letting Anne-Marie ride the previous week. It was as though an invisible barrier separated them. They saw each other, spoke to each other and, in the dark of night, even sought each other out to satisfy the yearning need, the passion, that still held them tenaciously together. Yet even then Marla's heart wasn't really in their lovemaking, and she began to wonder about the crassness of her own desires, which *would* be satisfied regardless of her state of mind.

Her relationship with Anne-Marie had also deteriorated. Gone was the hard-won intimacy, the camaraderie that each had come to cherish. Anne-Marie had retreated into her shell of self-consciousness and subdued resentment, avoiding not only Marla but everyone else. Roy had inquired severa. times about her well-being. It was obvious he, too, had developed a special fondness for Anne-Marie and wondered what had happened to make her keep herself at such a distance.

So far apart had they grown that Marla was startled to hear Anne-Marie call her name one day as she was leaving the house for the stable. Marla stopped at the back door, about to get her parka, and turned suddenly, surprised to see Anne-Marie only a few feet away. She hadn't even heard her approach.

"Good morning," Marla said, smiling gently She began pulling one sleeve of the parka over her arm. "What are you doing up so early?"

Anne-Marie looked down for a moment, and Marla caught the telltale frown that creased her smooth brow. As she looked up again, she was chewing awkwardly on her lower lip.

"I—" she began, one hand suddenly coming up to press beneath her abdomen. "I don't feel so well."

Marla's eyes widened before she remembered to disguise her alarm. Lord, what if.... But Anne-Marie wasn't due for another three weeks. It could be something else.

"When did you start feeling like this?" Marla asked, removing the parka and slinging it for the time being over the back of a chair

"Only a little while ago," Anne-Marie said. Her luminous brown eyes flickered with worry, and Marla hastened to soothe her.

"I don't think it's uncommon to start experiencing discomfort about now. Why don't you lie down on the couch, and I'll phone Dr. Sloan and tell him what's happening."

Anne-Marie moved slowly and awkwardly to the couch and lowered herself, squinting with obvious discomfort as she did so. Eileen walked in just then, hesitated, then moved quickly to join them.

"Is something wrong?"

"No, nothing to worry about," Marla quickly inserted before the older woman's concern could alarm Anne-Marie. She glanced meaningfully at Eileen. "Anne-Marie doesn't feel too well. I'm going to give Dr. Sloan a call, though, and just let him know what's going on."

"Sure. That's a good idea." Eileen turned to the young girl. "Would you like me to get you something, honey?"

Anne-Marie shook her head, calmer now. "I feel better."

"Well, here," Eileen said, bustling around in her usual fashion, "sit forward and I'll put this behind your back."

Anne-Marie did so, and Eileen said, "Would you like me to turn on the television?"

"No. I'd rather read."

"All right." Gathering up a stack of magazines, Eileen handed them to her. "Here you go. Take your pick." She paused, adding, "I'll be in the kitchen if you need anything, okay?"

Anne-Marie smiled and nodded, and satisfied, the housekeeper left the room.

Marla was hanging up the telephone when Eileen joined her in the kitchen.

"What did he say?"

"Well," Marla began, perching on the edge of a barstool and looping a strand of hair behind one ear, "essentially he said just to keep an eye on her. It's not unusual for her to experience a few contractions at this point—in fact, she could even go through false labor—but we should be alert to any regular contractions." Marla paused. "How is she now?"

Eileen shrugged and turned both hands palm upward. "Back to normal as far as I can tell. I think she'll probably—"

Both women stared at each other in alarm as a loud frightened cry emanated from the living room. Instantly Marla was on her feet, hurrying out of the room, Eileen at her heels. They reached the living room to find Anne-Marie in a half-sitting position, her dark hair spilling across her face and one hand clutching her back, the other her lower abdomen

Marla sat on the couch next to her, placing an arm around the girl's shoulders. There was nothing to do except wait until the spasm eased, sympathizing in the meantime, with the anguished and frightened girl.

Beads of sweat dotted Anne-Marie's forehead as she looked up in bewilderment at Marla, taking a deep breath. "It was worse this time," she told both women. "Before it was only in my back. Now the pain is in my stomach—down here."

Marla glanced at her watch at the same moment that Eileen looked at the wall clock. The housekeeper moved to straighten the pillow behind Anne-Marie's back once more, then casually asked Marla, "Would you like me to call Roy and tell him you might be a little late?"

Marla nodded briefly. "Yes, I think so. I'll stay with Anne-Marie for a while longer."

"Something is wrong," Anne-Marie said, her brown eyes glinting with fear and worry.

Marla smiled, trying to hide her own worry. "No, nothing is wrong. I just spoke to Dr. Sloan, and he told me everything to expect at this point. We'll give it a little longer, and if you keep having contractions, then we'll call him back."

Anne-Marie relaxed somewhat, apparently appeased for the moment, and, settling back on the couch, began turning the pages of the magazine still lying in her lap.

Ten minutes later she was stricken by the same pain she had described earlier, and Marla held her hand, wincing at the girl's cries of distress. When Eileen stepped into the room, Marla signaled that she should phone Dr. Sloan again. There was no doubt in Marla's mind that Anne-Marie was going into labor, and all her thoughts were trained now on that probability. She left Anne-Marie for a moment to join Eileen in the kitchen and discuss what the obstetrician had said, then rejoined the girl as Eileen went to Anne-Marie's room to pack a suitcase for the trip to the hospital.

An hour elapsed before they were ready to go. Anne-Marie's contractions were coming as regularly as before, but Dr. Sloan had assured them this was to be expected and could—indeed probably would—continue for several more hours. Marla called the stable to tell Stefan what was happening, but Roy informed her that he'd driven into town earlier. He had no idea when Stefan would be back. As soon as he returned, Roy promised, he would tell him.

After waiting another half hour without hearing from Stefan, Marla decided they should go. Notifying Dr. Sloan's office that they would be arriving at the hospital in about twenty minutes, she and Eileen bundled Anne-Marie up and set off in the car.

MARLA TURNED at the sound of a light rapping. Eileen stuck her head around the door, and at her questioning look, Marla nodded and released Anne-Marie's hand.

"I'll be right back, okay?"

Anne-Marie agreed and closed her eyes, weary from the rounds of contractions.

"Why don't you go downstairs for a cup of coffee and something to eat," Eileen suggested. "I just had some lunch. It's your turn.

Marla glanced back worriedly at Anne-Marie, and Eileen said, "She'll be fine. I just spoke to the nurse, and she said everything is progressing as it should. It could take several more hours."

Marla arched her torso slightly and rubbed her lower back. "I am pretty hungry. You'll stay?"

"Of course," Eileen assured her.

Marla glanced at her watch and frowned. "I don't understand where Stefan could be. Did you speak to Roy again?"

"Yes. He said he still hadn't returned, but Roy remembered something about a meeting with his accountant."

Marla lifted her eyebrows. "And that could take a while. Well, there's nothing we can do.

All right, I'll be back as soon as I've had something to eat.''

"There's no need to rush.''

Marla smiled wearily and bent to pick up her purse from the chair, then stepped into the hallway. "See you later,'' she whispered.

In the hospital coffee shop Marla downed a grilled-cheese sandwich and two cups of steaming coffee. Despite Eileen's urging not to rush, she was reluctant to dawdle over the meal. By the time she'd finished, visited the rest room and returned to the obstetrics ward, only half an hour had elapsed.

As she stepped off the elevator and started down the short hallway to the waiting room, her stride faltered briefly, for she caught sight of Stefan's dark head. He was sitting on the edge of a couch, his elbows propped on his knees as he thumbed idly through a magazine. Marla's footsteps drew his attention, and he turned suddenly, tossing the magazine on the table.

"How is she?'' he asked. Marla looked at him steadily for a moment, then sat down on an adjacent chair. She should ignore the fact that he hadn't even greeted her before inquiring about Anne-Marie. Determinedly thrusting her personal feelings aside in the present situation, she informed him calmly, "She's doing fine. Eileen is with her now. I just went down for some lunch."

"Where is Dr. Sloan?"

"He went back to his office to see the rest of his patients. When—"

"What?" Stefan asked incredulously. "Why the hell isn't he here? She is having the baby, isn't she?"

Marla straightened, her features stiffening. "Stefan, lower your voice," she insisted. "There is absolutely no reason to get upset. Anne-Marie is doing fine. She's in labor now, but it may be several more hours before they wheel her into the delivery room. The nurses intend to call Dr. Sloan as soon as the time is right, and he'll come right over. His office is in the medical building next door."

Stefan said nothing as he studied his hands for several minutes. Then once more he reached for the magazine. As if suddenly struck by the fact of his wife's presence, he asked, "How are you doing?"

Marla summoned up a tense smile and a shrug. "Fine. A little tired, I guess, but I'll make it."

Stefan said nothing but returned the smile rather stiffly before settling back into the couch and opening the magazine. Marla stood up and walked through the set of double doors separating the labor and delivery rooms from the lounge. She had been given permission to attend at the birth.

The next twelve hours seemed interminable. Marla and Eileen rotated an hour at a time, staying with Anne-Marie and helping her through the taxing, tedious, sometimes nerve-racking process of labor. Shortly after one o'clock in the morning the following day Anne-Marie was wheeled into the delivery room.

Marla went in with her, and Eileen returned to the lounge to wait with Stefan. Marla's heart went out to the young girl as she panted and groaned. She felt Anne-Marie's agony almost tangibly in her hand as she squeezed it, trying to impart some of her own strength. When the first resentful wail pierced the sterile tile walls of the delivery room and Dr. Sloan held up the new-born boy, Marla's heart caught in her throat; tears ran unashamedly down her face. She bent down to kiss the thoroughly exhausted yet relieved girl and smoothed back her damp dark tendrils as Anne-Marie slowly sank into the peaceful restoring oblivion of sleep.

Marla returned to the labor room to get her purse and remove the scrub garments she'd been required to wear in the delivery room. As she walked back into the corridor, the door to the delivery room swung open and a nurse stepped out, holding a small, blue-blanketed bundle in her arms. Marla rushed up to meet her and smiled broadly as she peaked at the tiny reddish face of the infant.

''Please,'' she entreated the nurse, ''my husband, Anne-Marie's uncle, is waiting outside. I know he'd love to see the baby before you take him to the nursery.''

The nurse glanced down, then smiled knowingly. ''I hear that one a lot. But all right.''

Marla walked briskly forward to push open the doors to the waiting room, and the nurse walked through, hesitating for a moment as she scanned the few visitors.

''Mr. Gerhardt?''

Marla, moving forward toward her husband and Eileen, suddenly stopped dead in her tracks behind the nurse. Instinctively she knew she would never ever forget the scene being played out before her. Stefan had turned abruptly as he heard his name spoken; it was clear he had abandoned his patient wait on the couch and had been pacing the floor, no different from any other expectant father.

He walked tentatively toward the nurse, his haggard features revealing all too clearly the extent of his own ordeal

''It's a boy, Mr. Gerhardt,'' the nurse informed him as she held the infant out to him.

Marla's heart sank and her stomach lurched as she saw the look of absolute joy that spread across her husband's face, a joy for something he'd wanted for so long, that meant everything in the world to him.

Unobtrusively she slipped past him, noting with a hurt that penetrated to the very core of her being that he didn't even know she'd come or gone.

CHAPTER EIGHTEEN

DURING THE WEEK FOLLOWING Anne-Marie's return from the hospital, Stefan's disposition brightened considerably. Everyone, of course, was relieved that Marcus's birth had been uncomplicated. He was a strapping healthy infant.

But for Stefan the event held a far greater significance. It seemed as though a tremendous burden had been lifted from his conscience. At long last he could lay to rest the deep remorse that had haunted him those long years. The first time he had taken little Marcus into his arms and stared down in wonder at the tiny wrinkled face, his forefinger caught within the surprisingly powerful grasp of that miniature hand, something inside him clicked. For the first time in years, with sadness but no guilt, he said good bye to his brother

In spite of the difficulties, in spite of the circumstances of his birth, Stefan experienced a deep surge of love for Marcus that would, in its own way carry on what he had thought lost forever when Rolf died. He would see to the infant's welfare as he had finally done with Anne-Marie. At long last he could truly pay back the debt he owed his family after all those years.

MARCUS JOSEPH GERHARDT flailed his tiny arms and legs and gurgled happily as Eileen dusted his little bottom with a generous portion of talcum powder before fastening both corners of the fresh diaper. The infant was growing rapidly—that was certain—had gained almost two pounds in the past three weeks. She picked him up and, securing him in the crook of her arm, snatched up the bottle of warmed milk she'd placed on the dresser earlier.

Crossing the room, she sat down in the Bentwood rocker and positioned the baby across her lap.

"Okay, okay, little fella," she said softly, smiling as Marcus's lips began to smack in anticipation. He took the proffered rubber nipple greedily, closing his eyes and sucking loudly on the prepared formula.

Eileen watched him for a moment, then leaned back in the cane-bottomed rocker, laying her nead against the cushioned pad. The nursery, a converted guest bedroom in the east wing of the house, was easily the most cheerful place in the Gerhardt household of late. Most of the decorations in the room—mobiles, stuffed animals and necessary items such as bassinet, diaper holder, changing table—Eileen had bought herself. Stefan had told her to use whatever money she thought necessary to provide for the tiny babe, and she'd done just that.

In fact, the housekeeper, along with Marla, had assumed almost full responsibility for the care of the child upon Anne-Marie's return from the hospital. Marla was concerned about placing this additional burden on Eileen, but the housekeeper had assured her that she enjoyed immensely taking care of little Marcus, in spite of the fact that some of her chores had been placed on the back burner as a result.

Anne-Marie, sweet as she was, wasn't exactly one's image of a model mother, Marla had agreed. She knew virtually nothing about babies, and although Eileen tried to teach her a few things, it was obvious the girl's mind was on other matters. She had regained her youthful figure in record time and had shown a distinct inclination to pursue teenage activities once again. Her interest in stable matters was almost as great as Marla's and Stefan's, and she spent most of her day there, helping out in some regard.

Marla, who had been marvelously giving in her support during the delivery, seemed to draw more and more into herself each day. Stefan's behavior, however, was quite the opposite. Oddly, the more relaxed, indeed the happier, he appeared, the more isolated Marla became.

Oh, she made an effort to camouflage her feelings, was polite and careful to join in with the others fairly often. But still there was something missing. Gone was the familiar sparkle in the lovely blue eyes, just as absent as the good-natured bantering she used to initiate with Stefan.

Marcus sucked eagerly on the half-empty bottle, his dark gray eyes innocently surveying the newness of the world surrounding him. His birth had been quite an event. Yet it had had a distinctly upsetting effect on everything, everyone. . .even more so as the days went by.

"Marla, come here!" Roy's voice called out eagerly, and Marla turned, not seeing him immediately as she looked into the aisleway. She peered around Rudi's stall door, and Roy waved to her from outside the opposite end of the stable.

"We're out here," he yelled.

"Okay," Marla called back. "Be there in a second."

She walked into the tack room and hung up the bridle she'd been using on the overhead cleaning hook. Stopping at the door for a minute before leaving, she lifted her hands to her face, running her fingers along the slight depressions beneath her eyes, a telltale sign of the weariness she had been trying in vain to fight off lately. There seemed to be nothing she could do about it, however. Despite her efforts to combat the bothersome physical problem she was having a great deal of trouble sleeping lately.

Insomnia plagued her virtually every night; she slept for no more than three or four hours at a time. Her appetite had also been suffering, and there was little she could do about that, either. Still she forced herself to carry on as usual with her training schedule and had even attended a local schooling show with Rudi. Outwardly she was maintaining a normal mien. Inwardly it was an entirely different matter.

She lifted one hand to shade her eyes as she stepped out of the stable into the bright early-afternoon sunlight. Roy was gunning the motor of his brand-new BMW motorcycle as Stefan looked on. Anne-Marie was seated behind him, her now slender figure flatteringly attired in tight jeans and a short-cropped sweater. As soon as he looked over his shoulder and saw her, Roy thrust the bike into gear and flew out of the parking area onto the road, continuing almost to the highway before turning back and returning to the stable.

"He rides it well," Stefan commented as Marla moved to stand beside him.

"When did he get it?"

"Yesterday." Stefan chuckled lightly. "I think he stayed up all night getting used to riding it so he could show off today."

"Well, there's definitely one person he's impressing," Marla said, smiling wryly as she watched Anne-Marie lean her head slightly to the side as if to speak, her now almost shoulder-length dark hair streaming out behind her. There was something about the sight of that dark head, carelessly leaning back into the wind, that brought a frown to Marla's brow.

"Shouldn't they be wearing helmets or something?" Marla asked.

"What for?" Stefan wanted to know, his eyes still on the couple.

"For safety. What if something goes wrong?"

Stefan laughed lightly and looked down at his wife. "Like what?" He hesitated, studying her worried expression. "They're only going to the highway, then coming right back."

"Yeah, I guess so..." Marla said absently, puzzled as much as Stefan by the strange inexplicable concern that had crept over her so insidiously.

Just then Roy and Anne-Marie roared up on the BMW. Anne-Marie swung off the back and exclaimed delightedly, "Oh, I loved it! When are you going to teach me to drive it, Roy?"

Roy laughed at her choice of verbs. "You mean ride, don'cha kid?"

Anne-Marie clucked her tongue in exasperation. "I'm serious. I want to learn." Suddenly remembering her uncle standing there, she looked at him uncertainly with that same defiant gleam she reserved especially for him. "I've ridden before at home many times. I'm sure I could manage this motorcycle."

The barb didn't go unnoticed, but Stefan merely placed both hands on his hips and shook his head slowly from side to side. "Is there anything you don't want to do, Anne-Marie?"

Her brown eyes widening guilelessly, she answered, "No, I don't think so."

Stefan and Roy chuckled, and Stefan said, "Well. . .don't look at me. It's up to Roy."

Roy glanced from his employer to Anne-Marie and held up one hand to silence the plea about to burst from her lips. "I'll *think* about it."

"You will?" Anne-Marie clapped her hands together in a childlike gesture, satisfaction written all over her face.

"How about a spin, Marla?" Roy suggested.

Marla shook her head briefly. "No. Thanks anyway, but not today."

"Why not? It's just to the end of the road and back. Come on, I'll—"

"No, really. I . . . I have to get back. I just left Rudi standing there, and he's still hot."

"So have Stan take care of him and—"

At the obvious look of reluctance on Marla's face Roy let up. "Well, all right, we'll do it later. How 'bout you, Stefan? You game for a turn?"

Stefan's perplexed expression remained as he watched his wife turn and walk back inside. "No . . . no. Thanks anyway, Roy. Maybe later."

"Sure," Roy said, grasping both handles and swinging onto the bike, Anne-Marie cheerfully planting herself behind him once again.

Marla's slender form was disappearing into the shadowed aisleway of the barn, and Stefan strode quickly in the same direction. He caught up with her, grabbing her by the elbow in more of a jerking motion than he'd intended.

Marla turned around, staring at the hand on her arm, then up into the dark eyes studying her curiously.

"You don't have to grab at me just to get my attention." Her full lips became a rigid line as she spoke the words in an arid tone.

"Really?" Stefan cocked one eyebrow. "There are times lately when it takes a hell of a lot more than that. It seems like the only place we communicate at all these days is in bed."

Marla's jaw twisted as she focused her blue gaze past his shoulder. Trying to control the sudden shudder that swept through her, she replied in a somewhat softer tone, "What is it you want, Stefan?"

Stefan hesitated, then released her elbow. "I would appreciate knowing what in the hell is bothering you."

"I don't know why you think something's bothering me," Marla replied evasively.

"It's fairly easy, actually," Stefan replied, his voice tinged with sarcasm. "Your attitude just now with Anne-Marie and Roy, for instance."

Marla's blue eyes flashed as she looked directly at him. "My attitude!"

Stefan was surprised, but at least he'd got a reaction out of her. "Yes," he said more quietly. "Look, Marla, it's more than a little obvious that you're not yourself lately. You barely have time for anyone but yourself nowadays."

"Well, I'm sorry to disappoint you and the others, but as you can see—" she made a backward sweep with her hand "—I'm keeping fairly busy around here. This is what you hired me for remember?"

Stefan stared at her incredulously. "Come on, Marla, don't be ridiculous. You're my wife—not my employee."

Marla simply shrugged and glanced impatiently at the floor. "It's still my work."

"Of course it is. All I'm saying is...." Stefan hesitated, frustrated that she refused to look him in the eye. "It just seems to me that you could pay more attention to those around you—your family especially."

Sparks reappeared in the wide blue eyes, and a flush swept across her face as Marla shot back, "Marcus especially, right?"

Stefan was stunned by her brusque tone. He'd only heard her speak to him that way once before. Nodding slowly, he answered, "Marcus, also, of course."

"Oh, yes. Of course." Suddenly Marla brought up her wrist to check her watch, her tone brightening falsely as she added, "Look, Stefan, can we talk later maybe? I've still got three horses to school yet, and it's already three o'clock."

Stefan's jaw tightened. He studied his wife for a moment before answering. If she insisted on being so damned bullheaded, then he'd let her. "Yes, of course. Don't let me stop you."

Marla rubbed one shoulder absently, then

drew in a deep breath. "I'll see you back at the house for supper."

Stefan muttered something in reply, his brow furrowing deeply as Marla turned on her heel and strode quietly away from him. He stood for a long while in the same spot, wondering what, if anything, he'd accomplished just then. He no more knew now what was on Marla's mind than he had before. Indeed, the only thing he was certain of was that this conversation—a damned loose description for what had just passed between them—hadn't solved a thing. He turned away as Marla approached the washstand, where Stan had just finished giving Rudi a hose-down.

"Where would you like me to turn him out?" the groom asked as he removed excess moisture from the horse with a metal "sweat scraper."

"That's all right, Stan. I'm going to walk him till he's cooled down." She was far too uptight at the moment to school any of the other horses just yet anyway. Accepting the lead rope from the groom, she led the horse outside and onto the hoof-trodden path that wended its way among the various turnout paddocks and broodmare pastures.

The cool spring air still held a hint of a nip in it, but it felt good against Marla's face. She walked rather slowly, occasionally stopping to let Rudi indulge in a crop of new grass. She watched as the horse arched his long neck down to snap off a long sheaf of timothy. Lifting one hand to loop an escaped strand of hair behind one ear, she closed her eyes, stretched her neck and leaned her head backward, soaking in the warming rays of the sun.

It had a soothing effect, perhaps all the more so because the sensation was in such direct contrast to the feeling deep within her, a sinking feeling, a painful reminder of all the things she'd left unsaid a few minutes earlier with Stefan. It was the same feeling that had seized her the moment she'd walked out of the delivery room to witness Stefan's reaction to the sight of newborn Marcus.

The meaning of that incident had struck her full force then, placing everything else that had occurred from that moment on in a dramatically altered perspective, the perspective she should have been aware of long before . . . from the very beginning.

She oughtn't to feel this way, of course; none of it was tiny Marcus's fault. But the very fact of his birth had wrought a change in Stefan that was too obvious, too hurtful, to ignore. That he loved the child was understandable. That Marcus filled a need within him that she herself could never satisfy was undeniable.

That knowledge seemed to sear Marla to the depths of her soul. Here was the child he had always wanted, the "progeny" he had spoken of so revealingly in that one conversation in the days before their engagement. His overprotectiveness toward Anne-Marie had reflected more than simply a stodgy, old-fashioned attitude toward pregnancy. His hopes, his dreams had unconsciously rested on the birth of his niece's child—the child who would take the place of his own unborn one.

She knew what was bound to happen now, and a knot of dread twisted inside her at the thought. They had discussed the subject shortly after Anne-Marie's return from the hospital. The question of whether she would keep the child had of course come up, and it had been a foregone conclusion, had been assumed, that the baby would be raised within the family, raised at Morning Meadows. Marla couldn't bring herself to protest, and she and Stefan had never privately discussed the matter.

It wasn't the fact that not only Anne-Marie but also little Marcus would be living with them that disturbed her so. She loved them both very much. But to live every day with the child who would remind her of what she could never give her husband was too much to endure.

Rudi lifted his head, and she tugged on the

lead rope, walking ahead to the farthest pasture, the one with the pond. Despite the distraction of the beauty surrounding them, Marla's brain allowed her no respite. As she stood beside the clear natural pond and watched Rudi drink his fill of the cool water, she thought about how much she would miss all of this. A dry sob caught in her throat, and she bit her lower lip painfully. She had known it all along, of course, those past several weeks but hadn't consciously acknowledged her intentions. As she just had.

Funny, she thought on a long sigh. *Funny how it all comes full circle.* She had been thinking this very thing a mere nine months ago, before she'd ever met Stefan: how she would miss it all. And then she had had only a small part of what she had now.

But this time there would be no acceptance of an offer to stay. She would leave. She had to. There was no other way she could see to avoid what would surely develop into days, months, even years of resentment and misery on Stefan's part. Having Marcus now, he would eventually come to realize, as she did already, the extent of the sacrifice he had made for her. And he would grow to hate her. He would want his freedom to attain that very thing that could make his world complete.

It was better that she leave now and take the

part of their love that still lived than wait until nothing was left of it. The constriction in her throat became unbearable. As she stood watching Rudi while he grazed on the high-growing grass around the edge of the pond, her body shook with racking, soul-wrenching sobs for what she was about to lose.

A WEEK PASSED before Marla found the opportunity to act on her decision, a week in which she went through the motions of everyday living, masking the pain that was with her night and day. It was a Saturday morning, and Stefan had left after breakfast to spend most of the day in Charlottesville, taking care of business-related matters. Anne-Marie had left shortly afterward for an outing with Roy on his motorcycle.

As soon as they'd both gone, Marla retreated to the bedroom and telephoned her mother. She chatted about various things for a while, refraining from mentioning the real reason for her call. She hung up after several minutes of amiable interesting conversation, satisfied with what she had learned—her mother would be at home that weekend. She mentioned nothing to Jillian about her intended visit, reasoning that they could discuss it, perhaps even argue about it, when she got there.

Willing herself to ignore the bittersweet emotions roiling inside her, Marla set about packing as rapidly as she could. The task was more difficult than she'd expected. Eileen interrupted her once, asking if she'd mind taking care of Marcus while she made her weekly trip to the grocery store. The trip had stretched into two hours, and Marla was growing impatient by the time the housekeeper returned. She wanted to get through packing and be on her way soon. Stefan might unexpectedly come home early, and she'd prefer to avoid any shattering confrontations.

Finished with her packing, Marla sat down on the edge of the king-size bed, running her hand absently over the smooth cover. God, was she really doing this? Her heart pounded ominously, and she stood up abruptly, straightening her back and drawing in a deep shuddering breath. She had to. There was no other way. She'd gone over and over it, and though he might be hurt in the beginning, Stefan would come to realize she'd done the right thing by leaving him.

Swiftly she crossed to the sitting room and sat down at the desk. Picking up a pen, she withdrew a sheaf of paper from a leather caddy and paused.

"Dear Stefan," she began. She waited, but the words wouldn't come. Lifting her eyes, she

stared straight ahead, a montage of scenes playing across her mind's eye, familiar loving
scenes, ones she would never ever forget. Involuntarily her chin began to move, and fat
tears formed in her eyes, spilling over and running down her cheeks. Suddenly she dropped
the pen, leaned her elbows on the desk and
buried her face in the palms of her hands. Quietly she sobbed her heart out, her shoulders heaving uncontrollably.

She sat that way for a very long time, unwilling to get up and fetch a handful of tissues,
which by now were sorely needed. The sound of
the front doorbell barely pierced her awareness,
so caught up was she in the anguish over what
she was about to do. When Eileen opened the
door, not bothering to wait for her knock to be
answered, Marla was startled. She hadn't even
heard her footsteps in the hallway.

"Wh-what is it, Eileen?" she asked, sniffing
and roughly drying her cheeks with the backs of
her hands.

Eileen was also clearly startled. She had never
seen Marla cry. But her earlier frown abruptly
reappeared, and Marla's preoccupation with her
own troubles momentarily receded as she wondered at the alarming expression on Eileen's
face.

"I'm sorry to bother you," Eileen said, "but

you need to come with me. There are two highway patrolmen in the hall.''

"What?'' Marla stared uncomprehendingly at the older woman. "What do they want?''

"I have no idea. They drove up just now. When I answered the door, they asked to speak to a member of the family.''

"What could it be about?'' Marla stood up, her concern overriding any consideration of her appearance. Hastily snatching a few tissues from the dispenser on her dressing table, she blew her nose, then quickly followed Eileen into the hallway.

The strongest sense of déjà vu she'd ever experienced crept over Marla as her footsteps slowed toward the end of the hall and she saw the two Virginia highway patrolmen standing in the entrance. Long ugly talons of fear gripped her, and it was all she could do to subdue her runaway imagination. Something had happened—she knew it. Oh, God, Stefan. . . .

"Hello,'' she greeted the two men in a surprisingly controlled tone of voice.

"Mrs. Gerhardt?'' The taller of the two men spoke up.

Marla nodded. "Yes?''

"Ma'am, my name is Sergeant Reitman. My partner, Officer Jargrove.'' He hesitated and cleared his throat. "Ma'am, do you think we could sit down?'' he suggested politely.

The icy fear gripped her even tighter, but Marla forced herself to retain a semblance of composure.

She gestured toward the living room. ''We can go in here,'' she said, then led the way. As the men each took a chair and Marla sat down with Eileen on the couch, any vestige of hope that this was just some routine matter quickly fled from Marla's mind. The younger shorter officer kept his eyes averted, carefully not saying anything, and the spokesman seemed to be having a difficult time continuing with what he had to say. He had removed his black leather gloves and began to nervously shift them from one hand to the other.

Marla sat anxiously on the edge of the couch. Why didn't he come to the point, for heaven's sake?

''Ma'am, first I need to clarify some informa tion. This is the home of Miss Anne-Marie Ger-hardt?''

Marla nodded. ''Yes, it is.''

''And you're the young lady's aunt?''

''My husband is her uncle, that's correct.''

The officer glanced down then back up, his hazel eyes squinting. He was obviously uncomfortable. Drawing in a deep breath, he let it out slowly. ''Mrs. Gerhardt, I'm really very sorry to have to inform you of this.... There's been an accident involving Miss Gerhardt and a Mr. Roy Valmire.''

Marla's hand came instantly to her throat at the same moment as she felt Eileen grip her shoulder. "What are you saying?" She barely heard the words she spoke. Strangely, it seemed as if she had heard all this before, hadn't she? The room began to spin around her.

Again the officer hesitated. His partner sat stock-still, studying the floor at his feet.

"Miss Gerhardt and Mr. Valmire were thrown from the motorcycle they were riding north on Highway 33 at ten-thirty this morning. Mr. Valmire is at Valley General in Charlottesville.''

Marla's eyes widened in shock, and she croaked, "Anne-Marie? Is she there, too?''

The officer hesitated for what seemed like an eternity. "Ma'am, she was pronounced dead at the scene of the accident.''

Marla felt rather than heard the deep primitive moan that rose up within her, was unaware of the arms surrounding her, holding on to her as if she, in her disbelieving anguish, were a lifeline. Vaguely she could hear Eileen's dry sobs mingling with her own as they clung to each other, rocking back and forth, keening with the grief that pierced them both. Unbidden, the girl's image came to her: Anne-Marie, sitting behind Roy on the BMW, laughing as they flew down the gravel road, her almost black hair streaming out behind her....

Please, dear God, not Anne-Marie, Marla prayed, her body suddenly icy cold, as if she were huddling naked on some frozen tundra. Oh, God, why her? Her desperate pleas were given voice by Eileen, who was now sobbing uncontrollably. Marla's anguish was soul deep, greater than anything she had ever experienced. Yet she could not weep as Eileen did.

Her thoughts immediately went to Stefan. He didn't know. He wasn't even home yet. Suddenly she pushed away from the housekeeper, turning to face the pained expressions on both of the officers' faces.

"My husband.... I don't know when he'll—" The sound of the kitchen garage door opening interrupted her, and she turned just in time to see Stefan stride into the room. He was removing his parka, and his expression was preoccupied, as it had been most of the time of late. Evidently he hadn't noticed the patrol car parked on the circular drive out front.

He stopped abruptly as he took in the scene awaiting him: his wife, distraught, Eileen sobbing unashamedly, two state troopers....

"What is it? What's happened?"

Marla closed her eyes as Sergeant Reitman stood up and walked across the room to her husband. She squeezed them shut, in fact, unable to bear the look that would be there on her husband's face as he heard the news of his niece's death. Releasing Eileen, she sat forward and folded her arms on top of her knees, trying in vain to stop the violent shaking of her body.

At last she looked up. Stefan's horrified disbelieving expression went straight through her. If only there were some way she could make it all untrue, relieve him of the agony that surely exceeded her own.

Placing her hand over her mouth, she closed her eyes again and sank back into the couch, not knowing how—or if ever—she would be able to get up again.

CHAPTER NINETEEN

MARCUS SQUIRMED on Marla's lap, his whimpering rapidly escalating to a piercing wail as the airplane began a decidedly choppy descent into New York Kennedy. Stefan put down the magazine he had been reading and glanced over at his wife.

"It's okay," Marla said, shifting the cranky baby as she leaned forward to extract a fresh prepared bottle from her bag beneath the seat in front of her. "Shh, Marcus. It's okay." Grasping the bottle in her right hand and placing the child's head in the crook of her elbow, she crooned softly, "Here you go, sweetheart. This will help."

Marcus's little hands grasped eagerly at the familiar bottle, and he sucked hungrily, the timely feeding effective not only in satisfying his hunger but in relieving the auditory discomfort caused by the change in altitude.

Marla cast a reassuring glance at her husband, then returned her attention to the baby in her lap. Marcus's eyes were shut now. He didn't seem bothered by the remainder of the landing process.

Customs was a tedious affair, and Marla was thankful that Marcus slept through all of it. Stefan relieved her often by holding the baby. He'd grown by leaps and bounds and was a strong little fellow by now, not the least inhibited about expressing his feelings about anything and everything.

As they boarded the connecting flight for the short hop to Charlottesville, Marla thought—gratefully, for once—about the inherent problems and all-consuming concerns of traveling, especially those involved in such a long-distance trip as the one she and Stefan and Marcus had just made—all of it within the space of one week. Very little time had remained in which to focus on the pain and sorrow that had rendered the trip necessary. *Someday,* Marla thought, not without a pang, *someday perhaps I'll get that romantic trip to Europe I've always dreamed of.*

This time, her first, had been devoid of any glamorous overtones. It had been the saddest, most heartrending time of her life. Anne-Marie's funeral had taken place just four days earlier, and still it ran through her mind in constant replay.

The cemetery on the outskirts of the beautiful university town of Würzburg was tiny, yet fastidiously maintained. Anne-Marie had been laid to rest next to the graves of her parents as Marla, Stefan, his parents and a few relatives and friends looked on. Marla had held tiny Marcus in her arms, the big brown eyes staring up at her innocently, his chubby arms unwilling to be confined by the blanket swaddling him. Grabbing a piece of Marla's hair, he'd pulled it loose from its neat chignon, and Marla had reached down to loosen the ferocious grip of those powerful little fingers. Already he had such a distinctive personality, just like his mother.

A muffled sob had escaped from her at that moment, and she'd lifted the baby to her chest, burying her face next to his small one as her grief overcame her. She had loved Anne-Marie like a sister. She would love her son as her own. It was the very least she could do to repay the kindness and warmth Anne-Marie had brought into her life.

The rest of the week had been spent at Stefan's parents' home in Würzburg. Despite the rather limiting language barrier, the older couple were quite gracious and kind to their new daughter-in-law. Stefan's father looked to be in somewhat better health than Stefan had described earlier. Yet Marla could only wonder what this blow would do to him. She would speak to her husband later about the possibility of bringing his parents to Virginia to live with them if the situation warranted it.

As she looked down now at the sleeping baby in her lap, she thought of how very much everything, all her plans to leave Stefan, had changed with Anne-Marie's death. Her assessment of Stefan's true feelings about her inability to bear children was irrelevant now. The motherless little fellow demanded that she not leave—not now—even, she reflected sadly, even if it meant enduring what would only be a sham of a marriage.

IN VIVID CONTRAST to the harsh frigid winter, the refreshing warmth of spring gave way to scorchingly hot summer days. The sloping verdant pastures of Morning Meadows were dotted now with an abundance of grazing broodmares and three- and four-month-old foals. Between training sessions, Marla busied herself with Marcus, taking over for Eileen, who usually saw to the child most of the day.

Marla's days were filled like never before. She would never have dreamed that caring for an infant, even with regular help, could be so time-consuming. But she was grateful for the diversion. She, like everyone else at Morning Meadows, was dealing with her grief in her own way. Time, she'd discovered, really did work miracles in healing the pain and anguish one suffered over the death of a loved one. Yet not nearly enough of it had passed. Although it had been almost three months since the accident that had taken Anne-Marie's life, too often it seemed like only yesterday.

But somehow they were all making progress, carrying on with their lives. Marla had spent many painful sessions with Roy, who, feeling tremendously guilty that he'd only been injured in the accident that had killed Anne-Marie, had not wanted to come back to work for her and Stefan. Gradually she'd made him realize that he couldn't run away from his grief—he'd have to deal with it, as they all would. It wasn't his fault that he and Anne-Marie had been hit by a careless driver. There was nothing he could do now but go on, and she and Stefan really needed him. So he came back

Eileen, being generous loving Eileen, dealt with her sorrow openly at times, breaking into tears at certain sensitive moments. But day by day she was adjusting, too, undoubtedly finding solace in the delights of helping to raise young Marcus

Stefan, unfortunately, had retreated further

into a protective unemotional shell, one Marla could neither fathom nor penetrate. More than anything, she would have liked to share with him his feelings of loss, anger, hurt—anything just to be able to talk to him. But he was so much like a stranger to her now, focusing his attention on his work, hardly sleeping at all at night, then avoiding her most of the day. Even the times he spent with Marcus, which were frequent enough, were organized in such a way as to exclude her. He wasn't the same man she'd married, and she had given up hope of bridging the ever-widening chasm between them.

STEFAN'S THOUGHTS on the death of his niece had run the gamut from guilt to a resigned sorrowful acceptance that she was never coming back. The guilt in time had faded, as had the anger over the senseless unnecessary accident itself. He was grateful that at least Marcus had been spared the tragedy. The sparkling exuberant youngster was the one light in his life. Stefan could ill afford to lose him by letting his grief keep him from showing his affection.

Still, this new bond did not replace the even greater unexpected loss of a once passion-filled, loving relationship with his wife. At a time in his life when he wanted her, needed her desperately, he was unable to approach her. His confusion and hurt went beyond any amount of suffering or grieving over Anne-Marie's death.

Indeed it had begun the day he'd found the police officers sitting in his living room, waiting to inform him of the accident. Later, after returning from the hospital, he'd been terribly distraught, as they'd all been—but not to the point that he hadn't recognized his wife's packed suitcases placed next to the bedroom door, or the notepad with airline and flight number jotted down. He hadn't had to ask; he'd known right then that she'd been prepared to leave him.

They'd never spoken of it, and Stefan's bewilderment became buried in the traumatic aftermath of Anne-Marie's sudden death. Through it all, though, he had never forgotten. Still, he was loath to bring the subject up. Was he simply afraid of what he might hear—that she intended to leave him at some later date? He supposed so.

Even now, as he lay listening to her soft even breathing, the fear gripped him. She lay on the far side of the king-size bed, so close yet so far faraway. It had been months since they'd made love, and had she been sleeping in another room there could not have been any greater distance between them. There were times, such as now, when he ached with a desire for her so intense, so consuming, it was everything he could do to keep from reaching out and pulling her to him, making pure uninhibited love to her, with her...the way it used to be between them.

But nothing was the way it used to be. Everything had changed. Not only had he lost his niece, but he'd lost his wife, too. Oh, she was still there; she'd taken over with young Marcus in a way he'd never have expected, never had a right to expect. But she was a different woman from the one he'd married, the one he loved, would always love. He had no idea anymore of how to reach her, and it killed him by inches to think of spending the rest of their married life this way. Night after night and day after day he racked his brain, trying to figure out some way to get them back to where they had been.

But always the memory of those suitcases stopped him. The fear that he would say something wrong, drive her even further away, prevented him from making any move at all. The only thing he could do was hope, pray, that someday, somehow they could put whatever was so wrong between them behind. For good.

MID-JULY brought the most intense heat wave Marla could remember living through as an adult. High humidity made the days, even the nights, sweltering, and Marla had to alter the training schedule she normally adhered to year-round. Riding in the middle of the day was impossible, both for her and the horses, so she began schooling them in the very early morning or late evening. The rest of the day was spent with Marcus. Often she would take him outside under a large spreading oak, where she'd installed a small plastic wading pool.

One particularly scorching day Marla was sitting in the circular pool, dressed in her briefest bikini, supporting Marcus and watching the playful cooling little splashes he made. A gentle merciful breeze picked up at one point, and Marla was about ready to extend their normal period of playtime. But Marcus began to fret, rubbing his fisted hands against his face in a familiar gesture.

"Okay, little fella," she comforted him, scooping him up and wrapping him in a towel. "Time to go beddie-bye for you."

After changing his diaper and feeding him, Marla settled him down in his crib for an afternoon nap. She returned to her own room and took a long refreshing shower, then put on a pair of white cotton shorts and a sleeveless T-shirt. The sun had worn thin her normal resilience, and she yawned widely, thinking how nice an afternoon siesta would be. The house was quiet. Eileen had gone into town for some shopping, and Stefan was at work at the stable. The steady drone of cicadas and katydids was a lulling invitation to simply lie down, forget everything and fall peacefully asleep.

Picking up a novel she'd just begun, Marla went to the kitchen and poured herself a large glass of iced tea, then continued on into the den and sank gratefully onto the comfortable couch. Propping up a few pillows behind her back, she settled down to start reading.

Neither the book nor the tea went very far, however, in holding her attention. The overhead ceiling fan seemed to beckon her with its wafting coolness, and within a few minutes she had drifted off to sleep.

Marcus's wailing cries awakened her abruptly. Sitting up and blinking rapidly, Marla had to struggle to overcome her feeling of disorientation. A glance at the wall clock, however, indicated she couldn't have slept for more than fifteen minutes. Swinging her feet to the floor, she drew her arms up over her head, stretching out the last of her sleepiness

"Coming, Marcus," she called out cheerily. She frowned, though, as she neared the nursery. Marcus's crying sounded different for some reason; she couldn't put her finger on exactly how. More plaintive, perhaps.

And it was no wonder, she thought worriedly,

picking up the fretting child. "You're hot as a firecracker, baby doll," she said, placing Marcus against her left shoulder as she patted his back and checked his diaper. Gently she continued to stroke his tiny head and back. He *was* hot as a firecracker.

A streak of alarm shot through Marla as she walked quickly to the chest of drawers and located the baby thermometer among a host of other supplies. Making certain it was sterile, she shook it down and began taking the baby's temperature. Her alarm was well founded: Marcus's temperature was one hundred and three point eight.

Crooning soothingly to the whimpering child, Marla made her way to the telephone in the den, thumbing quickly through the personal directory until she located the pediatrician's phone number. Marcus lay his head against her shoulder as she rocked him from side to side, nervously tapping her fingers on the desk, listening in growing irritation as the other end of the line rang endlessly. Finally the receptionist answered, and she told her story. A nurse was put on the line, and she went through it all again before she was told what to give him for the fever, and to continue administering the dosage on an hourly basis.

Throughout the afternoon Marla stayed with

Marcus, taking his temperature frequently and noticing with relief that, indeed, it was beginning to come down. Probably some sort of virus—hopefully the twenty-four-hour kind. Eileen returned late in the afternoon, and Marcus was sleeping quietly by then.

At supper Marla recounted the day's events to Stefan, adding that she'd better stay with the baby that evening instead of making her routine trip to the stable.

"Does he still have fever?" Stefan asked, returning his coffee cup to his saucer.

"A hundred and one," Marla informed him. At Stefan's expression of alarm she hastened to add, "But it's coming down. Dr. Josephson's nurse said to phone if there was any further problem."

"His nurse? You didn't talk to him?"

"Stefan, really, it wasn't necessary. She's a physician's assistant. She's well equipped to handle situations such as this."

Stefan said nothing for a moment, just raised his eyebrows ruminatively and sipped his coffee again.

"I'm going to check on him now," Marla said, standing up and picking up her empty dishes to return them to the kitchen first.

Stefan watched her walk out of the room, the seductive sway of her hips stirring a primitive, long-ignored impulse in him. God, she was so beautiful. What was keeping them apart? Was it a matter of mutual pride? He'd always had an overabundance of that, he thought cynically. Or were their differences so great now that nothing could overcome them?

But what were the differences? He was so confused, so befuddled by everything. He didn't know what to think anymore. He could hear her soft voice coming from the nursery as she spoke to Marcus, who had started to cry again. This was not unusual, however, since it was his dinnertime.

Despite all that was wrong between them, he could feel gratified that at least one thing had worked out. Marla was devoted to Marcus, more than he could ever have hoped for. It meant a lot, of course, that one fortunate aspect of their marriage. But would it, *could* it, be enough?

MARLA TOSSED AND TURNED, half asleep and uncomfortable in the rather hard single bed in the nursery. She longed for the comfort of her own but had opted to spend the night with Marcus. His fever had not gone below 101, and she reasoned that it would be better to check on him periodically.

She bolted upright suddenly. The plaintive

cry that had alerted her was like none other she'd heard since the baby had taken ill. Finding her way with the aid of the two night-lights, Marla crossed the room to the crib.

"It's all right, sweetheart. Shh." Taking the child in her arms and lifting him, Marla knew in a split second that it wasn't all right—at all. Marcus was burning up. Quickly she placed him in the bassinet and took his temperature, noticing as she waited that he was lying differently, as if he couldn't or wouldn't turn his head. The reading on the thermometer really frightened her: one hundred and five degrees. It couldn't be!

Picking up the baby and cradling him in her arms, she hurried out of the room, through the quiet house to Eileen's room. Knocking sharply on the door, she called out, "Eileen? It's me—Marla."

The door opened seconds later, and Eileen stood there in her robe and curlers, obviously still struggling to wake up. The sight of the baby, however, brought her rapidly to her senses, and she asked in a worried tone, "What's wrong?"

"He's much worse. His fever has risen to 105! My God, Eileen, what could it be? And look, he won't turn his head."

Eileen frowned deeply as she felt the baby's

forehead, then rushed out of the room, calling back over her shoulder, "I'm going to phone Dr. Josephson. Get dressed and pack a few things for the baby. As soon as I dress, we're taking that child to emergency!"

Marla's heart seemed literally to knock against her chest as she stared after the older woman. Then, like one possessed, she rushed to do exactly as she'd been told.

MARLA PEERED INTO THE MIRROR above the sink and studied the whites of her eyes. They looked like roadmaps. Turning on the taps, she bent over the sink and splashed cold water on her face. It helped. A little.

But how she looked at the moment was the least of her concerns. Nothing could help the way she felt inside. If only it didn't take so long, she thought for the hundredth time in the past half hour. Dr. Josephson had arrived at the hospital at the same time as she and Eileen. Now, an hour and a half later, she still knew nothing about Marcus's condition. They'd had to wait until the neurologist the doctor had called in on the case arrived. Both were inside one of the treatment rooms performing a spinal tap—an absolute necessity in this particular case, they'd told her.

Marla had prayed almost constantly for good

news ever since she and Eileen had been told to wait outside, but the hope that whatever was wrong would not be as bad as she feared died slowly with every passing minute. Why was it taking so long?

Eileen was waiting for her in the visitors' lounge outside, two steaming cups of coffee in her hands.

"Here. I went down the hall and found a vending machine."

Marla shook her head and collapsed into the vinyl upholstered chair next to the housekeeper.

"Thanks, but I don't think—"

"You don't know what to think," Eileen interrupted her gently, proffering the cup. "You haven't slept in heaven knows how long, and it's after 5:00 A.M. anyway. You need *something*."

Marla sighed wearily and accepted the cup. "I guess you're right." She sipped the dark liquid for a moment, then cast a curious glance at Eileen. "What did you mean by that, anyway?"

"What?"

"That I hadn't slept in heaven knows how long? Why do I have the feeling you weren't just talking about last night?"

Eileen shrugged. "Well, it's true, isn't it? I'm not blind, you know. You haven't been yourself for a very long time. Want to know just how long?"

Marla frowned slightly and studied the other woman for a moment. "No," she admitted softly. So her cover-up had been that transparent. What difference did it make, though? Her own unhappiness was insignificant compared to what was happening at the moment. Suddenly another disturbing thought occurred to her, and she started, almost spilling her coffee.

' How could I have forgotten to tell Stefan! I'll have to call him right away—''

Eileen placed a restraining hand on Marla's arm. "I also found a telephone where the vending machines were. He should be here shortly."

"Oh,' Marla muttered, sitting back down again. How sad, she thought miserably. Stefan hadn't even entered her mind during the crisis. Things between them had deteriorated even more than she'd thought.

The depressing realization was interrupted by the sound of a door opening and voices coming from farther down the corridor.

"Mrs. Gerhardt?" Dr Josephson said as he appeared in the doorway.

Marla got up immediately and walked toward him. "Yes?"

"I'd like you to meet Dr. Raymond Kelsey."

Marla nodded her head toward the tall, middle-aged doctor. She should have shaken hands, she thought, but her arms were wrapped around her chest in a vain effort to stop the shaking that had started up again.

"Mrs. Gerhardt," Dr. Kelsey spoke up, getting right to the point, "I'm afraid your nephew is seriously ill with spinal meningitis. I've already made arrangements with nursing to transfer him to intensive care."

Intensive care, Marla thought wildly. It couldn't be that bad....

"We're starting him on an aggressive program of antibiotics," Dr. Kelsey was continuing. "Hopefully he'll respond within the next twenty-four hours."

Marla swallowed hard, her throat dry as sandpaper. "And...if he doesn't?"

Dr. Kelsey's expression was unreadable. "There are other avenues of treatment we can explore." He summoned up a sympathetic expression and patted Marla on the shoulder. "Now if you'll excuse me, I'll need to write some orders and—"

"Wh-when can I see him?" Marla interrupted him.

Dr. Kelsey hesitated, noting the look of intense worry on the young woman's face. "I'll speak with the nurses about it. You can talk to them when you get to the waiting area."

Marla nodded and watched as both doctors

left. Vacantly, like a mannequin, she turned, staring as she saw the outer doors to the lounge open and Stefan stride over to her and Eileen. The expression on his face was ominous.

Before Marla could open her mouth he demanded, "What in God's name is wrong with you? Damn it, how could you just walk out of the house and not tell me what was going on?"

"Stef...I—I don't know," Marla stumbled over the words, unable to control the quaver in her voice. 'I'm sorry. But you're here now, so—"

"You're goddamned right I'm here." The frown never leaving his face, Stefan stared at his wife for a long moment. She looked like she'd been through hell; there was no denying that. In a quieter tone he asked, "Where is he now?"

Marla began to speak, but Eileen stepped forward, and placing a hand on his arm, began to gently inform him of the baby's condition.

Chewing on her trembling lower lip, Marla turned and absently walked away to a corner of the waiting area. The remnants of her self-control suddenly shredded, and she threw her hands over her face, sobbing quietly and deeply.

God, what more could happen to them? How much more could they take?

CHAPTER TWENTY

"MRS. GERHARDT, would you like to come in now?"

Marla's eyes flew open, and she blinked rapidly, reaching up to rub the back of her neck. "Yes...thank you," she said hoarsely.

Straightening, she frowned curiously as she noticed the blanket that covered her. "Where did this come from?"

The nurse smiled and replied, "I put it over you a while ago. You've been asleep for almost two hours."

Marla's eyes widened. "I have?" She rubbed the dark crescents beneath her eyes wearily. "Well, I suppose I could have used it."

"I'm sure you could use a great deal more of it," the nurse commented wryly. She handed Marla a scrub gown and a mask and waited as she put them on. "Really, Mrs. Gerhardt, you should go home for a while. There's nothing much you can do at this point, and you need the rest. This is the second night in a row you've slept out here.''

Marla glanced ruefully at the plastic couch that had indeed been her bed those past couple of nights. As far as couches went, it wasn't too bad, although she definitely would have appreciated the comforts of her own firm bed. But wild horses couldn't have dragged her away from there

She and Stefan had kept a constant vigil outside the intensive-care unit, anxious to make use of every precious minute of the visiting time allowed. Words between them had been perfunctory at best, each retreating into his and her own world of worry and desperate prayer that Marcus would make it.

Stefan could not imagine losing the baby after all that had happened; the thought of it was too much to bear. To speak of it was worse. Marla couldn't forget the times she'd thought, as she'd cared for or played with him, that if it wasn't for Marcus, she'd be gone, starting a new life faraway from the loveless marriage that never should have been in the first place.

And now there he was poised between life and death and it was impossible to forgive herself for any of those negative thoughts. She would not leave him. They were allowed fifteen-minute visits with Marcus four times a day, which included the middle of the night, and she refused to miss any of them.

Finally gowned, she followed the nurse into the intensive-care unit, quite familiar now with the forbidding sights and sounds of the place. A circular nursing station was positioned in the middle of the large room, providing an all-encompassing view of the twelve beds. Marcus was in one of two isolation rooms, surrounded by a wall of glass with one door.

He slept fitfully, as he had ever since being brought there, and Marla's heart twisted at the sight of his tiny vulnerable body, naked except for a diaper, an intravenous tube attached to his right arm. He awakened as she stood there, whimpering softly, throwing up his little arms, beseeching her to pick him up. He hadn't known her the first time she'd visited, and Marla had been beside herself until the nurses reminded her that she looked like everyone else with her face and hair covered with the protective garb.

She'd quickly identified herself, speaking to the frightened baby, and he'd readily recognized her voice. Now as she bent over the bed she crooned softly, and he waved his arms at her even more. Taking one hand in her own, she whispered, ''I wish I could pick you up, too, sweetie. You just keep being the little fighter you are and you'll be outta here in no time.''

Marla remained with him until one of the nurses came to tell her that visiting time was up. Fifteen minutes was infinitesimal, she thought, even as she realized the prudence of such restrictions. Stepping outside into the waiting area, she removed her scrub garments and handed them back to the nurse. The lounge was empty, as was usual, judging from her experience of the past couple of nights. Stefan had elected to go home for at least a change of clothes and a couple of hours' sleep. Taking up her vigil once more on the couch nearest the set of double doors, she lay down and closed her eyes, weariness overcoming her as she drifted off almost immediately into a deep sleep.

STEFAN GLANCED AT HIS WATCH as he drove the Mercedes along the darkened country highway. Glancing at the lit clock on the dash, he was surprised to note it was already past midnight. But that was not unusual, he supposed. His normal concept of time had been altered drastically ever since the moment three days earlier when he'd learned Marcus was in the hospital.

He'd stayed late, waiting until the ten-thirty visiting time, trying to convince Marla to come home with him. But she'd absolutely refused to abandon her watch over the baby. There was precious little she could do, he had argued repeatedly, by spending every waking moment— and every sleeping one, for that matter—outside in the waiting area. He'd even gone so far as to consult with the hospital administration, who had offered the use of a private room for her to sleep in. She'd used it, but only to shower and change into the fresh clothes Eileen had brought her.

She was like a zombie by then, and nothing— no one—could get through to her. The knowledge of her unbelievable devotion to Marcus overwhelmed him. He loved her more than he could ever express—of that he was certain. Yet he grew more and more frustrated by the hour. In her intense concern for Marcus she had shut him out, refusing to share the waiting with him at a time when they needed each other the most. It was as though she couldn't hear him. He wasn't even sure she saw him.

The kitchen light was still on, he noticed as he pulled into the driveway. As it was every night until he got home from the hospital. Eileen was having a tough time of it, too, bless her. Entering the kitchen, he slung the keys on the bar and said hello to her.

She greeted him with the same question she did every night. "How is he?"

Stefan sighed and pulled out the barstool to sit down. "The same—no worse, but no better."

"Fever still?"

Stefan nodded. "Dr. Kelsey doesn't want to change the antibiotics, though. He wants to keep Marcus on the one he's getting for another day."

Eileen finished preparing a plate of leftovers and handed it to Stefan, who merely looked at it without interest.

"Thanks, but I'm not really hungry."

But Eileen was adamant. "You're hungrier than you think. When was the last time you ate?"

At Stefan's frown of perplexity she said, "See? You don't even know. You barely touched breakfast this morning. It's not doing any of us any good to ignore our own health."

"I couldn't agree with you more on that," Stefan conceded, pulling the plate closer and taking a bite. It was good, and he *was* hungry, he quickly discovered.

Eileen prepared herself a cup of herb tea and sat down opposite Stefan. "I take it you're referring to Marla."

Stefan chewed slowly and nodded.

"Mmm," Eileen said, sipping her tea. "What did she have to say tonight?"

"Same thing she always says. She won't leave until Marcus pulls out of this—period."

"Stefan?"

"Hmm?"

"Can you stand a little frankness from your employee? I don't know. You might even call it meddling."

Stefan forked up another biteful, then hesitated as he looked directly at her. "You're more than an employee to me. I think you know that. One of the family, if you don't mind the label."

"Label?" Eileen waved a hand dismissingly. "That's no label. I consider it no less than an honor to be a part of it."

Stefan continued eating, apparently pleased by her response, and Eileen gazed into her cup for a thoughtful moment. "However," she began finally, "family or not, you might object to discussing what I have in mind."

"You'll never find out unless you ask," Stefan said.

Eileen drew in a breath and let it out slowly. "All right, then—here goes. I think Marla's behavior now is due to more than Marcus's illness."

Stefan raised one eyebrow questioningly.

"It's just that...well, Marla hasn't been herself for some time now," Eileen continued. "I...well, I've been noticing the—"

"State of our marriage," Stefan finished for her.

Eileen blushed. "That's not really how I would have put it."

"It's all the same any way you phrase it." Stefan pushed back his plate and wiped his mouth with a napkin. "Do you want to know the truth? I'm as confused as you are." Leaning forward, he put one elbow on the counter, resting his chin in his hand. "I can barely remember when it all started." Stefan rubbed his jaw absently, his brown gaze focused unseeingly on the countertop. "But it doesn't really matter, I suppose. It all led to the same thing." Suddenly he cast a hard stare at Eileen. "Did you know she was leaving me?"

"What?" The housekeeper sounded incredulous.

"The day Anne-Marie was killed. She was going to leave me."

"But . . . how. . . . ?"

Stefan shook his head. "We'e never discussed it, but I know. She was packed, had flight reservations. Of course, she never went through with it."

Both were silent for a long while, each lost in his own thoughts. Finally, softly, Eileen spoke. "Well, one thing is certain—I've never seen anyone so devoted to a child. You'd think he was Marla's very own."

The barest hint of a frown appeared on

Stefan's brow just then, but he merely picked up his fork and began to eat once more.

Eileen drained the remainder of her tea and stood up as she picked up her cup and saucer. "I think I'll turn in now. Is there anything else I can get you?"

"No—thanks anyway. I'll see you in the morning."

"All right." Eileen rinsed out the cup and saucer and hung up her apron. "Good night, Stefan."

"Good night, Eileen."

It was a very long time before the kitchen light was doused, though. Stefan sat alone with his thoughts, most of them triggered by that one phrase of Eileen's: "you'd think he was Marla's very own...." The implications were so obvious it seemed impossible he'd never considered them before. How blind could he have been all this time not to realize that she hadn't ever left those personal doubts, that sense of inadequacy, behind?

With the dawning realization a slender thread of hope unraveled, the hope that there was still a chance for the two of them .. a very good chance.

MARLA HAD SLIPPED INTO yet another sterile scrub gown and was pulling the paper cap over her hair, when the door was pushed open and the night-shift head nurse appeared.

"I'm just about ready," Marla said, stopping as she noticed the grin on the nurse's face.

"Good news," the nurse said. "How does 98.6 sound?"

Marla simply stared at her. "You're kidding. When did it come down?"

"His fever broke about an hour ago. We've telephoned Dr. Kelsey for orders. He's on the phone if you want to talk to him."

"Yes. Yes! Let me just finish here." Before the words were out of her mouth Marla had pulled on the sterile mask and was through the door.

She waited impatiently as the nurse had first turn with the physician, scribbling down his orders on Marcus's chart. Marla took the phone from her eagerly, listening intently to everything he said. He would be there soon, he told her, but from the results of tests and, more significantly, the break in his fever, it did appear as though Marcus was out of the woods. The doctor even mentioned moving him to a private room.

Hanging up the phone jubilantly and crossing the unit to the isolation room, she verified that Marcus indeed looked quite different. He was sleeping, but it was a peaceful sleep now, and his complexion had lost the deceptively healthy-looking flush the illness had produced. After staying the allowed length of the visit, Marla spoke with the nurses for a few minutes, thanking them for their dedication and support.

Back out in the waiting room, Marla just stood for a moment, staring straight ahead, intense relief flooding through every fiber of her being. Reaching up, she rubbed her face, realizing how grubby she felt from staying up most of the night. How she would love a long hot soak.

Coming back to the present she remembered suddenly that she should call home, let them know that everything was all right—Marcus was going to be okay! Tears formed suddenly in her eyes. She couldn't believe it—he really was all right! Then what was she doing crying like a fool!

Forcing herself to get a hold on her emotions, she gathered up her things from the couch and began walking down the long corridor toward the elevators. She could call Stefan and Eileen from her private room. While she stood alone on the elevator as it made its slow ascent, a bone-deep weariness washed over her. When and if she ever did get to sleep, she was certain it would be for at least twenty-four hours.

Shutting the suite door behind her, she walked over to the bedside telephone. She was about to pick it up when her attention was caught by the single window; she didn't remember leaving the curtain pulled back. Drawn by the first pinkish gray shafts of early-morning light, Marla forgot about the phone call for the moment and walked over to stand beside the window.

Folding her arms across her chest. she looked out into the distance, her gaze wholly captivated by the faint silver blue line o⸋ the Blue Ridge Mountains. How beautiful they were, how absolutely wondrous. She would never get over the sight of them.

Slowly, magically, the pinkish gray light took on warm golden highlights. Sunrise, Marla thought wistfully. What a majestic thing it was, so promising. As was this certain sunrise.

The creak of the door opening did not startle her—probably one of the nurses coming to check on her, she thought. But the familiar footsteps arrested her, and she looked around to see Stefan walking in.

She turned completely then and faced him Her breath caught in her throat as she became swept up in the pull of his magnetism. *He's your husband,* some tiny voice spoke from inside her. Now what did that mean? Of course he was her husband. She'd never lost sight of that fact—or had she? What had happened to their marriage those past few months? Ignoring such crazy thoughts, she said, "I was just getting ready to phone you. Marcus is going to be all right."

"I know. I was just there, looking for you."

"The nurses told you?"

Stefan nodded, then smiled gently. He was standing next to her by then, and Marla was more than a little disturbed, though it was a familiar disturbance, one she had missed for a very long time.

"He finally responded to the antibiotics," she went on, filling in the uncomfortable silence with words, unnecessary ones. "Dr. Kelsey even mentioned moving him to a room soon." Still Stefan said nothing. Yet his eyes never left her face.

Marla frowned in consternation. "Stefan, why are you looking at me that way?"

He glanced around the room, and seeing the small piece of luggage she'd kept there, he suggested, "Why don't you get your things together now? I'm going to take you home."

Marla swallowed and ran a hand through her disheveled hair. "Yes, all right." Silently she began to pack. By the time Stefan held the door open for her a few minutes later, she was ready to go.

A SINGLE CREAK signaling the opening and closing of the bedroom door brought Marla out of the semitrancelike state she'd been drifting into. The hot water had quickly worked on her exhaustion, and she'd come very close to falling asleep.

"Marla?" Stefan called out her name from the sitting room.

"Yes? I'll be out in a minute." Yawning uninhibitedly, Marla finished with her bath a few minutes later, donning a cool pink-and-white-striped seersucker dressing gown. Coming into the bedroom, she stopped suddenly, surprised to see Stefan seated in one of the sitting-room chairs, obviously waiting for her.

"I want to ask you something," he said suddenly.

Marla's blue eyes widened as she took in his serious expression, his tense demeanor.

"Why were you going to leave me?"

She blinked, taken off guard, then tried to turn. Stefan rose and quickly covered the distance between them, placing a hand firmly on her shoulder.

"What are you talking about?" Marla asked, swallowing uncomfortably.

"No more games, Marla," Stefan chided softly. Slowly he turned her around, and his gaze also told her she couldn't avoid the issue any longer. "I know you were going to leave me the day Anne-Marie was killed. I suppose you were too upset to remember the luggage you left by the door, the flight number you scribbled down.''

Suddenly she did remember. She *had* forgotten that day. Everything had been such a blur. . . .

''I want to know, Marla,'' he repeated. ''Why were you leaving?''

Marla avoided his demanding look and struggled for words—any words to answer his question. What could she say? She would never have thought she'd have to express the pain that had lain so heavily on her heart all this time.

Reaching up, she ran her hand along the side of her neck. ''I. . .I thought it was the only thing to do.''

''Why?'' Stefan queried, clearly baffled.

''Be-because there was really no reason for me to stay at that point. I—'' She broke off and stared past him.

Stefan placed both hands on her shoulders and forced her to look at him. ''Honey, you're not making sense.'' He hesitated for a moment before he added, ''It had to do with Anne-Marie and the baby, didn't it?''

Reluctantly Marla shifted her gaze to meet his. She said nothing, but her answer was there in the shimmering light of her blue eyes.

Stefan winced and shook his head slowly. ''Oh, honey, what a mess we've made of things—*I've* made, I should say. Come here.'' Taking one of her hands in his, he led her to the bed. They sat down on the edge of it, facing the window, which revealed a sky drenched in a soft golden glow.

Marla was too choked up to say anything. The emotion of the moment was too over-whelming. His hard thigh felt good nudged up against her own, and she looked down at her own small hand captured within the largeness of his.

''You thought I was still upset about your inability to have children, weren't you?''

Marla nodded, keeping her eyes fixed on their hands.

''Oh, darling, you should have talked to me about it. Why did you keep all that to yourself?''

Marla looked up at him then. ''You kept a few things to yourself, too, Stefan.''

At Stefan's frown of incomprehension she went on. ''I practically begged you to tell me why you were going to Germany last fall, but you wouldn't reveal hardly a thing. Then when you brought Anne-Marie back I was shocked, to say the least.''

Stefan groaned as he rubbed his thumb across the back of her hand. ''Yes, that. Well, I can't deny it, can I?''

Marla shook her head. Several seconds passed before she summoned the courage to ask, her voice very small, very diffident, "Well? Doesn't it make a difference? My not being able to give you children?"

Strong, terribly missed arms wrapped around her then. Stefan tilted her chin upward. "I don't ever want to hear you ask that again. Do you understand?" Marla's eyes misted over, and she gave a barely perceptible nod. "Because you give me enough all by yourself," Stefan went on softly. "A child would only be a luxury, and we have that luxury now, too."

"Marcus?"

"Mmm-hmm."

"Stefan?"

"Yes?"

"I want us to adopt him—officially."

Stefan smiled slowly and planted a soft kiss on the tip of her nose. "We will."

"And Stefan?"

"Hmm?"

"We haven't done too well in the communication department, have we?"

"I've never been much on words, Marla."

Marla chuckled softly. "That's true enough. But why?"

"As you've said before, we come from very different backgrounds. I guess you can blame it on that. But I think it's something we can manage, don't you?''

Marla studied her lap thoughtfully for a moment. "You know, Stef, I remember thinking at the time, when you sprang that trip to Germany on me, how very naive I was. I thought I knew everything about you. I knew so little.''

"Yes, well, I suppose that does deserve a bit of explanation,'' Stefan admitted. Quietly, haltingly, he told her about the years of grief over the loss of his brother, the guilt when he'd discovered what a difficult time his parents had had trying to raise Anne-Marie, then his joy when Marcus was born and the overwhelming feeling of coming to terms with it all, the sense of peace that at last he'd put the guilt over Rolf's death behind him, made up for all those years of shirking his responsibility.

Marla listened, humbled by his words. She'd assumed the worst, never dreaming he was capable of such sensitivity.

"I really didn't know much about you,'' she said softly, reveling in the touch of his hand on her hair. She hadn't known that sensation in so long! It was a sin, the time they'd wasted

"The same is true of me,'' Stefan replied. "I knew I was getting a little hell-fighter, but I never dreamed she'd possess such a stubborn streak.''

"Me, stubborn! Talk about the pot calling the kettle black!"

"It's true, though. You were too stubborn to open up and tell me how little you trusted me."

Marla grimaced. "That's an odd way to put it."

"Well, that's the way it was. You didn't believe that what I told you before we got married was the absolute truth—despite whatever came after and despite whatever will happen in the future."

"What do you mean?"

"I mean," Stefan explained in a low voice, "that I meant it when I said it doesn't matter—at all—that you and I will never have our own children. I love you for you alone I always will."

Marla turned, bending one leg at the knee as she reached up to throw her hands around her husband's neck.

"Oh, Stefan, you don't know how long I've wanted to hear exactly those words." She lay her head on his shoulder and whispered, "I've missed you...more than you can imagine."

"I think I can imagine very well," Stefan said hoarsely. "God, all those weeks of lying there beside you. I could hardly stand it." Cupping her face tenderly in his hands, he lowered his lips to hers.

Their kiss was deep, searching, probing—all the things Marla remembered so well and responded to now with a fervor she had never once forgotten. As Stefan's hand glided down her back in sensuous suggestive strokes, Marla instinctively moved toward him. She felt his readiness, shared it, matched it with her own.

Slowly his arm slipped down to her waist, and together they glided onto the bed, stretched out fully against each other. Deftly, with hands that ached to perform the ritual they'd so long been denied, Stefan removed her robe, raising her slightly to slip the long sleeves from her slender arms.

She lay naked before him, and as his eyes traveled down the length of her sweetly curved body, he began to shed his own clothes. Impatiently Marla helped him, desperate to remove this final barrier between them.

Her heart caught in her throat as he lowered himself onto her. Wrapping her arms around him tightly and pulling him close, she eagerly accepted the love that would fill the aching void within her.

They came together slowly, tenderly, with serenity that belied the yearning impatience that filled them both. Marla was astounded by the depth of her response to him, and as her fingers plied through Stefan's wealth of hair, she moaned softly into his ear, feeling his own need and passion intensify as her warm breath, her caressing hands, teased him even further.

Holding himself back this time seemed the most difficult thing Stefan had ever done in his life, but he would wait for her, go with her as they moved against each other, stoking the fire of passion that drew breath from their long-neglected desire.

And as at last fulfillment became theirs and theirs alone, Marla knew with certainty that the love they shared and nourished was indeed enough. More than enough for one lifetime.